Margaret's Faith

Beth Durham

ISBN: 978-1790750054

Cover design by Dany Zamora

Chapter 1

Beneath a clear blue October sky, Margaret Elmore painstakingly rubbed clean her family's clothing and bedding. Mama's standard for her chores was long since drilled into Margaret's mind so she worked quickly yet thoroughly. Her lifelong familiarity with the view from the family's mountain-top farm caused her to nearly miss the breath-taking beauty of the fall colors sweeping across the distant valley.

Home had never meant anything other than this little piece of rocky ground on Tennessee's Cumberland Plateau. The Elmores had very little in the way of material things, but Papa was always quick to say they had 'tolerable plenty'. And recently, rumors had drifted up from the deeper south of people in great need, so the family thanked God daily for His provision and the protection that their seclusion offered from the cruelties of war.

This morning, there was a touch of frost still in the air, for Margaret had started her day's work at the first sight of sunlight kissing the distant mountains. She preferred her solitary laundry chore over working with her siblings in the barn as they fed the stock, milked the cows and gathered eggs. There was always persistent chatter as Papa gave directions that each child had heard dozens of times. And all the children were constantly bantering. Most days their only human contact was within this little family. Therefore, their best friends were their siblings.

Since Matthew married Lou, there was a voice missing

1

from this chorus and they all missed him no matter how much they loved Lou. After he marched off with the Confederate Army, Lou had often filled his spot at the table and in chores. Margaret knew that Paul missed Matthew especially since he was now the only help Papa had in the fields. Little Jesse, just ten years old this fall, was still not able to do a grown man's work, try though he may.

However, Margaret's mind did not hear her family's friendly joking, nor her Mama's joyful humming as she focused on today's chore. Having lived all of her eighteen years in Cumberland County and rarely leaving the plateau, she could scarcely have named the distant land to which her mind traveled, but this land was far from home and very, very different. She dreamed of big cities and ladies in fine bonnets and gentlemen who bowed when she passed. She longed for ballrooms glowing with the light of a thousand candles and flowing skirts whirling about her ankles as she glided across a polished floor... she blushed as she came back to reality, knowing that Papa did not approve of dancing.

It was sixteen year old Catherine's voice that wrenched her back to reality. Returning to the house with a pail of milk, Catherine's sharp eyes spotted a figure striding toward the farmstead. "Who's that comin'?" she asked.

So rare were callers at this hour that both sisters froze in their work to watch the approach. As the form moved closer, their focus grew sharper and they could make out the haversack on his back, a bedroll slung over his shoulder and the tell-tale rifle at the ready in his right hand.

Although the uniform was covered in dust, the Union blue was unmistakable. At the realization that it was a soldier approaching, sudden fear crept along Margaret's spine –

although there appeared to be only one, they would have to assume him to be part of either a scouting or scavenging party.

In an instant, Margaret's alarm ran a gamut wondering, *Will the raiders take all of the stock? Do they know that the family's oldest son is serving their enemy or is this man injured and seeking our help knowing this is a Christian home and could scarcely turn him away?*

Her pondering stopped as little Jesse joined them and, following his sister's stares, also saw the man. "Who's that?" he echoed Catherine's question.

Margaret wrapped her arms protectively around him.

"You two go into the house," Margaret ordered them, knowing their curiosity would tempt them to stay with her. She pushed Jesse into Catherine's arms propelling the pair toward the back porch and Mama's protection. Instinctively she turned toward the barn and Papa, knowing he would want and need to protect the whole family. Yet as the soldier's long strides brought him ever closer to her, she could not tear her gaze from him.

Now, he was close enough to speak by raising his voice and he called to her. "Haaalo" His voice was strange to her. She had heard northerners speak and knew they sounded different than her Tennessee neighbors, but this sound was foreign to her. She realized she was staring at him without moving and urged herself to respond.

Without fully realizing she was answering him she heard a voice that sounded almost like her own respond, "Mornin'."

He continued moving toward her and now she could make out his features clearly. He was long and lean; even at a distance he appeared quite tall. Beneath his tattered forage cap spilled jet black hair. His face was very slender with a long nose that almost gave him a hawk-like appearance. His dark eyes seemed to bore into Margaret's very soul. Somehow she felt vulnerable beneath his gaze. Yet she still could not tear herself away. A voice deep inside her was screaming, *Run to Papa*, yet her feet were rooted in place.

The man seemed to have assessed the girl and the farm and all of her surroundings. "Is *theez* your home? Are you all alone?"

Now this sounded like a challenge. That same voice in her head urged Margaret to counter his question with the sure knowledge that Papa was just a few yards away in the barn and that her nearly–adult brother Paul was there as well. Perhaps she should tell him that they were armed. After all, Paul had his very own squirrel rifle and Papa had Grandpa's musket as well as a Richmond rifle he'd acquired through some unknown trade. However, this was not what she offered to his challenge.

"No, the family's around," and she unconsciously dipped her head and smoothed the damp apron. The moistness reminded her momentarily of the pile of unwashed laundry but the call to return to her responsibility was overwhelmed by embarrassment that this gallant gentleman had caught her in such a mundane task.

Missing Catherine's return, Lawrence Elmore stepped from the barn to find a soldier chatting with his daughter. In an instant he noted the Union uniform, and made a hunter's scan of the surrounding area as he wondered if there were others with him. "Howdy," he called to the soldier - his dedication to kindness and gentleness tempering the fear and anger that initially welled within him. "Can I he'p ya?"

"My name is Philip Berai," the soldier replied. Margaret blushed at the feeling his melodic accent sparked. Philip continued, "I am headed north, tried to camp a few miles back;

however, the morning's chill got me moving early."

Papa must have decided the danger here was minimal for he continued talking to the young man; nonetheless he needed to move his daughter to safety. When he sent her to help Paul in the barn Margaret knew he was both telling Philip that there was another man on the place and also sending her to warn Paul of this soldier's presence.

Although the family had never actually practiced what they would do should they be visited by soldiers, many times Margaret had listened to her parents talking quietly at night when they thought the children were asleep and she knew of her parents' fears of invasion.

The Elmores found themselves in a blessedly remote part of America, nestled between the predominately Union East Tennessee and the pro-Confederate Middle Tennessee. They were not close enough to any big cities to feel the changing political pressures or to fear large-scale invasion first by the Union Army after Tennessee chose to secede, and later by the Confederate Army attempting to re-take lost territory. Still the family feared straggling soldiers as well as scavenging guerillas. Until the appearance of Philip Berai, they had scarcely seen Union blues, a fact that Lawrence remembered each day in his prayers.

Now he found himself face to face with a Yankee soldier. For the fear it wreaked, it might as well have been the whole union army. Lawrence rediscovered his voice and asked again, "Then you're just passin through?"

Philip Berai had been a long time marching south and had fought in battles across Tennessee. He heard the children in the barn, smelled fresh bread in the house and couldn't miss the glint in the daughter's eye. "Could I work out a *meeeala*? That aroma, it is bread, no?"

Lawrence could never send anyone away hungry, and this rail-thin man could surely use one of Bessie's meals. Margaret heard his response as she eased back from her mission in the barn, "I think we can manage that. Come out to the barn and put down your things. We have corn shocks ready to harvest and we'd be happy for the help."

Margaret lifted her eyes enough to catch the wink Philip Berai tossed her way and she immediately blushed. He disappeared behind Papa into the relative darkness of the barn's interior. Margaret was still looking around, somehow unable to orient herself to the chore on which she had been working just a few moments before. Only Mama's gentle voice brought her back to reality. "Margaret, we need to get them clothes finished. I'll need your he'p if we have an extra mouth to feed today. "

By mid-morning, Margaret had completed the washing and then turned to household chores to ease her Mama's load a bit. At forty-three years old, Bessie Elmore was still beautiful in Margaret's eyes. Her life had been hard on this rural farm, but Papa did everything he could to give her ease. Still, the lines around her eyes and deep creases in her forehead seemed to tell a story of lost babies, harsh winters with scarce provisions and, now, of her oldest son fighting in a war. These woes she kept close to herself though; she was always ready with a smile for her children and praise to her God for his myriad blessings.

Bessie had the bread cooling beside the stove by the time Margaret joined her in the kitchen. Flour was a precious commodity on this mountain plateau that did not easily lend itself to cultivating grain crops. Cornbread was the family's regular fare; nonetheless, today she had splurged and used some of their precious flour to make soft bread which was a family favorite. The kitchen seemed overly warm after Margaret's time in the chilly morning air with hands immersed in wash-water. The big iron stove warmed more than Margaret's skin. This was the heart of their home. The scarred eating table pre-dated Lawrence and Bessie's marriage, probably made by Grandpa Elmore more than 50 years ago when he built the cabin that formed the center of their house.

Mary was already at the table in front of a pan stacked high with apples. They would all pitch in to peel and slice the apples for drying. It was laborious, but each one could practically taste the fried pies Mama would make this winter. The heavy beam behind the stove was already lined with bunches of leather britches – green beans from the summer's garden that they tied there to dry. Their strong taste would be welcome this winter along with the vegetables stored in the root cellar, salt pork and whatever meat the woods yielded to Paul's careful aim with his aged rifle.

The Elmore ladies worked like a choreographed team, each knowing what needed to be done from years of repetition. Margaret took the handmade broom from its home in the corner and swept the rough floor. They would scrub these floors on Saturday so a thorough sweeping was all that was necessary on this mid-week day. Glancing out the window, she noted both the gentle flapping of sheets on the line and the sun's position in the sky. Papa would keep Paul, Catherine, Jesse and the stranger in the field until the sun was straight above them. He may even send Jesse to bring their dinner back to the field. Guessing that papa would prefer to keep the soldier out of their house as much as possible, Margaret pulled out a large basket and began to pack the cold side meat and cornbread.

"What's the basket for, Margie?" Mary asked, barely

lifting her eyes from the fruit in her hand.

"I thought I'd take lunch to Papa in the field. It'll save them some time not having to come in to eat."

Mary nodded her head, "He'll appreciate that, what with having that soldier with him."

All three of them had carefully not mentioned the stranger's presence. Even Mary's quick reference caused Bessie to tighten her lips and scrub more vigorously on the pot she was cleaning. Margaret knew she too should be nervous because his presence was a stark reminder of the war raging around them. Instead she kept thinking of his dark, piercing eyes, and she felt somehow drawn to him. She had to admit to herself that her trip to the corn-field had more to do with this visiting soldier than helping her father.

From Mary's unpeeled bowl, Margaret added fresh apples to her basket and snagged a pewter pitcher as she headed to the back door. She would fill the pitcher at the spring as she passed by it.

"I'll be right back," she called as she backed out the screen door.

Stopping at the spring to fill the pitcher with the cold water, she was anticipating another meeting with Philip Berai. Maybe she could learn something about him. Why did he sound so strange? Where was he going? She had so many intriguing questions about him. It just didn't seem fair that Papa would have the whole day in the field to learn all about him.

The corn-field was beyond the vegetable garden. Mostly brown now, the garden was surrounded by a split rail fence in an ongoing effort to keep out the milk cow, as well as any neighbors' stock that chose to visit. Margaret did not enjoy the time she was required to spend weeding and picking here, but

Mama always liked to say that garden dirt was good for the soul. Mama thought lots of stuff was good for the soul!

Margaret found her family and their visitor in the hillside field. She met Paul first. At fifteen years of age, he pulled the load of an adult man. And he longed to be a part of the war just as his older brother Matthew was. He could easily have fibbed his way into the ranks as many others his age had done. Especially now, two years since the beginning, the Confederacy greatly needed men and they would be happy to accept Paul. And yet his dedication to family, and submission to Papa, won the internal battle with youthful wanderlust. So, he stayed at home and helped Papa, and together they protected the women, his baby brother and their property.

Paul called to her as she approached, "Margie, have you brought cool drinking water for us? Bless you!" He used her childhood nickname and she cringed slightly. She thought it undignified; she couldn't bear the stranger to hear it. As she poured water for Paul into the pewter cups she'd brought along, she looked about the field strewn with neat shocks awaiting the short trip to the farmstead.

"Where's ever'body got to?" she asked her brother.

Paul's eye twinkled as he realized she could easily see all of her family. "Just who are you lookin' for?"

Margaret blushed. She had been caught one time too many daydreaming of exciting places and her siblings well knew that she would be looking for any opportunity to meet, and even impress, anyone who hinted at having a fascinating life. Choosing not to answer Paul, she squinted her eyes at him, mutely warning him not to tease her and moved on toward the rest of the family.

Only when she approached her father did she hear

Philip Berai's melodic voice as he worked on the far side of the wagon, shielded from her view. Catherine stood atop the wagon, feet spread far apart to brace herself from the lurching motion as the horses started and stopped. She held the driving lines loosely in her hands. Margaret couldn't help thinking how unlike a lady she looked, and she was ashamed that the girls would be seen working.

"Margaret, God bless you for bringin' us some refreshment. And a basket of food too? It'll be good to eat our dinner here and not lose the time of going to the house. I'm thinking we need to haul as much as possible today." Papa talked as he took water from her and peeked into the basket on her arm. "Philip, come 'round here and get a cup of cool water. It was a chilly start to the day but a man warms up fast in the field."

As she filled another pewter cup and handed it to the soldier, Margaret smiled shyly, scarcely meeting his eyes. Her childhood teaching made it difficult to look in his eyes and smile brightly, as she wanted to do. Still, she found her voice to ask, "Are you hungry yet, sir? I've brought side meat and bread – got some apples too."

"Thank you, I am *veeery* hungry" Philip Berai responded, "and you can call me *Pheleep*". This allowed Margaret to look into his face, dipping her head to acknowledge the name and smiling at the gentle *uh* he added to almost every word. She thought how the most mundane talk with this man was like beautiful poetry.

"Mr. Elmore, you are right, the day warms quickly in the field. It is good to work hard though, without mini-balls whizzing by. On the battle field, there seems to be a constant wind as the air is cut by lead." He referred to battle as though it were commonplace.

"When did you join up with the army?" Margaret asked, not daring to glance toward Papa, knowing he would neither want to pry into this stranger's affairs, nor would he want to know too much about a Union soldier lest Confederates question him.

"I joined in '61 as soon as Mr. Lincoln put out the call to arms." Whether Philip saw Lawrence Elmore's slight grimace or simply felt the tension, he checked himself on the mention of the U.S. President. "Living up north, there was little mention of joining the Rebs. My brother and I had hoped when we came to America we would finally be able to earn a good living without wars, but work had slowed down just before the call to arms. And I thought the army was a good chance to bring in some money."

Oh, thought Margaret, I knew he was from a foreign land. "When did you come to America, Philip?" Margaret slightly emphasized his name, enjoying the freedom to speak so familiarly with him. "And where'd ya' come from?"

Philip seemed happy to talk about himself, and regale this lovely young lady with tales of his adventures. He swallowed the meat and bread he was chewing, washed it down with another gulp of water and settled back against the wagon wheel to answer all her questions. Papa seized the moment's pause to break this too-comfortable exchange, "We'd better finish this food and get back to the work at hand. Paul, you and Philip take the horses over to the branch for their own drink of water."

Paul needed only seconds to unhook the trace chains and double-tree that held the horses to the wagon, and then he and Philip were headed to the branch. Margaret knew that Paul could have handled the horses alone for he did it almost every day. This was just Papa's way of sending the stranger away. As she picked up the cups and helped ensure Jesse had eaten enough, she waited for a word from Papa.

Lawrence was well aware of his second daughter's imagination and her dreams of excitement far beyond the Tennessee mountains. He looked at her, admiring the beauty that she inherited from her mother and the height his own family genes passed to her. She was beautiful and all of the local boys agreed. Of course most of those boys had marched off to war, along with his Matthew. And Papa knew that these war years were hard on his older daughters who would have planned to be marrying and settling into their own homes by now. Instead, they were still at home and making do with very little as he tried to protect his family from all aspects of the war that raged around them.

"Margie, you remember your raisin' with this man. We know nothin' about him and anyway, he'll be on his way northward in a day or two." Margaret didn't even bristle when Papa used the nickname. She knew that the gentle chastening was offered with deepest love. She also felt certain that Papa had never known any real adventure and couldn't appreciate her need for such excitement. Still, she well understood the "raisin'" to which Papa referred. Mama had schooled each of her daughters in the proper comportment of a lady. Margaret felt they should have learned the ways of fine ladies like she read in books; however, Mama's teaching focused on humility and modesty. She forbade them to be 'forward' with any gentleman, never speaking too familiarly or too quickly. They were always accompanied by Papa or their brothers on the rare occasions they were in town, allowing them to protect the ladies in their family.

With an inaudible sigh, Margaret picked up the now-empty basket and began her short walk home. She took her time, rehearsing the little bit she had learned about Mr. Philip Berai, and reveling in the melodic sound of his voice. "I never did learn where he came from" she mused aloud. "Maybe I can get that at supper."

Chapter 2

The western horizon was streaked with orange and red when the jingle of the horses' harness announced the return of the workers from the field. "Come girls, we need to get the food on the table" Bessie Elmore summoned Mary and Margaret from their brief respite back to the warm kitchen.

Just a moment ago, Margaret had watched her mother on the porch's split-bottom chairs, allowing the fading sunlight to illuminate her Bible. She wondered how her mother could spring from such quiet meditation into this flurry of activity. Mama never seemed to use her quiet times to dream the way Margaret did. Instead, during most spare moments she could be found with that battered Bible in her hands.

Papa could not read so well as Mama, but he had much of The Bible memorized. Each evening Mama would read to the family and Papa would close his eyes, trying to write the words on his heart. Almost every evening would end with Papa's deep voice, head bowed low, praying over his family and sending them off to bed in this quiet spirit.

The wagon disappeared around the barn as Catherine and Jesse hopped off and raced to be the first in the house. Mary already held her position at the back door with clean rags in hand. The youngest Elmore children would have to fill the wash pan with spring water and clean grimy faces, scraping dirt from fingernails and shaking loose corn fodder from skirts and trousers before they would be admitted to supper. They knew the routine well. Margaret could remember when Mama's kitchen stood across the dogtrot with only dirt floors. Even then, no one came in without first cleaning off the remnants of field and farm.

Papa worked harder than any of them, but he respected Mama's rules inside her home. And she repaid his respect with tender loving care. There was always food awaiting his return. She would rise earlier than him in order to have coffee, or chicory when that's all they had, waiting on the stove. As was the custom of their people, they did not show much affection in front of their children, yet Margaret often caught Mama's hand gently resting on Papa's back. And Papa always held Mama's hand when they prayed, seeming to join himself to her as their marriage vows joined them as one.

As the family filtered one by one into the kitchen, they each found their place around the table. Papa came in with their guest soldier and directed him to the end of the table. Each child sat with head slightly bowed, waiting for Papa to return thanks to the Lord for his provision. They did not question whether they could eat first. This ritual never wavered and they had known it from their earliest remembering.

Margaret noticed that Philip eyed the plain fare on the table while inhaling the myriad of fragrances. There were fresh green beans, probably some of the last their garden would produce and slices of fried pork. A glass of milk sat before his plate and bright orange sweet potatoes steamed in the center of the table. He started to reach for the plate of sliced bread – undoubtedly what he'd smelled baking early this morning – only to notice that none of the family had started and he checked his reach.

As Bessie sat down, always the last to the table,

Lawrence reached gently for her hand and lifted up his voice, "Lord God, we thank thee for thy blessings on this day. We thank thee for this food which thou hast provided. We beg thy blessings upon my dear wife who's prepared it; bless my girls who've worked beside her. We thank thee for Philip Berai, who breaks bread with us today. Please bless this food to the nourishment of each one here. In the name of our Lord and Savior, Jesus Christ, we pray. Amen."

Margaret noticed Philip raising his hand to his forehead making some kind of strange movement across his chest.

"Mrs. Elmore, this looks delicious" Philip said to Bessie flashing her a charming smile. "I do not know that I have eaten this well since I last planted my feet beneath my own mother's table."

Margaret saw an opportunity to learn more about him, but knew that she should allow her parents to lead this conversation. Thankfully, Mama was as curious as she was. She asked, "Where's your Mama at?"

"Well, she is still in Italy, Falerna is the name of our village."

"Italy?" Her head jerked to look more closely at him. "Well you've come a fur piece I'll reckon." Bessie surveyed every plate and ensured all her family's plates were well filled. "How long ya' been in America?"

Margaret noticed that her Mama didn't question what brought the young man to Tennessee as she carefully avoided speaking of the war.

"I came in 1857. My brother *Ju-zep* came two years before. I haven't seen him since we fought in Manassas, Virginia."

While Margaret knew Papa would have learned a lot

during the day's work, this seemed a new fact to him and he wasn't as hesitant as Mama to discuss the battles. "1861? You haven't seen your brother since the fighting started?"

"No Sir, summer of 1862 – there were two battles in Manassas. Joseph was not quite as quick as me to join the army. We will meet back now that I am, uh, out and I know he'll be returning home soon too."

"And where's 'home' for you?" Margaret jumped into the conversation with as much poise as she could muster. She tried hard not to sound overly-interested but her eyes showed that she was about to burst with questions.

"Chicago, Illinois," Philip responded, raising his head enough to push his chin out in a show of pride for his adopted hometown.

The family chattered on and while Margaret wanted badly to follow every word, her mind was spinning. *Here at our very own table is a man come all the way from Italy. And he was on his way to that glamorous city, Chicago! I can only imagine what his life must be like traveling that way and living in the big city.*

She resolved to find a way to learn more from him. However, she knew that her parents would tolerate no prying questions. She was drifting back to the current conversation when she realized Philip was speaking.

"...such a delicious meal. You ladies are very good cooks." Philip looked directly at Margaret, seeming to caress her with his eyes. "This meat, it has flavor like from my home land. The meat in the army was rotten."

Margaret blushed, dipping her head and mumbled some kind of thanks for the compliment. Lawrence cleared his throat and asked Bessie for another glass of milk, offering his guest some as well.

As he poured from the dented pitcher, Lawrence explained the food. "My Daddy taught me to cure meat. He never liked smokin' it too much so he mostly salted his meat."

Philip placed a bite in his mouth and closed his eyes as he savored the taste. "Yes, the flavor is not the same as in Italia but the essence, that is the same."

As the plates emptied, Mary served the cake with apple butter but Margaret's piece sat untouched before her. The Elmores did not waste food so she knew she'd better eat quickly, or everyone would leave her at the table. It was a delicious treat and one of the family's favorites, however on this evening Margaret could hardly swallow it. After taking an extra half glass of milk, she finished just as Lawrence pushed back his chair and asked Bessie to bring her Bible to the table for the family's devotions.

"If you will excuse me Sir, I will leave your family to their worship. I will toss my bedroll in the hay like we talked about. I guess farming is harder than soldiering because I am very tired." Philip strolled out of the house, tossing a coy smile toward Margaret.

Several mouths were agape as the visitor stepped out the kitchen door. Margaret felt like he'd left for good and she despaired that she had not learned more from him. Papa was shocked that he would walk out before their time of worship. Mary, Catherine and Paul were stunned that anyone would even leave the table, much less the house, without Papa's express permission.

Lawrence Elmore recovered quickly, he knew that not everyone was as committed to these daily devotions as were he and his wife. Margaret saw him quietly nod at Mama who opened her trusted Bible to the book they had been studying.

Usually, the family read slowly through the Bible, about one chapter per evening. Tonight's reading was Luke chapter 14.

As Mama's clear voice read through the familiar words, Catherine occasionally interrupted with questions. Papa always allowed these interruptions because he knew they would learn best what they understood fully. And, he preferred to explain the scriptures to his children rather than to allow them to go into life with erroneous beliefs.

Margaret listened to the words Mama read, waiting for the hymn the family would sing. She was eager to have this meditative time past because she was intent to find a way out of the house to see her new friend. She mused, Could I call him a friend?

After the family's devotions, the sisters moved upstairs to their common bedroom. Mary went directly to loosen her long hair and begin the evening's brushing ritual. Margaret saw Catherine pick up the pitcher from the wash stand to fill with water for the evening. "Cathy, I'll get that for you. I need to run to the privy anyway; might as well save you the trouble." Margaret smiled at her little sister knowing she would be happy to avoid the trip to the spring house.

Margaret descended the steep stairs with slow care, avoiding alerting her parents. Mama was already in their downstairs bedroom, and she could hear Papa's boots on the front porch as he enjoyed a few minutes of the chilly autumn evening. She stole out the back door.

Outside, she made her way toward the spring house, but her eyes searched the shadows surrounding the barn, searching for any sign that their intriguing visitor was still awake. She saw the glow of embers in a pipe, moving slowly as Philip made his way toward the spring house. Margaret's breath caught in her

19

throat! For a split second she thought of quietly hurrying back to the house for she was sure her presence was as yet unknown to him. In the end, her longing for this man's attention and her hope for excitement won out over better judgment and she continued toward the spring house as though she did not see him.

Still several yards from the spring house, Margaret realized Philip had seen her. He did not call out; instead he spoke in a soft, quiet tone. He was so quiet that she knew Papa would not hear even if he were still on the front porch. Her pulse raced and, hidden by the evening shadows, Margaret smiled broadly.

"Good evening, Miss Elmore," Philip greeted her. "It's cooling down fast don't you think?"

When he spoke her family name it seemed to slide from his tongue as Ela-mora and she wanted him to say it again and again. Combined with the sofe 'uh' he added to many words, she couldn't help but feel like he was singing to her. Margaret took a deep breath trying to respond to him politely as her mother had drilled into her mind for her whole life. "Yes Sir, once the sun goes down the heat just seems to rush right off the mountain's top."

Ooh, she thought, *Why did you call him 'sir'?* Years of Mama's repeated coaching came out even when she wanted to cultivate familiarity with this man.

"I sure enjoyed hearing about your adventures at supper and I'd love to know more. There just was no way for me to get all my questions out, what with ever' body at the supper table."

He stepped closer to her, still keeping his voice low. She could smell the pipe tobacco and stifled a sneeze. "You may ask anything you would like; I enjoy talking with you."

Margaret was thrilled, yet she was unaccustomed to speaking with boys alone, and this was no boy. She tried to count how old he must be; despite years, he had fought in the war and Papa said that made men out of boys overnight. She didn't even care to think that his bullets may well have been aimed at her brother. All she wanted to think about right now was how to prolong this conversation.

She heard her own voice begin to prattle about his coming to America from Italy. Was the trip exciting? What must Italy be like? She stopped herself, embarrassed to have bombarded him with so many questions. She caught his eyes as he drew on the pipe, brightening its glow. He was staring at her and his gaze made her mildly uncomfortable as though he were looking deeper than she dared reveal. Yet her discomfort was paralleled by excitement. She gave a little shudder.

"There now, you are getting cold." Philip wrapped his arm around her.

She believed that gentlemen did not touch ladies unless they were promised to marry. Mama had talked to her and her sisters many times about this. Mama had never mentioned what were the rules in the dark of night, outside the spring house. Margaret was frantically trying to think of the proper thing to say as Philip continued.

"So you want to know about my journey to America, do you? My home is in the southern part of Italy. It is balmy warm there – there are no October nights like this one. The weather does cool some about now though."

He was very close to her, but Margaret was no longer uncomfortable with it. She was trying to see his eyes in the moonlight for they seemed to be looking far away now, almost as though he could see his Italian home.

"When the army marched south, I was happy because it felt more like my home. The mountains here are rounded; our mountains are steep and make sharp lines in the sky. And the sea is too far from here."

"It sounds so lovely why ever would you leave there?" Margaret's words came out as a whisper and she feared he had not heard her. He was slow to respond.

Philip inhaled deeply and took a small step away from her. "My home land is very poor and the living hard. Like here, there is war in our land. My mother did every kind of work she could find to save money enough to buy passage to America for me and my brother. She did not want us involved in the wars. I don't imagine she is very happy that we have joined the Army here in America. And that is why I must be finished with war and return to Chicago to make my fortune."

Margaret knew she should make her way back into the house. *How long have I been out here? I certainly do not want to explain myself either to Mary or Mama and Papa.*

Suddenly, she was aware of the pitcher she held in her hands. Lifting it slightly, she tried to excuse herself from Philip. "I should be gettin' back inside with the water."

She filled the pitcher and as she stood from the spring, she turned to see him still staring into the night sky. Impulsively she said, "Thank you for sharin' it with me".

Philip cocked his head slightly, "Sharing what?"

She could barely whisper, "Your heart." As she turned toward the house, she wished she could run but the heavy pitcher would not allow it. She felt she had seen into this stranger's very soul and it embarrassed her slightly.

Margaret slipped the back door open as soundlessly as possible. There was still a candle burning in Mama and Papa's room; the door stood ajar. She was creeping toward the stairs when she caught their voices; the strain in Papa's made her stop and listen.

"This man is not like the boys from Isoline and Crossville who went north to join the Yankees. I'm worried about having him here with our children."

Bessie added, "Especially Mary and Margaret. Mary is twenty years old now. She's naturally beginnin' to think of marriage and family. Were it not for the war, she would surely've already married. And Margaret, well, her head's so far above the real world that there's little knowin' what's goin' on in there. I b'lieve I worry more about her than any of our children, including poor Matthew who's off at war."

"Ah Bessie, you've done a fine job raisin and teachin your girls. We've prayed for them every day since they were born. And you've talked with 'em so many times about men and marriage that probably even Catherine could teach the lessons. Now we have to entrust them to The Lord and His promise that when they are old they will not forget their training."

"Thank ye Lawrence," Margaret heard Mama answer him as her voice became muffled, no doubt in his shoulder.

Margaret continued her quiet climb to her room, but the joy from her time with Philip dimmed as she considered her parents' words. Papa's faith in his daughters made her smile. And she certainly knew the teaching that he referred to, for Mama had talked so much about how to conduct yourself with boys that each of the daughters could repeat it verbatim.

As she slipped into bed beside Mary, she convinced herself that her parents had misjudged Philip. He was such a gallant man. He certainly showed a tender concern for his mother who was still in Italy. And surely his bravery in the army proved he possessed the strong character the Elmores considered so important. Mama was certainly right that he was not like the boys in Crossville. Margaret thought she could never be satisfied with one of the local boys in their humdrum acceptance of farm life. She whispered to the night, "Why can't they see that I want excitement and glamor from life?"

Dismissing her parents' concerns, Margaret drifted quickly to sleep and into her dream world that now included Philip Berai.

Chapter 3

Thursday morning dawned bright and clear. From her window, Margaret saw a hint of sparkling white tipping the grass in the light of the rising sun. She could smell the chicory coffee from the kitchen. Real coffee had always been something of a luxury for her parents, and since the war, all store-bought supplies had been in short supply. Not only were the stores sparsely stocked, but Papa was not eager to go into town. Mama had learned from her own mother and grandmother how to grow, dry and grind the bitter chicory root. She then boiled it for a hot drink which she and Papa enjoyed.

The children were fed strong chicory coffee a couple of times each year as an antidote for worms. Although it was a familiar scent in Mama's kitchen, she could never bring herself to enjoy it as others did. Somehow, it always seemed like medicine that she had no choice in taking.

As she moved to the tiny mirror to put up her hair, Margaret noted that Mary's bed was already empty. Catherine was still softly snoring so Margaret gave her a little shake. Margaret's fingers moved quickly to pile her dark hair on top of her head. The smooth bun that her sisters so easily accomplished was never easy for her. The waves in her thick locks made the bun much more time-consuming. With the job done, she gave Catherine's shoulder another shake and moved down the steep staircase.

Mama had the big iron skillet on the stove for eggs and

there was corn bread already in the oven. Margaret automatically picked up the plates and began placing them around the table. She put a plate at what was normally Matthew's end of the table and paused, why would they set a place for Matthew? Distracted by the routine of the morning, she had almost forgotten that Philip Berai was still with them. This plate would be for him.

Immediately, she surveyed the kitchen, the breakfast fare and mentally her own appearance. It all seemed far too mundane for this exciting Italian soldier.

Her hand went to the bun she had formed on her head and she was mortified at her own plainness. She had only three blouses and the one she had chosen today was badly stained. She nearly dropped the last of the plates in her haste to return to the loft and improve her appearance.

When she re-entered the kitchen wearing her Sunday blouse, Mary took immediate note. "Margaret, what are you wearin'?"

This caught Bessie's attention as well. She said nothing, only made a careful appraisal of her daughter's Thursday morning appearance. "Margaret, please change into your working clothes. You know there will be little chance of getting new things anytime soon. We need to take care of what we have."

"But Mama, we have company and I can't wear that stained blouse" she begged.

Bessie's eyes widened, "Margaret, I would not really call that soldier company. He'll be leaving very soon, maybe even today. 'Til then, we should be kind to him, but wary. Remember, we don't know a thing about his character."

Margaret took a second to consider her mother's words.

"Well I b'lieve he has a fine character. And just think of everything that he's seen and all the adventure he's known. He crossed the Atlantic on a great ship – how elegant must that be?"

Bessie took a slow, deep breath to temper her retort, "The stories I've heard from folks that came from the old world weren't one bit glamorous. The ships were packed with people; the food was scarce and stale. They were just tryin' to get to America where they thought they could build a better life. And I guess it is better at that. Just you remember Margaret Elmore, keep your distance from that man. He won't be here long enough to do any proper courtin' and he don't seem the type to do his courtin' by letter, now does he?"

Why does she keep talking about him leaving? She even said he might leave today, Margaret bit her lower lip to keep the thoughts inside.

Suddenly, Margaret's world seemed to shrink around her. He seemed so interested last night. *Why, he acted like he would've talked late into the night. Surely he knew what a risk it was to talk with me alone; didn't he know that Papa would be enraged if he knew we were out in the dark together? Is it possible that his character is, like Mama said, not exactly sterling?* Margaret suddenly realized that Mama had continued to talk even as her hands kept to their breakfast tasks.

Margaret tuned back into her mother's words in time to hear, "Satan can send a perty messenger when he's temptin' you. He knows we would never foller along behind an ugly one. We need to always be askin' if the path we're choosin' leads toward God or away from Him. Now Margaret, get on upstairs and change out of them Sunday clothes. Your Papa will be in here any minute and we don't want to ask him to wait on his breakfast."

As Margaret made her way upstairs, her mind was so full of the seeds Mama had planted that she forgot to worry about the stain on her everyday blouse. All of the ladies of the Elmore house had often talked about courting and praying for a godly husband. She knew this was Mama's prayer for all of her daughters. She wondered though, *Does Mama pray for a chivalrous man? Does she care if her daughters have wonderful advnetures in their lives? Surely she don't expect me to spend my whole life on some farm in the Elmore community, or one of the surrounding areas. Surely God wouldn't expect that!*

When Margaret returned to the kitchen, Papa and Philip were already at the table. Philip had taken the same seat he held last night, at the end of the table, with his back to the wall. From this position, Margaret faced him as she descended the stairs. For a moment, she imagined she was gliding down a polished staircase in some grand hall she'd read about in stories from the old country. Her posture mimicked her imagination, straightening her back and lifting her chin unconsciously. And she saw that Philip looked at her, watched her as she made her way into the kitchen. There was a slight smile on his lips, a glint in his eye that she could not quite read. Was he truly pleased to see her this morning?

A quick look around the kitchen told Margaret that everything was in order for the morning's simple meal. She took her place at the table, not daring to look again at their guest. Papa was talking about the day's work and it was apparent that he had agreed to allow Philip to stay a few more days. Margaret caught a quick look that passed between her parents and she knew that Mama was frightened by Papa's decision.

Margaret smiled at her plate when she heard the news,

still not daring to look up.

Breakfast always found the Elmores planning their day. Lawrence believed that wasted time was poor stewardship. He would lay out a plan for what he wanted accomplished and Bessie would add whatever household chores that the children were expected to help complete.

"We have to finish bringin' in the corn. I think we can get the rest of the shocks on just one more wagon load. Then, we'll have to lash them tight so the winter winds don't spread 'em all the way to kingdom come." Lawrence already knew what he expected from the day. "Philip, you and Paul can head on out to start loading them shocks. Me and Jesse'll be on out there when we've finished what needs doin' in the barn."

Bessie joined them at the table and all planning was set aside in order to return thanks to God for His blessings. As Lawrence said Amen, Bessie turned to him, "We should get the pun'kins into the cellar. There was a bit of frost again this morning. If we wait much longer we may lose some of 'em."

"You're right Bessie; do you think they'll fit on that little sled?"

She closed her eyes with a spoon of grits half-raised, seeming to count the fruit that lay in her garden. "Yeah, I think the sled would hold 'em."

Papa already had a plan for the most efficient use of their limited resources. "Philip can pull the sled over to the garden right after breakfast. Then, when we have the team back from the corn-field, we'll hitch up 'ole Molly and pull it to the cellar door."

Margaret took a deep breath hoping it would calm the sound of her voice as she volunteered for her day's chores. "Mama, I'll load the pumpkins on the sled for you." She hoped

29

to accompany Philip to the garden as he pulled the empty sled.

By the time his planning was finished, Papa's plate was empty. "Bessie, thank you for that delicious meal" he squeezed her hand from his position at the head of the table. Margaret looked at the remains of grits and eggs and wondered, How can Papa be so thankful when we're eating such common food. She'd asked the question before and chose to avoid the lecture today so she quietly picked up her plate as well as Jesse's and Mama's and moved to begin cleaning them.

With the kitchen work left in Mama's hands, Margaret headed toward the garden with a quick check in the barn to see if she was needed there to help with milking and feeding.

The little garden patch was in many ways the lifeblood of the family although the sight wasn't very pretty this late in the year. The green vegetation had mostly turned brown. The light orange of the pumpkins stood out and reminded Margaret of how much work she had volunteered for.

She sighed as she noticed that the small sled was already positioned just outside the fence and realized she'd missed Philip's delivering it. While the family had a wagon with big iron wheels, the horses were very accustomed to pulling the homemade sleds. Every farm in the community had these vehicles that were simple boxes mounted on runners made of bent saplings. Without the resources to buy the iron foundation for a traditional wagon, these sleds served most every need the farmers had.

Today, the familiar sled seemed to mock her as she walked around it, as though these strips of wood somehow knew what her plan had been this morning. With a sigh, she bent to retrieve the first round melon. Her mind was temporarily relieved of the Philip Berai concern as she thought of the work before her not only to move this crop to the root cellar, but also every time this winter when she, Mary or Catherine would be sent down to retrieve one for pumpkin pies, pumpkin bread or even the seeds which would be roasted into a crunchy wintertime snack. Mama had taught all of the children to temper their work with thoughts of the end results. Now Margaret could hardly enter the garden, cellar or kitchen without automatically thinking of dozens of good things to come.

With the last pumpkin loaded, she looked at her sad appearance. Her apron was streaked with dirt; wisps of hair had freed themselves from her bun and now hung about her face. Unwilling to ruin her shoes, she had come to the garden barefoot, and now her feet were the same color as the rich garden soil. *Well, maybe it's best that handsome soldier didn't see me in this state. I could hardly make claim to being a lady today!*

Making a futile swipe at the dirt on her apron, she moved toward the backdoor planning to be clean with her hair re-pinned before lunch. As she rounded the corner of the house, she caught a glimpse of Jewel tied outside the barn.

Oh no, she thought. Either she had misjudged her time or they had finished early with the corn. Then she heard the splash from the wash pan – Philip was there, towel drying the water he'd splashed on his face.

Margaret froze, wondering where she should turn. Finishing, Philip lowered the towel and immediately saw her. The smile he offered hinted mischief. "Did you bring the garden back with you?"

Blushing, Margaret sought for a witty reply but her words failed her. Nodding her head with a soft 'uh-huh', she tried to step around him to fill the wash pan with fresh water.

He didn't move out of her way and the porch was small.

"I'll just take this water to the flowers. I don't enjoy carryin' water from the spring to water them and they'll stay pretty a few more weeks if we give 'em a little care. Don't you just think flowers make a place into a home?" Once she opened her mouth, she seemed to prattle endlessly. She felt his eyes following her as she moved to the flowers surrounding the porch. And she smiled, enjoying the knowledge that he was looking - and not caring what his motive might be.

"Did you get your pumpkins loaded?" Philip asked her. "Mr. Elmore asked me to take Jewel or Jenny down to get the sled after dinner. Maybe you could come with me?" Philip was rolling down his sleeves. Today he wore his uniform pants with a plain work shirt rather than the wool sack coat he'd arrived wearing yesterday. Margaret realized this was more serviceable in the warm sunshine. It seemed somehow intimate to see him like this. He seemed to become less a soldier and more a man.

She blushed again, realizing he was looking at her, waiting for her to reply.

"Yeah, they're loaded on the sled." The wash pan clinked against the rough table as she reached around him to drop it on the table. She reached for the water bucket but Philip took it from her and refilled the pan. His head was so close, the coal black hair curling out where it's ends had gotten damp. Margaret took a deep breath and cast about her mind for something to say, some way to regain control of the moment.

"I don't s'pose you're accustomed to such dirty work, are you? I mean, before the war, living in Chicago you must have worked in some office or maybe a bank?" Margaret asked, as she rolled up her own sleeves in an attempt to control her shaking hands.

"Well I've got to get some of the garden out from my nails if I'm to be permitted at Mama's table".

Philip stepped back from the wash stand to allow her to pass. However, he did not move quite far enough and she was sure he would have touched her as she passed, had Jesse not bounded through the crack of the kitchen door. Philip cleared his throat and stepped off the back side of the little porch as Margaret blushed and plunged her hands into the soapy water. She began scrubbing so briskly she felt the sting of the coarse bristles on the tips of her fingers.

Philip went on into the house, leaving Margaret nearly breathless.

With dinner complete, and a brief rest behind the whole family, Papa pushed back his chair signaling everyone to begin their afternoon's work. Margaret hoped to follow Philip out, but Mary had already begun taking warm water out to the back porch where she would wash her hair reminding Margaret that she had promised to help her sister. With a deep breath Margaret grabbed a kettle from the stove and bit back the complaint that this was causing her to miss time talking with Philip

Mary arranged the big wooden tub beside a bowl in which she'd shaved slivers of lye soap and crushed dried lavender. During more prosperous times, Papa would bring home sweet-smelling store-bought soaps for his girls. They had not had any of that for many months but since Mama always kept a good supply of homemade soap, the girls scarcely noticed that their store-bought variety was gone and Mama had long ago taught them to mix in herbs or rose petals to add a nice scent to their hair. Each daughter seemed to prefer a specific scent from among the herbs Mama grew and gathered;

lavender was Mary's preference and she liked to tie up sachets filled with the fragrant dried plants into the folds of the Sunday dress. She already had sprigs of lavender in the soapy water.

As Margaret lathered the long, light brown locks that Mary tossed over her head into the tub, she was torn thinking that maybe she too should take advantage of one of the last warm afternoons and have her hair clean and ready for the cold weather that would surely come quickly now after these frosty mornings. The girls would not often wash their hair during the winter months since Grandma taught them to fear sickness if their head was allowed to be wet and chilled. So, each one would thoroughly brushed her hair each night, a ritual Mama had taught them from early childhood. Mama would often still come upstairs at bedtime to brush for them. Each slept in a long, loose braid and pinned her hair up before starting each day's activities. And they would wash it again when the weather was warm enough, or there was enough time to sit beside the winter fire drying wet hair.

Since Mama considered it indecent for a nearly-grown girl to be seen with her hair loose, Mary would have to spend her afternoon working upstairs so their visitor would not see her. Realizing this, Margaret decided she'd rather take the chance that they would have another sufficiently warm day to wash her own hair, rather than risk missing a few minutes with Philip Berai.

She found herself always mentally speaking his name, rather than thinking of 'the soldier' or 'the visitor' as Mama, Mary and Catherine referred to him amongst themselves. And she was even now trying to devise an opportunity to chat with him alone like she had at the spring house last night.

"I declare, Margaret, are you planning on drownin' or

boilin' me?" Mary had clearly been talking to her for several minutes. "That water is awfully hot; can't you temper it with some of the cool water in that bucket? And where's your head these days? It seems like I'm talkin' to myself even though you are standing right beside me."

"Oh honey I'm sorry I got it too hot," she scooped a dipper full of water from the fresh bucket and added it to the rinse tub.

"Mary, I was thinkin' about Philip Berai and all of the adventures he must've had. Can you even imagine what his life would'a been like in Italy?"

Mary's voice was soft as she tried to call her sister back to reality. She knew from long hours listening to Margaret's dreams and imaginings that the presence of this stranger would be fascinating to her. "Margaret, I 'spect his life in Italy wasn't a great deal different than ours is here. I heard him tellin' Papa that his people were farmers. Only his family didn't own a farm like we do. They had to work for another man, and I don't think it was a very easy life for them."

"Hmm, and we're fightin' a war here on account of makin' people work on other peoples' farms."

Mary patted her hair in a piece of toweling, "Well I don't think he was a slave, more like hired help."

Margaret shrugged, "Either way I'm glad he's come to America and I can't wait to hear what he dreams of doing here."

Mary cocked her head and looked so deeply into Margaret's eyes that the older sister began to squirm. "Why would you care about this Yankee's dreams? Surely you don't think he would be suitable to court do you?"

Again Margaret could only shrug.

"Don't you remember how often Mama has said she

would not trade Papa's humility and faith for the plantation homes down toward Nashville or the finely dressed gentlemen in Memphis? No Margaret, this man is not courtin' material." She looked another moment at her sister seeming to weigh whether she should say more. "Well, I had better get upstairs and brush out the tangles or they will dry in there. Plus, we don't want to be standing out here with my hair down this way."

Margaret truly felt the love Mary was trying to show her. She opened her mouth to try again to show Mary her heart. Surely, if her sister, who loved her so much, could see that God had created her for excitement, that he had built her for adventure, then surely Mary would understand. Surely Mary would urge her sister to leap at the God-given opportunity that Philip Berai represented. She opened her mouth to say, "I have to follow my heart." Yet as she looked at Mary, she could see that she would not understand. Instead, she offered, "You go ahead; I'll put the cool water on the flowers and wipe up the wash stand."

Chapter 4

The big wash tub was far too heavy for her to move alone, so she dipped out pails of water and carried them around the side of the house. Movement caused her to look toward the path to the garden and she realized Philip was leading Jewel to the pumpkin patch to move the sled. Carrying the empty wooden bucket with her, she walked quickly to catch up to him. As she approached the back of the familiar horse, she spoke gently to her, reaching out to put a calming hand on her side.

Philip was whistling and did not stop as she fell into step with the horse and continued along at their pace. As they reached the loaded sled, Philip backed the horse up and Margaret automatically reached for the single tree and attached it to the sled's pulling chain. She was so accustomed to helping in every aspect of the farm that she had the device in her hand before she thought perhaps this would not be lady-like so she gently lay it on the ground hoping he hadn't noticed. Philip reached for the trace chain on his side without a word.

Rubbing her hands free of the dirt one inevitably picked up from the horses, she mentally searched for a conversation topic that would cast a favorable image of her. "Tell me about Chicago. I'd just love to see it. I'll bet there's a lot of interesting people there."

Philip had moved around to her side of the sled to attach the trace chain there. "Well, there certainly are a lot of people there. My brother Joseph came to America two years before me and he had word that good work could be found in Chicago. So he wrote to me and when I arrived in this country, I went straight to find him there. We were working on the docks when Mr. Lincoln put out the word that he wanted troops."

"Oh, you were on the docks! Did you get to see all of the ships comin' and goin'?"

Philip gathered the long reins in his hand and stepped behind the sled. "Well, yes, there are always ships in the port. Of course right now most of the shipments are for support of the army."

Margaret motioned the direction to the root cellar where most of the family's winter provisions were stored. "Don't the river boats come in there that carryin' the fine ladies and gentlemen? They've got real crystal and bone china tea cups you know. I'd just love to see it all!"

Philip clucked to the horse and Jewel obediently took a step forward. As the sled made a bit of a lurch with its first movement Philip concluded their conversation, "I would not know about the passenger boats."

Margaret could see that Philip was finished with the discussion. She walked in silence the rest of the way to the cellar, speaking only when he needed direction and help opening the big cellar doors. Their job was obvious and Margaret gave minimal instructions as they found an open bin to store the pumpkins and began unloading them.

Her mind raced with questions about his life in a big city. She sensed he was tired of talking and she feared she would seem childish if she continued. Margaret was accustomed to whiling away hours of menial farm labor while she dreamed. She retreated to that dream world now. She scarcely noticed the silence or how long they had worked until she saw the floor of the sled and realized they had unloaded a large portion of the crop.

Mama had already filled crocks with pickles and buried heads of cabbage in moss and the hole that was filled with Irish potatoes was well covered with hay. While the cellar smelled of the hay and earthen walls, the provisions stored there assured Margaret the family would not be hungry during the coming winter months.

Philip's voice brought her abruptly back to reality. "You have been quiet a long time. Surely you did not run out of words?" He grinned mischievously and winked at her.

Boys did not wink at her, as a rule. "I guess I's just daydreaming." Another blush crept up her neck. In part, she hoped he couldn't tell that he was the center of those daydreams. On the other hand, she longed for him to know how she was feeling and how very attracted she was to him.

"My but you've made quick work of this load job. It would've taken me all evenin'. I can hardly remember what we did on this farm without you." As she said it, she realized it had only been a day since he arrived.

Why does everything sound so clever in my head and so silly when it comes out my mouth, she wondered?

Philip continued his steady pace carrying one melon after another into the cellar door. "Well, you will remember soon enough; I will be leaving tomorrow or the next day."

Margaret sat down abruptly and unceremoniously on the large wooden stump that was used to tightly secure the cellar doors. She reminded herself to breathe and inhaled deeply. Her thoughts were coming so fast, she could scarcely sort them out. Finally she muttered, "When?"

Philip had not stopped working and he answered her now in short sentences as he passed in and out of the cellar door. "I do not know for sure. No later than Sunday. I have to meet a friend at the provisioning camp in Pleasant Hill on Sunday night. Have you ever been there?"

While Margaret didn't know what a provisioning camp was, she well knew the small community of Pleasant Hill. "Of course I've been there. It's a good long way though. It takes nearly a half day to walk it. Ann Cox married a man from Pleasant Hill; I went to visit her two summers ago with Mrs. Cox. She had just given birth to a beautiful little girl. I think she has another baby now. You know, I don't remember whether it was a boy or another girl."

"You say it is a half of a day's walk?" Philip asked, ignoring the neighborhood news she'd included.

Realizing he had stopped and was looking directly at her, Margaret unconsciously straightened her back despite the pumpkin she had been holding now for several minutes and the terribly uncomfortable stump on which she sat. "Well, yes. If you took the Kentucky Stock Road into Crossville then the roads are better and we always take the opportunity to pick up anything we might need at the general store. Of course, you could go straight along the ridge and it's shorter; then just at the end you get in those hills so the walking is tougher."

Philip seemed to speak almost to himself, "Not knowing the country that might be a hard trip. And I might encounter the Rebel scouting parties anywhere." Then, almost as though he just remembered Margaret was there he asked, "Could you take me there, along the ridge, I mean?"

Margaret nearly gasped. Was he asking her to accompany him? Was this how a man proposed? Surely he meant to whisk her away from the melancholy life this mountain offered. She immediately began planning, scarcely aware that she spoke aloud. "Oh, I would need to do some sewin'. I think Mama has a piece of finely woven ivory she's been saving for one of us. And the church will want to celebrate. We'd want to do it before the winter, of course, since we'll be travelin' to your home in Chicago."

"Winter! Didn't you hear me say that I was leaving in a few days? I have a man in Pleasant Hill who is helping me get the necessary... Uh, he is helping me get home."

"Oh, I don't think we can plan a proper weddin' in two days."

Philip made a slight gulping sound that ended in a quick cough. Lost in her own thoughts, Margaret completely missed the long pause before he said, "Maybe you could just get me started on the right road."

He stepped behind the sled and picking up the cotton driving lines he clucked to the horse and walked off to the barn leaving Margaret speechless and confused.

She sat on the stump, lost in her thoughts, for longer than Mama would have thought reasonable. Mama was always telling her to get her hands working while her head was dreaming. *Well! Why do you reckon he just stopped planning? How will I know what he's wantin' in our wedding? Maybe he'll just leave it up to me. I think the bride usually chooses everything for her wedding. I s'pose he wouldn't want to be married in that dinky little at Clear Creek Baptist Church though.* She felt a pang of shame referring to their precious church as 'dinky'; she had so many sweet memories there. She pushed aside the moment's shame and turned her thoughts back to the beautiful wedding she must plan. *He'll want to go into town to one of the stone buildings with the pretty stained-glass windows.*

As she re-entered the cellar to deposit the last pumpkin, she wondered what kind of churches Pleasant Hill had. After all, she had not really gone into the town when visiting Ann Cox. Only with a quick, fleeting thought did she wonder whether he had really proposed. *What else could it be? He asked me to go with him, so I'd have to be his wife.*

She spent some time tidying the cellar, ensuring the pumpkins were stacked well and that any of the family could easily move around within the small room when they needed to retrieve their stored foods. Then, Margaret joined her mother and sisters in the kitchen just in time to make the final preparations for their evening meal.

As she worked alongside her family her mind whirred with thoughts of Philip Berai and plans of a life with him. Yet something kept her from mentioning it to her mother. She didn't brag to her sisters about the dashing man she'd caught.

She moved about the kitchen automatically, out of step with the normally well-choreographed team. Then she bumped into Catherine with a bowl of steaming beans in her hands, sloshing juice on Catherine's bare feet as well as the spotless wooden floor. Catherine squealed in pain and Mama rushed to her side, "Margaret Elmore, where's your head, child?" In a flash, Mama was grabbing her honey pot and dabbing at Catherine's red skin.

"Oh Cathy, dear Cathy, I'm so sorry. I simply didn't see you there till I was right on top of you. Mama, please let me help her."

Mama's kind eyes rose to look deep into Margaret's. She saw immediately that Mama was not angry with her as she probably should have been. "Margie, you've just got to get your head out of the clouds and focus on the life you've got to live here on earth." She turned back to her doctoring and continued speaking to her children in general, "I have prayed every day of your lives that you'd be focused on our Lord and His work. It is wonderful to dream, but the work God has for you is here right now. And so long as He keeps you alive on this earth, you can rest assured that there'll be work left to do." Satisfied that Catherine's foot would heal, she wrapped a clean rag about it and moved to wash her hands in the tub of warming water. "Well children, we still have to eat, don't we? Margaret, are there enough beans left in there to feed us?"

Margaret still held the kettle, "Yes, Mama, I really only spilled some of the juice off the top. I guess they should've cooked down a little more anyway."

Bessie moved close enough to put her arm around her daughter's shoulder and said, "Margie we just have to get your head down here to earth with the rest of us. You have the sweetest spirit and I know that God has wonderful plan for you. He created this adventurous spirit in you so He surely knows what to do with it."

Margaret's eyes lit up at her Mama's words. Surely she was beginning to understand. She turned to Mama to tell her about Philip's proposal and all of the adventure they would have. However, hustle of the kitchen resumed as Mama cared for Catherine and Mary continued getting the meal together. There was no more chance to talk about Margaret's adventurous spirit.

Mary had seen that the cornbread didn't burn while Mama worked on Catherine's burn. Now, she removed the turnip greens that had been cooking all afternoon from their place on the stove, and the simple meal was ready; it was time to call the family to the table.

Chapter 5

Dawn broke on Sunday morning with a heavy fog over the mountain. As Margaret tried to orient herself to the morning, she slowly realized it was Sunday. She lay there pondering all that had been happening in her world. Her head had been so filled with dreams that she had moved through her chores in a fog as thick as the one hanging over the mountain today. She had been so busy imagining the life she would lead as Mrs. Philip Berai that now she could scarcely remember the last couple of days.

She smiled now, as memories flitted through her mind of moments when she was able to exchange a word with Philip or steal a few minutes alone with him. He had grown bolder with his affection. Margaret caressed her right arm as she remembered his touch as his hand brushed it.

Rising, Margaret looked out the little window. She thought to herself that after the beautiful, clear weather they had been enjoying this fog would certainly roll away shortly, probably before their walk to church. She splashed her face with water chilled by the night in the unheated bedroom. Patting it dry, she peered into the small mirror, thinking how she might arrange her hair beneath the straw hat she kept for her Sunday best.

Disturbed by Margaret's movements in their small bedroom, Mary and Catherine began to stir. She could hear Paul and Jesse in their room as well. Margaret always thought the whole house awoke with a brighter spirit on Sundays. All of the children quickly dressed in everyday clothes and moved downstairs for breakfast before the necessary morning chores.

The first one down, Margaret grabbed a basket and tossed words over her shoulder to her mother, "I'm gonna' to run to the holler and get some of them beautiful purple and gold flowers for the church house."

"You'd have done well to pick flowers while the sun was shinin' yesterday." Mama hardly looked up from her work table as she cut side meat to fry.

Margaret chose a path that would take her right by the barn, hoping that Philip Berai would already be out in the barnyard. Instead, she saw a familiar horse, tied by the back porch rail. She saw Papa and Mr. McCormick leaning against the board fencing. Mr. McCormick was the Sunday School Superintendent and took his responsibilities very seriously. He was usually headed to church at first light to fire the stove, open the shuddered windows and sweep off the front porch. He always had the church feeling warm and welcoming by the time the congregation began to arrive. And he often made this stop at Lawrence Elmore's farm, sometimes sharing a cup of chicory coffee with his neighbor.

She had no intention of eavesdropping on these two old friends' chat, but she caught the word 'soldier' in their conversation and knew immediately they were talking about Philip Berai, so she paused.

"...headed out nearly before daylight" she caught from Papa, and she froze. "He said he was headed back into Crossville; I'm pretty sure he was lyin' to me though. There was just something about him I couldn't 'xactly trust."

Margaret was not interested in hearing more of his

slanderous talk about this wonderful man that had passed through their lives. With the flowers forgotten, she turned back toward the house. What would she do? What could she do? How could Philip be gone? She remembered their chat at the cellar and knew that he had told her he would be gone by Sunday. She had been so busy enjoying him that she had not thought again of the deadline.

Now, she couldn't understand why he had left without a word of good-bye. And why hadn't he taken her with him? He had proposed to her, hadn't he? And then the thought occurred to her that maybe she had not accepted his proposal with the warmth and excitement he had hoped for. Perhaps she had even made him believe she did not wish to marry him. In fact, now that she thought about it, she couldn't remember actually *accepting* his proposal at all! And they had never decided on a time and location for the wedding ceremony.

As thoughts flooded her mind, she felt close to a panic. She would have to act – do something, anything. She couldn't let this man just walk out of her life. Surely, God had sent him here to fulfill all of her dreams. Surely, God intended her to have a life of glamor and adventure and He knew she could not get that life in the Elmore Community. Even as her heart cried out, *Stop him, Lord,* she knew that Philip would not stop, would not return to the farm. She felt hot tears behind her eyes and bit her lip to hold them back. For the briefest moment, she wanted to scream at God, demanding to know why he would ever let Philip leave. She stopped herself. As frustrated and angry as she felt, she feared railing against God.

Margaret decided she would just have to handle this herself.

She was on the move, now. Refusing to consider the

repercussions of her actions, she was simply acting. She would do anything necessary to hold onto this man. She rushed into the house, dropping the basket in its familiar place behind the door. Without a word to Mama or her siblings, who were now working and visiting in the warm kitchen, she charged upstairs. It took her only moments to change into her best blouse. She pinned on her homemade straw bonnet without another thought about her hair. Her thoughts were purely practical now. How long had he been gone? Would she be able to catch him? Which direction was he traveling? He couldn't have been gone very long for the sun was only now showing a bit of light through the thinning fog. Surely she could catch him.

She didn't know how long she would be gone; she didn't care. She knew she would need some things so she grabbed the only travelling bag that either she or her sisters owned. She pulled out her two remaining blouses but discarded the more stained, work-day garment. She shoved the clean blouse in the bag with her hairbrush and, remembering no lady should be without a handkerchief, she pulled a couple from the basket on the girl's dressing table.

Descending the steep stairs, her haste almost made her forget to be stealthy. Hearing Jesse, Paul and Catherine bantering at the table reminded her that she did not want to answer their questions about why she was carrying Grandma's carpet bag this morning. She stepped softly, nearly skipping the last stair. She turned toward the front room instead of following the familiar route through the kitchen. Out the front door, she rounded the house, stepping onto the back porch where Mama's cheese house hung high to keep it safe from mice. She took out a big chunk of cheese and grabbed two apples from the pan sitting on the railing.

Heading toward the road, she saw Mr. McCormick's horse awaiting the end of his chat with Papa. Without a second thought, she untied the reigns and stepped into the saddle. Unladylike though it may be, she was perfectly familiar with riding the plow horses bareback. So she scarcely noticed the inconvenience of riding astride the saddle in her long skirts. In one smooth motion, she made a cluck with her tongue in her cheek, pulled the horse's head around and kicked his ribs. All of this being familiar to the animal, he knew just what his rider was asking. They were out of the yard in a moment, with the sound of Papa and Mr. McCormick in the background. She knew they were yelling questions; there was just no time to explain. Philip was getting farther away with every second.

Now she had only to decide which way to go. She planned to head toward the Kentucky Stock road which led into Crossville. Knowing he left on foot, she felt she could surely catch him before he reached the little town. And what if he opted to try the more difficult route across the ridge? Well, she'd think about that only if her first plan failed.

She rode as quickly as she dared in the fog. This horse well knew the road, but he would still be prone to putting his foot into a hole when travelling at a running walk so she held him back in a flat foot walk. Margaret said a quick prayer of thanksgiving for the smooth gait common among the local saddle horses.

She was right upon Philip before she realized it. She had been watching for the church to come into view, trying to gauge her progress by the familiar landmark. So, when she saw him, turning to face the approaching horse, it almost spooked her. She pulled the horse to such a quick stop that she nearly lost her balance. She recovered because she intended to dismount quickly anyway. She dropped to her feet a bit out of breath and lifted a face alight with her broadest smile.

"Oh, I've found you!" she practically panted. "I didn't realize the day. I thought you were goin' to take me along. I…" She had so much to say. Somehow she found herself unable to get it all out.

Philip looked genuinely glad to see her. "Well, you did not say anything about it so I did not think you wanted to come along. And you've brought us a horse to ride. That will make the journey easier."

"Oh, it's Mr. McCormick's horse. We couldn't take him all the way to Pleasant Hill – that is where you said you had to report, right? Mr. McCormick will be headed to the church, so we can leave the horse there. The church house is just up at the crossroads." She pointed only a few more yards to the little white building.

Philip's eyes followed her finger and he stared at the little white building. He was flattered that this lovely girl had come charging after him on a stolen horse. Yet he realized that either her father or this McCormick man might come chasing after them at any time. He knew it was essential that he get to Pleasant Hill as quietly as possible. He looked again at the girl who stood within arm's reach and he longed to reach out to her. There had been something in Mr. Elmore's eye that kept him in check while they were on the farm. He smiled at her now, happy to have the company. "Well, I suppose the last thing we need is a bunch of men out to retrieve a stolen horse." He took the horse's reigns and resumed his steady pace.

By the time they'd reached the church and Philip tied the horse in front, Margaret had caught her breath and begun to sort her thoughts. "I'll leave a little note for Mr. McCormick. I s'pose I need to apologize to him for causing him to walk from our farm this morning."

She located a scrap of paper in her bag and Philip pulled a piece of pencil from his uniform blouse. Margaret jotted a quick note saying each word aloud as she wrote, "Sir, I thank you for the use of your horse. I do apologize for forcing your walk this morning. Mr. Berai and I are on our way to his home in Chicago to marry and begin our life there together." She folded the note just under the saddle without offering it for Philip's approval.

Having unhooked her carpet bag from the saddle's pommel, she turned to Philip, "Well, Mr. Berai, we are ready for our journey." She turned east toward the sunrise and the Kentucky Stock Road.

After a quarter hour's walk they had met no one on the Clear Creek Road. Margaret knew that the early hour on a Sunday morning had all of her neighbors completing the work the farm required each morning, before heading to church. The road seemed particularly quiet and though she'd tried to encourage Philip to talk to her, he seemed solemn. Trying hard not to annoy him, Margaret attempted to be quiet. Still, if she was to guide him to Pleasant Hill, he would have to make a decision on their route.

"That's Keyes Road up yonder. If you wanted to go 'cross the ridge, that would be the road to take."

Philip looked intently toward the dirt road fading into the overhanging woods just ahead. "And this is the way we would go to avoid the town?"

"Well, you wouldn't go through Crossville unless you went on to the Kentucky Stock Road. 'Course it's a hard walk. You have to cross a tough ridgeline to get through here."

Philip had quickly made his decision despite Margaret's attempt to shed a brighter light on the Crossville route. He had his eyes set far down Keyes Road and she saw no choice but to follow him.

After about an hour, Margaret saw a group moving toward them having just come off the Plateau Road. With a smile, she raised her hand in greeting and called out a cheery, "Hello". She did not yet recognize anyone in the group, still her childhood teaching demanded she greet them.

"Good morning" called an adult woman in the group. "Well, I believe that's one of the Elmore girls, ain't it? You're Bessie's daughter?"

As the lady greeted her, Margaret searched her memory for a name. The lady was pleasant, smiling as she spoke to her. However, she did seem to have one eye on Philip, and Margaret was keenly aware of his Union uniform. Having made recognition of the lady, she tried to draw her attention away from Philip. "Why yes, I'm Bessie's second daughter, Margaret. And you would be Mrs. Blaylock, wouldn't you?" She had paused in the road as the two parties met and now she turned to Philip to introduce him but found him not at her side. He was several yards down the road. He had not stopped when she did, just continued on his way. She blushed slightly and turned back to the Blaylock family to excuse herself, "Pardon me please; I have to catch up to my fiancée."

By running just a short way, Margaret caught Philip. "We really must be friendly to the neighbors we meet. That has always been Papa and Mama's rule."

She received no answer. She was surprised that Philip wasn't a more pleasant traveling partner. Whenever she and Mary, or she and any of the neighbor girls walked these roads, they had a marvelous time talking together. She tried to reason why Philip wasn't more fun and decided he was probably making plans in his head. That always seemed to be why Papa would be quiet.

Thereafter, when they met families walking along the road, Margaret simply made a cheery wave and called greetings to them. Although she was very disappointed not to be able to introduce her handsome fiancée to the distant neighbors, she did not again attempt it.

Sighting pooled water at the side of the road, Margaret said, "Philip, I'm getting awfully tired and hungry. We left before breakfast you know. I've got some apples and cheese here, why don't we sit at this spring and eat a bite?"

Philip agreed they needed a break and threw down his haversack. He rolled his bedroll halfway out to allow Margaret to sit without soiling her skirt. From the haversack, he pulled a pone of cornbread wrapped in what Margaret recognized was her mother's kitchen towel. They made a lunch of the bread and a portion of the cheese. "Better not eat everything now, we will need something later on."

Margaret didn't understand him. "Surely there will be supper ready at the inn."

Philip did not answer. He'd dipped his canteen into the spring and drank the cold water. Un-strapping a tin bucket from his belt he passed it to Margaret.

"What's this?" she asked him.

"The army calls it a mucket. You can drink your water from it."

Margaret was fascinated by the utensil which had a lid on hinges and both a handle like a mug and a bell like a bucket. She did fill it with the spring water and truly enjoyed the drink, realizing only when she felt the water against her parched lips just how thirsty she'd become. The dampness of the fog had made her feel colder than was comfortable. Now, however, the sun had pushed all sign of the mist away and warmed her cheek. By its position in the sky, she knew it was about 10:00. She guessed they were half way to Pleasant Hill, and noted their progress aloud. "I guess we're halfway there now. If we keep this pace, we'll be just after dinner time getting' there. You have friends we are meeting, is that right?"

"Yes, there is a man who will help us get on our way back to the north." Philip was willing to answer her questions although he never gave any extra information.

So Margaret ate her snack, enjoying cold cornbread as much as she could.

The following three hours were spent in quiet, quick walking. Margaret guided Philip through the crossroads onto the Plateau Road and continued onto the Tanner Road. The sun was high in the sky when Margaret began to notice landmarks of Pleasant Hill. She turned to Philip to tell him so, but he was already on the alert. They had not seen a soul along the way for the past hour or two and Margaret knew that all of the local folks were in their respective church services. So, when they heard the familiar clop of horse hooves and jingle of harness chains their attention was quickly turned to the coming wagon. Philip however did more than turn his attention. He grabbed Margaret's sleeve and pulled her off the road into a small thicket at the side of the road. Putting his finger to his lips, he motioned for her to be quiet. As her mouth formed a question, he put his hand over her mouth to silence the question. Unwilling to move even her head, she rolled her eyes to the roadway to see a loaded wagon surrounded by a half dozen uniformed soldiers pass. Margaret knew nothing about the armies, their individual units, or their uniforms. Still, those men appeared to be dressed the same as Philip, and not at all as she remembered Matthew when he left two years ago.

The pair remained hidden several minutes after the wagon had passed. Only when Philip straightened did Margaret dare look deep into his eyes with the unspoken questions. He understood her.

"I am in no mood to answer their questions," was all he said and after double checking the road, he again began walking toward Pleasant Hill.

Margaret followed.

Shortly after noon, they arrived in Pleasant Hill. She knew they had arrived because she saw the Pleasant Hill Methodist Church and the general store with a sign for the post office over a small door on the side. She realized that Philip, too, knew they had arrived. He clearly was no longer looking to her for direction. And neither did he seem to care whether she was able to keep up with him. He walked very directly toward the general store, making his way to the side. Thinking that he was going to the post office door, Margaret quickened her pace to reach him and remind him that today was Sunday and therefore the post master would not be in. Before she could reach him, he passed the post office door and slipped behind the general store building. Now, Margaret saw a small, log building, probably a corn crib although it seemed to no longer be in use. It appeared to be empty, and surely everyone would have their corn out of the fields by this time. She was at his side when they reached the structure and Philip stepped inside.

"Philip, are you gonna to tell me what we're a'doin' out here?"

"There is a man who will meet us here but not until after dark. He has made... uh, he has my traveling orders."

"Why have we have gotta wait out here? Where is your camp, couldn't we just go there and get your orders?"

Philip first looked frustrated, but his face softened and he reached out to touch her shoulder. "Now you know I could not take a lady into a Union camp, especially a southern lady. Anyway, are you not tired as I am? We will just rest here and maybe we can move again in the evening."

Philip took off his haversack and bedroll. With the side of his foot, he pushed the corn husks into a pile and shook out his blanket over them. Realizing he was settling in for a long rest, Margaret felt she must remind him that they had not taken care of critical business.

Margaret continued to gently press the issue. "Philip, we could probably see the Methodist minister, I saw the church just a little ways back. I'm sure he'd marry us, even though it's Sunday and we ain't from his congregation. I wonder if he knows Ann Cox. I b'lieve she married a Methodist man."

Philip had pulled his forage cap down low on his brow so that she could scarcely see his eyes. Unsure what she should do, Margaret paced a few steps in the tiny building and made a quick turn to face Philip. She wrung her hands as she turned from man to door, and looked from face to floor.

For the first time, she began to realize that this morning she walked, no she ran, away from everything Mama had taught her. She found herself whispering, speaking to herself, *What must I do? Should I try to get back home? I don't think I can make it back home before dark and Papa has strictly warned us not to be on the road after dark, what with all the soldiers and foragers around. I wish I could remember where Ann Cox lives. I know, I'll go to the Methodist church and ask their minister where she lives. I'm sure he'll know and I can go stay with her until daylight tomorrow. Ann will let me stay there, I just know she will.*

Philip pushed back his cap with one finger, "Why are you pacing about like that and acting so nervous? Why don't you stretch out and get some rest?"

Margaret's eyebrows shot as high as her voice, "Mr. Berai, I can NOT sleep here, alone, in this barn with a man I ain't married or kin to. I understand if you want to be married in your home in Chicago, but I'm gonna have to stay somewheres else 'til we move on outta here."

Philip had been watching Margaret closely over the last few days at her family's farm. And she had given him every opportunity to study her. However, this was a side he had not seen. She suddenly exhibited a strength of character that his plan had not anticipated. He needed to meet a man after dark. Until then, his only priority was to stay out of sight until he could get the papers that would give him safe passage out of the war zone. He had mainly needed Margaret to get him to Pleasant Hill as directly as possible; she had done that and now he no longer required her help. However, he certainly couldn't let this girl sound alarms that would bring the sentries down on him before he got his papers. He leapt to his feet and grabbed her wrists, immediately loosening his grip but his tone remained as gruff as that first touch. "I will not have you going to the minister and raising a lot of questions. We cannot let anyone know that we are here."

Confused, her voice softened as she asked him, "I don't understand why? You're here to meet your Army group, they wouldn't care just when you arrived, would they?"

Philip dropped his hands and in almost the same

motion flopped back onto his corn-shuck bed, "No, Margaret, I am meeting a single soldier. I arranged for him to bring papers and possibly a horse to this barn."

Her eyes widened, she'd heard of the covert work some soldiers did. "Oh, are your orders secret then? Well, I'm sure if we explain that you are on a secret mission for the Union army then the minister will not tell anyone."

Philip saw the firm set of her jaw and something about the light in her eyes assured him that she would not be relaxing there with him while they waited for his buddy to arrive. "Tomorrow I will try to find the Justice of the Peace. I'm sure Pleasant Hill has one." Hoping this would buy some time before she left, he shut his eyes again.

"I am sorry Sir. That just won't do. I'm a'goin' to find me somewhere to stay the night." With that, Margaret turned to open the door.

Chapter 6

With the first creak of the wooden door and its rusted iron hinges, Philip was on his feet again and reaching for her. "Wait, *Maagherete*..."

Margaret couldn't help but pause when she heard him speak her name in that lyrical way; she felt like he was singing it and she turned to him waiting to hear the rest.

Philip saw her shoulders relax as she turned to him and he softened his voice, We will have to find another way. I suppose we can go talk to that minister."

Philip pulled her behind him and peered out the cracked door. Seeming satisfied, he stepped out and moved to cross the field rather than returning to the road in front of the general store. Margaret followed. It was only a matter of a few yards to reach the small house sitting beside the whitewashed church building. The little house was neatly painted and Margaret saw gingham curtains at the window. There was a wisp of smoke coming from the rock chimney. Philip walked to the back porch but Margaret stopped him. "We can't go into the back door when we are visitin' a minister that we don't even know." And she walked around the house to the front door without looking back to see if Philip followed.

As she raised her hand to rap on the door, she heard Philip stepping onto the low porch behind her. She closed her eyes to breathe a quick prayer of thanksgiving and stepped aside to allow Philip to take the lead in summoning the minister. The door was promptly opened by a small lady with a soft grey bun atop her head. She greeted Margaret with a warm smile then turned her eyes to Philip, "Hello. Oh, you are one of the soldiers. Have you been to our church?"

"Ah, No Madame, I have not had the pleasure. I would like to speak with your husband."

The graying head dipped an acknowledgment and she stepped aside to allow the couple to enter. Theirs was one of the warmest, most welcoming homes that Margaret had ever known. It was simple and sparsely furnished with a small fire burning in the fireplace and an aroma that combined the familiar scents of chicory and apples.

"Please have a seat. My name is Hattie Lowe, please call me Hattie. My husband is Thomas and he's in the back room. He often lies down for a few minutes on Sunday afternoon, but he'll be happy to see you. Just have a seat at the table there, I'll be right back." She disappeared through a heavy curtain beside the fireplace. Margaret thought her voice sounded different than her own family's.

Doing as she'd been told, Margaret pulled out one of the split bottom chairs that surrounded a large table in the center of the room. There were two rockers placed at the front windows padded by cushions. And she noticed a brightly dyed chair mat covering the woven bottom of the chair she sat in. Philip continued to stand, his eyes turned to the front window.

It was only a moment before a small man with little round glasses stepped out of the curtained room Hattie had entered. She was directly behind him.

He looked from Margaret to Philip, "Hello children, I am Thomas Lowe. How can I help you today?"

Philip hesitated just a moment, then turned from the

window with his hand outstretched to the minister, "Good afternoon Father, I am Philip Berai."

Mr. Lowe took Philip's hand and gently corrected him, "I am only a humble servant of our Heavenly Father. You can call me Brother Lowe, or Mr. Lowe if you prefer."

"I beg your pardon, Sir. I was taught to call the priest 'Father'."

Mr. Lowe continued to smile up at Philip, who stood several inches taller than him. "What is your faith, son?"

"I am Catholic." He seemed to have momentarily forgotten that there was any other faith. "Again, I beg your pardon, Sir. In my homeland, few people are not of my faith. However, I have learned since coming to America, that there are many faiths here."

As the Reverend Lowe looked into the eyes of this young man, he saw a deep need. A quick glance to the young lady told him that she was not going to fill that need. He needed to learn more about the soldier standing in his front room. He pulled out the chair at the head of the table and motioned for Philip to take another chair. "And where is your homeland?"

"Italy, Sir. Falerna, Italy."

"Ah, yes. You're fighting in our civil war, but your home has wars of its own doesn't it?"

Philip seemed to relax more than Margaret had seen all day. "Yes Sir, that is why I came to America. My mother did not want her sons to die in war. She worked very hard to pay our passage to America. I am sure it hurt her very badly when she received my letter telling her I was going to war here."

"Well, we don't have a Catholic church in Pleasant Hill. I will certainly help you in any way I can though." Turning to Margaret for the first time, he smiled, "And what is your name dear?"

"I'm Margaret Elmore, Sir."

Philip seemed to recall for the first time their reason for visiting the minister as the man asked, "Elmore? Then you two are not married?"

Margaret blushed slightly and shook her head.

Her response pained the minister and he was almost sorry he'd asked. He had known the answer anyway.

Margaret spoke without looking at him, "No sir, fact is that's why we've come to you you today."

Thomas Lowe looked from one face to the other. "Margaret, do you live in Pleasant Hill?"

"No Sir, my family lives in Elmore community about half a day's walk east of here. I don't suppose you know of it, do you?"

"No, child, I'm afraid I don't know that community, although the Elmore name is familiar to me. I'm afraid I can't place it at the moment."

A fresh light touched Margaret's face, this man must know of her family. "One of my neighbors, Ann Cox, married a man from Pleasant Hill a couple of years ago. Do you know her?"

"Ah, yes, I do know her. They are a faithful part of my congregation."

Brother Lowe paused as he began to understand what they wanted from him. He breathed a quick prayer for guidance. The picture seemed obvious to him, at least it was growing clearer. This girl had run away from her home with the soldier. Now, they would ask him to marry them. If he said no, there would be almost no way to preserve her reputation or moral character – not to mention getting her back home to her family.

He was left to ponder the consequences if he agreed to marry them. He looked at Margaret and while he didn't know her personally, he was confident he knew the nature of her local upbringing and the religious instruction she would undoubtedly have received. A closer look at Philip told him this was not a young man; he appeared to be well into his thirties, if not beyond. An immigrant and a Roman Catholic, the reverend could only guess at his upbringing and his past.

Still hoping for a better outcome, he resolved that it would be better to marry them than allow this girl to leave with the soldier unwed, the reverend raised his head and braced himself against the unpleasant task.

During this brief pause in the conversation, Margaret had a moment of fear that Philip would make some excuse and leave without completing the marriage. She was resolved that she would stay here with the minister if that happened; surely they would help her.

Meanwhile, Philip looked at Margaret with that unspoken question of what he should do; his eyes conveyed a hesitation and also an understanding that he must continue on. He wondered if he left this young girl here with the Lowes whether she would cause trouble for his return to Chicago. As he looked at her, he saw again how beautiful she was. He smiled at the thought that it would be very pleasant to have her along instead of traveling alone. He had seen how her family functioned and knew that she would be an asset to him as he built his fortune. His mother had certainly taught him to marry carefully lest the woman break him.

Philip realized his internal debate had lasted a long moment when the old man's head shifted slightly for a different view of the soldier.

"Mr. Berai, is that your desire as well?" The Reverend Lowe asked.

Philip cleared his throat, "Uh, umm, well Sir, uh-yes Sir, we are wanting to be married. I am being ordered northward and Miss Elmore will accompany me."

"Oh, I see." Reverend Lowe's eyes darted to Margaret, "Miss Elmore, do you not have a home church and minister?"

Margaret blushed again, "Yes Sir, but we had to come to Pleasant Hill to get Mr. Berai's papers and, well…" Margaret wasn't sure how to tell him that she had run away quite suddenly and that only after she got to Pleasant Hill had she gotten around to urging Philip to take care of this crucial business.

The old minister blinked very slowly, seeking divine guidance on his next step. He looked closely at Margaret as though he would say more to her.

Margaret searched for a way to defend her moral character to this stranger. How could she make him understand that she insisted that Philip marry her before they set off on the long trip to Chicago? She desperately did not want him asking if her parents knew where she had gone or if they had blessed the union. She looked pleadingly at him, begging with her eyes that he not ask too many questions.

The minister looked sadly at his wife as he very slowly stood. He took the three steps to retrieve his prayer book from atop the mantle and said to her, "Mrs. Lowe, will you witness for them?" The couple had seen too many similar scenarios, especially in these war years. With death so near at hand for the soldiers, no one wanted to wait to pledge their eternal love and devotion.

With a nod of her head, she stepped behind Margaret

and gently pushed her up from the chair, she guided her to stand beside her intended and the minister began the simple vow.

As Margaret waited for her turn to speak in the ceremony she looked closely at Philip and tried to imagine what it would be like to spend the rest of her life with him. He was so handsome, and his voice was somehow exotic with the strange, melodic accent. She wondered if they would go to Italy for him to introduce her to his mother; whenever a girl was to marry any boy from neighboring communities, it was such a big deal when he introduced her to his family. Of course, no one from Elmore had ever gone to Italy to meet anyone's mother.

Mrs. Lowe's gentle touch on her shoulder prompted her to return her attention to the vows she was taking; she had missed her cue. "Yes," she responded to the minister's question scarcely knowing what he'd asked.

Philip answered accordingly and Brother Lowe pronounced them husband and wife. Philip looked deeply into Margaret's eyes and his whole face smiled as he gently kissed his bride. He turned to the minister, thanking him, and promptly asked what he owed for the service. With tear-moistened eyes, Mrs. Lowe embraced Margaret.

The sun was beginning to sink below the horizon as the new Mr. and Mrs. Philip Berai stepped out the door of the parsonage hand in hand. As he closed the door, Margaret tried to look deeply into Philips eyes; tried to read his thoughts and emotions. A few hours ago, as they walked into this house, she had felt desperate. Now a profound sense of relief washed over her. "Darling Philip" she began and realized how good it felt to bestow endearments on her husband, "Dear, were you wantin' to marry in your Chicago where you've got family and friends? I hope that won't be a disappointment for you."

Philip's focus had changed the moment he stepped outside. He was moving quickly back toward the little log building. He still held Margaret's hand, almost absentmindedly, and was nearly dragging her across the field. He didn't answer her nor even acknowledge her questions.

In the fading light, she saw a flicker of movement from the corner of the general store then heard the distinct clop of a horse's hoof. Philip did not alter his direction. Once they were in the little building, Philip positioned himself just in front of the door and Margaret noticed a revolver in his hand.

"Philip, are we in danger?" Margaret whispered.

Still he didn't answer; his eyes were focused on the approaching man. Following his gaze, Margaret saw a Union soldier approaching. He walked quickly and cast furtive glances over his shoulder, carefully watching the road which passed the general store. Margaret heard Philip take a slow breath and sensed that this was the messenger he'd been expecting. As the man drew closer, Philip stepped out of the building's shadow and offered an outstretched hand to the stranger.

Margaret did not move from the shadows and she was never sure the man even realized she was present. She watched and tried to listen, but their voices were so soft she could only catch an occasional phrase or stray word. She understood they were talking about a horse, yet Margaret didn't see a horse anywhere around. The man handed Philip some folded papers and Philip passed to him a sheaf of bills – even in the dim light she recognized it as money and she did not understand why.

The pair turned and she knew the stranger was preparing to leave. "Has there been any sign of the Rebs?" Philip asked.

"Some, just scavenging parties though. Probably locals trying to take advantage of the Union provisions here." The stranger stepped out of Margaret's hearing.

Several minutes passed. Margaret was tired yet she didn't dare move until Philip returned. She saw him before she really heard him so she knew he had not gone far, just out of sight in the now-dark night.

"Philip, was that money you gave him? Were you buying a horse for us?"

"No, he could not get a horse; we will walk to the train. We will leave at first light, it is a long walk I think." He reached out for her arm which he took with surprising delicacy. Without striking a match, he returned to the bedroll he'd left earlier and tugged at her arm to follow him. When she hesitated, he said, "It is okay Margaret, you are my wife now."

Her legs practically buckled beneath her, both from exhaustion and raw nerves. She had longed for this man's attention but now she felt somehow soiled by his touch. He touched her cheek and realized she was soundlessly crying. He wrapped his arms around her and reclined against the log walls. Margaret felt like a scared little girl comforted by her strong uncle. And with that comfort, she slept.

Margaret's first thought on waking was '*cold*'. It seemed to be the coldest morning she had ever known. She felt Philip stirring and turned as he spoke to her. It was still very dark inside the tiny building.

"We have to get moving Margaret."

She could barely see him. "It's not even daylight. Can we build a fire?"

"No, we have to get on the road, before the sun is up if possible."

"I don't understand…" Philip interrupted her protests, tugging at the bedroll and forcing her to either stand or sit on the dusty floor and corn fodder. In a matter of minutes, he had rolled his blankets, folding in his few personal items. He tied the ends of the blankets closed, then tied the two ends together and laid the woolen tube beside his haversack.

Margaret was shaking as she tried to restrain the stray locks of hair that tumbled about her face. Seeing her struggle, Philip handed her a small mirror which she could barely see in the dim light. From her own bag she retrieved her hairbrush and attempted to re-assemble the bun that she'd slept on. She remembered how often Mama had sat with her girls brushing their hair before bedtime and felt a pang of homesickness. She brushed at her skirts and straightened her blouse trying desperately to look like she'd come from anywhere besides a night in a barn.

Philip broke into her contemplation, "Are you ready? We really must go now." He was turning toward the door as he spoke and she felt he might walk right out while she was still composing herself.

"Yeah, I can go now. Where're we going?"

Philip was hoisting the haversack onto his back and arranging the bedroll across his chest as he answered, "A place called Sparta. We can catch the train there. Do you know that place?"

"Well, I know it. We had a map of Tennessee in school and our teacher filled in as many of the small towns as he could. I always loved looking at that map."

A small sigh escaped from Philip, "You have never been there? You do not know the road?"

As she stepped out the door he held open she answered

him, "No, I've never been there. Don't think Papa ever went there either. He went to Nashville one time; he often tells us about Nashville and I've longed to see it. There is a beautiful building where the government works, Papa went there. You think we'll go to Nashville while we're trav'ling?"

Ignoring her question Philip continued to talk about his destination. "Well that is too bad. It would have been good if you had known the way. The man told me we can just stay on the Old Stage Road and it will take us right to Sparta." Hitching the haversack higher on his back, he looked carefully up and down the road before he stepped from the field.

Watching Philip's careful check of the road, Margaret wondered if he feared being run over by a wagon and it struck her as silly. *No one is anywhere to be seen at this hour!* She kept silent because somehow, Philip seemed more serious right now than she had ever known him to be.

The walk to Sparta was as solemn as the last half of yesterday's trip had been. Her stomach grumbled and reminded her she hadn't eaten anything since Hattie Lowe had kindly offered them side meat and stewed potatoes with carrots. Thinking of the leftovers the reverend and Mrs. Lowe had shared, Margaret smiled. She had many times imagined welcoming neighbors into her own home and making a quick snack out of leftovers waiting on the stove's warming shelf. Now, she felt that dream was close to coming true.

She had so many questions about her new home. However, each time she asked Philip, he seemed reluctant to answer her. *He's just waitin' to surprise me,* she decided. The waiting was causing her imaginations to grow! For now, she was going to need to eat something.

"Philip, ain't you gettin' hungry? I've got some cheese

left, if you'll just stop a minute while I get it out of my bag."

Philip's pace did not slow, as he reached into the deep pocket of his sack coat and brought out a bundle, wrapped in a handkerchief. Unwrapping it, he handed her strips of jerky and shoved a couple in his mouth. "Here we can eat this."

"Thank you. Is it deer?"

"I think so. A friend gave it to me, said he took it off an Indian. I do not think that's true though. The Indians were removed thirty years ago."

Margaret could hardly talk as she tried to work the leather-like meat into something she could swallow. Seeing her struggle, Philip slipped his canteen from his neck and handed it to her. With enough water to wash down the bite of jerky Margaret was able to say, "Oh there are lots of Indians around. Grandpa had a friend in Crab Orchard who was Cherokee. He came to visit Grandpa when he was sick. I was very small and he seemed so tall and strong. Grandpa liked him a lot."

Philip had stopped abruptly as she talked. He first had a hard look as though he were about to fuss at her, but then a slow smile began at one side of his mouth then reached up to his eyes. "Do you ever stop talking?"

Margaret's eyes popped wide; she was afraid he was angry with her. When she noted the glint in his eyes she too smiled – a bright, beautiful smile. This was her husband and she had done something to please him, although she was not entirely sure just what she'd done. Without comment, she walked on chewing on the jerky.

Chapter 7

With the warming sun, the chill of the morning was forgotten and Margaret was soon breaking a sweat. They had walked for hours when she began to hear a strange hissing somewhere in the distance. She knew the time by the heat of the sun upon her back as well as the growing hunger in her belly. She didn't dare mention it again to Philip for fear he would offer more jerky. She'd drunk his entire canteen trying to swallow the dry meat and it had served to stave off her hunger for a while. Still, the longer she walked, the more her hunger grew. She thought, *Surely we will have a nice lunch when we reach Sparta. I wonder what kind of town it is. I've hardly heard of it; wish I could ask Papa whether he's been here.*

"Philip, you ain't got much to say today and I've got a million questions for you," she tried again to start a conversation.

He didn't even turn to look at her as he answered, "It is important to keep watching for our enemies."

Margaret's eyes widened and she looked deeply into the scrub brush on one side of the roadway then turned to stare across a field littered by brown corn stobs. She almost asked whether there was much chance they'd run into Matthew but thought better of it since she still hadn't mentioned her soldier-brother to him.

She was accustomed to long hours on her feet, even to walking for hours at a time but Philip had pushed her hard this morning, darting off the road anytime they heard someone approaching. She watched as a group of soldiers marched behind a handful of horses ridden by officers and was quite sure the men they hid from were wearing Union uniforms. She didn't understand this mission Philip had been sent on yet she chose not to question him. This was Army business after all. Exhausted, she was looking down at her feet, concentrating on the next step when Philip took her wrist. She expected him to pull her off the road again. This time he was only stopping her. She followed his gaze and realized they had reached a mining community.

She immediately saw the source of the strange noise she'd been hearing for miles. A shiny black engine sat on the rails seeming to breathe steam in and out; occasionally it would let out the high pitched 'hiss', as though the big engine were sighing. Margaret had never been this close to a train and the engine seemed somehow sad to her.

"Philip, is this our train? Is this what we will ride to Chicago?" She more questions with each passing moment and she realized her voice was squeaking like a little child's.

Philip seemed to relax just a tiny bit as they covered the remaining yards to reach the train. "I will try to get us on this train, if it is headed to the north."

As they drew closer to the train, Margaret realized there were endless cars behind it, filled with coal. In fact, she did not see any car that would carry passengers. Nor was there a depot sitting beside this parked train. She had visited Chattanooga as a young girl and knew that the trains stopped at a station. Builders still worked on the station she had seen in Chattanooga but here she didn't even see a partially-built station.

Philip was asking each man they met who was in charge

of the train. They pointed him toward the big smoking engine where Margaret could see two or three men moving inside; Philip started toward the train and Margaret hurried to keep up with him.

Margaret was filled with excitement to be so close to this iron horse. She had heard many stories from Papa and Grandpa about riding on the trains. Mama had ridden a train once from Nashville to Louisville, Kentucky when she was a very young lady. She told Margaret and her brothers and sisters the story like a fairytale. Now Margaret could almost reach out and touch a train. She reached her hand toward it just as a puff of steam escaped, causing her to jump. She moved farther away as her excitement and curiosity were tinged with fear.

As they reached the front of the engine, a tall man stepped out to greet them. He had the biggest mustache Margaret had ever seen and his cheeks showed streaks of black. "Can I he'p you folks?"

Philip stretched out his right hand to shake the man's. At the same time, he pulled folded papers from his bedroll and spoke in such a commanding voice Margaret shot a look toward him to confirm it was the same man she'd been following behind for the past two days. "I have orders and need a ride north toward Chicago. Where is this load bound?"

The man looked from Philip to Margaret and back. "Well, it's a'goin' to St. Louie, but it's all coal."

Without turning his head, Philip's eyes darted to the siding where a lone passenger car sat. "You do have a passenger car though, correct?"

The engineer looked straight into Philip's eyes; he cast a furtive glance first at the Union uniform and then at the rifle slung across his shoulder. "Millard, get the passenger car hitched," he called to one of the men in the engine. With that, he walked away from them.

Placing a guiding hand at her elbow, Philip moved Margaret away from the puffing engine and they found a relatively quiet spot still within sight and an easy walk to the train. "We will wait here, it may be awhile." Philip was untying his bedroll and laid it on the dusty ground for her.

Margaret realized she had been dozing when she opened her eyes and saw Philip walking toward her with his canteen dripping water. "I found their well and got some cool water for you" he said as he handed her the canteen.

"How long did I sleep? It looks like there are a lot more cars hooked there." Margaret surveyed the growing train.

"They have loaded a few more coal cars and hooked them to the rear. I don't think they are very happy about our riding because they sandwiched the passenger car between the coal cars. It should have been hooked right behind the tender car. Even though the train is burning wood, if we ride behind all that coal, we will look like miners by the time we reach St. Louis."

"St. Louis? Why, I've never even dreamed of going there. How long will we stay there?" Margaret cared little about the inconvenience of her car's placement when offered the prospect of visiting that great city. She had read of St. Louis, but had never known anyone to visit there.

Philip smiled, "We will not be seeing the city on this trip, only change trains there. It would not be wise to try to do any sightseeing right now."

Margaret tried not to let her disappointment show and attempted changing the subject to cover her over-eager reaction to the St. Louis stop. "Has there been fighting there?"

"No, I do not believe so. The Union has held the city since the beginning of the war. A lot of Negroes have fled there. But I think there are a number of rebel sympathizers. All in all, it is a pretty dangerous place to be, especially for us."

Margaret sat quietly, mulling over the 'especially for us' comment. She smiled to hear that Philip was concerned for her safety. She had listened to enough of Papa's political discussions with neighbors and family to know that Tennessee's presence in the Confederacy might not serve her very well in Missouri or Illinois. In the back of her mind she could hear Mama's voice teaching, "It's best not to tell everything you know," and she reminded herself to do just that as she and Philip traveled to her new home.

Margaret's pondering abruptly ended with the rising pitch of the steam engine. As she and Philip sat waiting, they had become accustomed to the constant hiss of the engine. She thought it seemed alive, breathing the gray smoke and allowing an occasional huff to escape. Philip had explained the 'huff' had to do with pressure although he could not answer more specific questions.

Now, the big engine seemed to breathe more heavily, like a horse panting after a run. The huffing sound seemed to come less often, but it was much louder when it did occur. Looking more closely at the curious machine, Margaret saw the big man with the mustache moving about inside, another man seemed to be frantically throwing wood at the interior of the engine. A third man, on the ground was dwarfed by the size and occasionally obscured by the steam escaping. It was clear that something was happening, and Margaret was drawn to the action. She stood to get a better view and had to restrain herself from rushing to the side of the big iron horse.

Philip noticed it too. He began to assemble his bedroll into the tube that he would wear across his shoulder. Margaret had been so engrossed by the activity that Philip was at her side before she realized it. "Come, I think we can board now."

He left a wide berth and positioned himself between Margaret and the hissing engine. When she stumbled over a big stick, he placed a firm hand on her elbow he chided, "Margaret, you really must watch where you are stepping or you will fall."

She nodded her understanding without looking at him. When she could tear her eyes away from the activity at the front of the train, Margaret realized how long the train had grown. And she saw their passenger car nearly at the end of the long line of coal cars. The big man with the mustache stepped from the engine as they passed, pulling a watch from the bib of his striped overalls. "Glad you're here. We'll be pulling out in five minutes." He snapped the watch closed and pulled himself back up the iron steps without another word.

Philip seemed unimpressed by the activity. "He does not seem happy despite his words. He must be a rebel sympathizer because I think he would just as quickly leave us as take us."

Reaching the passenger car, Margaret found a rough wooden step placed on the ground. Philip held her hand as she lifted herself up into the car, careful not to trip on her long skirt. Once inside, she gave her skirt a good shake and turned to enter the seating compartment.

As the train chugged its way to St. Louis Philip remained as quiet as he'd been walking along the dusty road. But Margaret didn't need conversation now. She'd never ridden a train nor had she ever left Tennessee. As the day wore away she stared out the window until the landscape was completely black. Even then, she was unable to sleep. Philip didn't seem to notice the hard, wooden seat or the constant jerking of the car as he slept. Margaret tried to close her eyes. Somehow, the combination of seat sounds and excitement seemed to chase sleep from her.

As her mind quieted a bit, she couldn't help but think about her family and what would be happening on the farm tonight. As she imagined their daily routine, it occurred to her for the first time that they might be worried about her. She dismissed the idea, assuring herself that they would somehow know what a great adventure she was enjoying.

Eventually, exhaustion won out and Margaret slept. She awoke disappointed that she had missed so much of the trip. Philip would have preferred to sleep the whole trip away. "Be happy that you weren't awake a little while ago. I made the mistake of opening a window and coal dust flew in like snow during a blizzard. And I think these seats get harder with every turn of the wheel."

"Oh Philip, how can you complain? This is a wonderful adventure." And she turned back to the window, admiring the flat lands they were now passing through.

She lost all track of time until the train began slowing noticeably. Philip roused and told her they were surely approaching St. Louis. In only a moment, he had all of his gear on his back and the rifle in his hand.

She had to ask him, "Are you expecting trouble at the station? Didn't you say your people are in control of the city?"

"No, there should not be any trouble – not from the Confederates anyway." He tried to sound unconcerned, but she couldn't help noticing the way his eyes were darting from one side of the train to the other, and his hand now rested on his belt where he carried the revolver.

The sea of people at the train station seemed to beg Margaret to stay and learn and enjoy this amazing place. Philip went directly to a window where a man in a striped vest looked at his papers and directed the couple to a nearby platform and another train. Margaret was hungry and exhausted, yet something in Philip's stride drove her to keep up with him and not make too many demands.

Margaret wanted to see the station and all of the interesting people moving about the platform. However, Philip pulled her toward the train and they were the first people to board their car so Margaret had to look at the station from the dirty little window.

Hearing movement, she tore her eyes away from the window to see Philip pulling a tattered overcoat on. "Why Philip that looks just like…uh, did you steal that from Papa's barn?"

"Well I am family now, surely your father would want to share it with me," he quirked a sideways grin at her as he tried to adjust the ragged garment over his uniform coat.

"But you can't wear that with your uniform can you?"

Philip just shrugged his shoulders, and slid low into the seat. He closed his eyes and didn't say another word to her until the train was well out of the station and headed north toward Chicago did he begin to relax.

Hours passed and the gentle rhythm of the train rocked Margaret to sleep despite her best efforts. When she opened her eyes for what must have been the hundredth time and asked herself again whether it was morning. Philip stirred in the seat beside her and she lifted her head from the cold window to rub the kink from her neck.

"We should be seeing Chicago before much longer," he said as much to the window as to his wife. The train was due to arrive at Rock Island Station at 8:10 that morning. Margaret had no way of knowing the hour, and since she was seated on the west-facing side of the train she was unable to determine how close the time might be to sunrise. Philip had given her the seat nearest the window and during every waking moment, her eyes were glued to the landscape that seemed to fly past in a blur. She had never moved this fast in her life and could scarcely believe it even now. She was very thankful that she was facing the front of the train and could see the sights as they approached instead of riding backwards as many people around her were forced to do.

Through the oily black fog of the coal smoke, she thought she could see lights and maybe some buildings rising up along the horizon, even in the pre-dawn light. She turned to Philip, her eyes lighting up with the prospect of seeing her new home. "I b'lieve I see it", her voice fairly squeaked. Philip had closed his eyes again in sleep and did not respond to her. Turning back to the window, she fastened her eyes on the horizon awaiting visual confirmation of their approach to the city, not giving rest another thought.

As other passengers began to wake, she heard soft voices and a baby crying somewhere in the car. She turned her attention back to the approaching city. She began to sense something different in the air, and then it grew to a stench. As she wondered what could possibly put off such an odor she wrinkled her nose involuntarily.

Margaret hadn't realized Philip was awake again until she heard him asking the conductor for the time and whether the train would be arriving as scheduled. "Five minutes till seven. We're always on time, Sir," the conductor answered with a snap of his shining pocket watch. Turning to Margaret, Philip smiled at the look on her face.

"You know butchering is big business in Chicago" Philip said. The train had begun slowing several minutes earlier and now they could clearly make out and even study the buildings along the rail. Philip pointed to big buildings with side tracks leading to their doors and explained these were meat packing houses.

"May be able to get work there, they'll be hiring now that it's cold weather again."

Margaret rubbed at her folded arms, "Yeah I been noticin' the chill; I b'lieve it's colder here than back home."

Despite the bodies packed into their rail car, several windows were open and she knew there was frost in the air that entered the car. She felt a pang of homesickness as she thought of the crisp air in Elmore community on the frosty mornings. "There'll be a heavy frost back home and milkin' will be cold business. But I always enjoy the walk to the barn or the spring on these mornin's." Turning back to the window, she pushed the memory aside before it could fully unveil itself, and turned her eyes toward this great new city she was entering. Surely these warehouses and stock yards were not what she could expect here. Her eyes searched beyond them toward the residential areas and wondered again about her new home.

Even as the train began to slow a long way from the depot, her new world passed Margaret faster than she could absorb it. She had known she was going to a big city, but somehow seeing all of the buildings and the people and, well it seemed like chaos out there and it nearly took her breath. She thought, *What have I got my fool-self into?* For just a moment, a mixture of fear and regret washed over her as the excitement and adventure were forgotten.

The appearance of the city had a very different affect on Philip. The train had not completely stopped before he was up and swinging his bedroll and haversack onto his back. He reached for Margaret and her carpet bag, "Come on Margie, we are home. Let's get out there and make our fortune." He grinned like a little boy and nearly pushed Margaret in his haste to exit the train car.

With almost no luggage, it took only minutes to wind their way through the depot crowd and out onto the city street. Margaret waited at the curb where Philip dropped his knapsack and bedroll at her feet and she sat her own tattered bag atop them with her hand looped through its handles. Despite her exhaustion, she could not stop her eyes as they darted from one scene to the next. She did not realize this many people lived in the whole country, yet they were all in this station coming or going or seeing folks who were on the trains.

She watched as Philip talked to a man behind a caged window, wondering what business they were transacting. He returned to her shortly with two small pieces of paper in his hand and retrieved his things. "We will take a horse-car to Lake Street then walk the last two blocks to the river – it sounds like the work is better on the docks than in the meat houses."

"Are we gonna live near the river?"

Philip smiled at her, "I hope to find something there. We will live close to whatever work I find. If there is nothing for me on the docks, I will still see if the meat-houses have any jobs to offer."

"Oh I sure remember hog killin's. Daddy and Matthew would get them big ole' hogs into the scalding pan and then scrape 'em down real good. That's when the hard work started. We'd have to cut everything up and get it packed in salt. Us girls, we'd render out lard from all of the fat. By the day's end I was about ready to give up meat for the rest o' my life. That is till we set down to supper and Mama had made fatty bread outta' the crispy cracklin's that were left over from the lard makin'. If you get work butcherin' maybe I can make it for you. Do you think you'd like that?" When she turned to see what he thought of the idea she found his face set in such a look of concentration that her question changed immediately. "Philip, what are you thinkin' about?"

"I am trying to make plans. Having you with me makes it a little harder. I could have camped out by the river for a few weeks by myself. But I do not think I can have you down there, it would not be safe for you. "

The stream of people moving from the train station seemed to be flowing toward a line of wagons. As Margaret looked more closely, she saw that they were unlike Papa's wagon. They had shiny steel wheels. The big horses stood patiently, occasionally blowing out a bored sigh or stomping a big hoof. Looking at their feet, for these horses were much larger then Jewel or Jenny, she realized the reason for the steel wheels. The wagons sat atop rails affixed to the road like the train tracks. Again, she turned to Philip with a question on her lips, "Why are the wagons on train tracks?"

Again, he smiled. Philip seemed to be enjoying her learning experience. He spoke to her almost as a child, "I keep forgetting that this is your first trip to our city. You know when I first arrived from Italy, I asked all these same questions. They are not train tracks, just rails for the wagons. It is a much smoother ride on the rails. Did you not notice on the train how there were no bumps?"

"Oh, I guess I did notice that, I was just so excited that I would not have minded any amount of rough road."

Philip placed a gentle hand at her back and guided her toward the step up to the wagon seats. She seated herself on the first empty bench and for the first time realized that she was chilled. Automatically she looked to the sky to check the weather and saw clouds amassing in the west. At least she believed it to be the west. Somehow, it was hard to keep her bearings in this strange new place. At home, she always knew from which direction the sun would come in the morning, across the distant ridge lighting the mountains first then sweeping over the plateau. In the evening, it would always set toward the west and the deep valley towards the Standing Stone community.

She closed her eyes and gently shook her head in an attempt to shake away the memory. She missed that setting sun. Shaking her head, she told herself she couldn't think of that now; she had to learn her new home as her husband had learned it.

"Philip, who taught you all about the city when you first come here?"

"My brother Joseph. He arrived in America two years before me. He found that Chicago was a good place to get work and find our fortune. So, when my ship arrived in America, I declared Chicago to be my destination."

The wagon lurched a bit as the horses began to pull their heavy load. Almost every seat was filled and Philip was forced in close to Margaret. She lowered her face from anyone who might see; even though she was a married woman now she found she was still embarrassed for him to be so close to her, especially among all these people. Philip didn't seem to notice her discomfort; in fact, he seemed so focused on the road that he hardly noticed Margaret at all. She turned her attention back out the dusty windows, taking in as much of the bustling city as she could see. The car drove through a maze of buildings that seemed to blot out the sky. It took Margaret's breath away.

"I never knew there were this many people in the whole world."

She didn't realize she had said it aloud until Philip responded, "The city has really grown since I left; it seems there are twice as many people here now."

"When were you here last, Philip?"

"1861. Your Johnny Reb didn't march this way, so neither did the Union Army." He winked at her as he said it.

Margaret blushed and turned back to the window. The car had stopped and many of the passengers, including Philip, stood and Margaret followed suit. Philip stepped into the aisle making just enough room for her to step in front. He kept his hand on her elbow and she was thankful for it when she felt the crowd would sweep her away. There were more of the horse-cars lined up along the street than Margaret could possibly count. Philip led her along without a word until he chose another car and lifted her up the steps.

"This car should take us all the way to the river, or at least within a short walk, maybe two blocks."

"What is a block?"

Philip looked decidedly like he expected that question. "That's how we measure distance in the city. As soon as I can find some work, we will walk around the neighborhood and I'll start explaining the city to you."

Margaret knew that she would have many more

questions. Since she'd seen the first hints of arrival this morning, she had a growing doubt about living in this strange new place. It was beginning to seem less like a glamorous adventure. The knot that she'd carried in her stomach was growing with every breath she took.

Chapter 8

Margaret was getting pretty tired as she stood on the street waiting for Philip to come out of yet another house. For hours they had walked up and down streets, stopping for him to check every building that said they had rooms. At each stop, he returned with a shake of his head. The first few he'd said they could not afford. At one point he even asked Margaret if she had money with her. She did not. Now, the buildings were looking more and more broken-down.

She turned her back to the dusty street and looked up and down the row of buildings. The homes were larger than any she'd ever seen in Tennessee. They were built so closely together that she almost thought they were a single building. Tiny front yards were bordered by fences in varying states of disrepair. Very few of the homes had porches and most of the tall windows were darkened by drapes shielding the interiors from her curious eyes.

She heard a gate creak and turned to see Philip returning to her wearing a small smile, very small. "We have a room."

Margaret let out a breath she felt she'd held for the last hour. Now, maybe they could get some food and rest. Both seemed to be luxuries she had not known for days and days. Philip read her thoughts.

Pulling a handful of change from his pocket, he said, "There is a market on the next corner. We will go see about getting some provisions."

Margaret was so tired. She was almost disappointed that they would not go to their room first; but her hunger tempered the disappointment and she followed without complaint.

She had visited the general store in Crossville with Papa many times, especially before the war. Yet the market that they entered was not like that store. There seemed to be no dry goods, no bolts of fabric or tools. She noticed a strong scent of raw pork and peered through a doorway to see hanging carcasses with a man working at them. Perhaps they could have pork chops for supper. Since leaving Elmore they'd been surviving on crumbs with Philip urging her to wait every time she mentioned food.

She turned to suggest the pork chops but Philip was already deep in conversation with two men, one behind a counter and he wouldn't turn to her even when she tugged at his sleeve. She stepped to the window and he finally came carrying a medium sized market basket. She did not dare ask what it contained.

As they made the short walk back to their rooming house, Margaret's head again flooded with questions. But the combination of exhaustion and confusion kept her quiet for the moment.

She didn't realize they had reached the rooming house until Philip nudged her shoulder to turn into the gate. She looked up at the tall house. It didn't seem to greet her as she had imagined her home with Philip would. They entered a tall, glass door. The hinges squeaked but at this point Margaret only noticed it was a heavy door that would surely keep out the weather. Without a word, Philip started up a carved wooden staircase badly in need of polish.

Margaret was trying to take in everything around her.

She heard the coughs of dozens of children and adults, yet she saw no one. The stairs were littered with bits of food and dust collecting in the corners of each step.

At the top of the stairs, she had no time to consider the long hallway, nor the tattered carpet and lack of furnishings. There was another set of stairs to climb. The light was so dim here she had to concentrate on her steps so as not to trip. She remembered the hour and knew the sun would be setting soon. On the second floor, she had noticed fixtures on the walls that would surely hold candles or lamps; they were all empty now. Perhaps the women of the house had not yet been able to light them. It was a large house; there must be many lights to put out in the evening.

Finished with the stairs, Philip led her down a hallway. This hallway was not as wide as she'd seen on the floor below but it seemed the carpet here was in slightly better condition. They walked almost to the end and Philip opened a door.

She stepped into a single room furnished with a slightly sagging bed and a dusty table. Two windows on the far wall seemed to promise light if the day were brighter and the hour earlier. The drapes hung limply open revealing another house just a few feet away. Three unmatched chairs sat around the table. A small table beside the door held a pewter water basin. There was no pitcher and a chamber pot stood below the table. The room also contained a tall wardrobe of dark wood and a sturdy shelf hung beside a squat little stove.

Margaret took in all of the elements of this room in a moment. She was still standing in the doorway when Philip pulled her by the wrist into the room, "You are going to have to come inside."

The door clicked behind her and she looked toward her

husband but he offered no words of welcome, neither apology nor explanation for the sad little room.

"The men at the market have told me who I should see at the docks tomorrow. I will be there at first light. There is plenty of work right now with so many men gone to war."

Philip had put the market basket on the table and she absently flicked through its contents. There were several large crackers wrapped in a paper and a chunk of hard cheese lying atop some eggs. Looking at the food, she remembered how sparsely they had eaten during the journey. Her mother's training unconsciously kicked in and she began to prepare whatever meal she could from these provisions.

The squat little stove in the corner caught her eye and she moved toward it. Still wearing her coat, the chill of the room assured her this stove would have no coals to help her. The door creaked loudly as she opened the firebox. There was a thick layer of ash and she knew she would need to clean the stove thoroughly before she could really use it. That would have to wait until tomorrow.

Margaret turned to Philip about to suggest a supper of cheese and crackers only to find him stretched out on the sagging bed, fast asleep. Sighing, she broke off a piece of cheese and somewhere in her mind, she thought, *I should return thanks to God for this meal.* Instead, she began to nibble at the cracker. She wanted to cry. She wanted to bury her head in Mama's lap and cry herself to sleep. The tears slowly ran down her cheeks as she realized crying on Mama would no longer be an option in her life.

Margaret awoke with a sharp pain in her neck. It was dark and she did not know what woke her; for a moment she did not even know where she was. Yesterday's events slowly came into focus and she heard movement behind her. Philip asked, "Why are you sleeping in the chair?"

"I must have fallen asleep here. I didn't realize…"

Philip lit a small candle and was moving around the room but she couldn't understand why. "Why are you up?" she asked him.

"I have to be down at the docks at first light. I must find work today."

Margaret's head was still thick with sleep. She looked to the tall windows and saw no indication of dawn's arrival. "It must be the middle of the night."

"No, it is later than we think. I hear movement on the street below, probably from the wagons that are making morning deliveries." He had wiped the dust from the wash bowl and poured water from his canteen. He splashed his face and combed his hair.

Moving to the table where Margaret still sat, he dug in the basket pulling out the remaining crackers and cheese. "Wish we could cook those eggs. I guess there was no wood in the room?"

"I didn't really look for any."

Philip moved to the stove and kicked a small box at its side. It moved very slightly indicating some weight inside. "I think there is enough wood here to make a cooking fire." He was already putting pieces into the wood box. Using a small shovel from his pack, he moved some of the ash into the chamber pot. With the first spark, Margaret stepped to the stove to soak up any warmth it produced.

"I'll boil the eggs for you." She was waking enough to help in some small way with his morning chores. She retrieved his canteen only to find it completely dry. "Wonder where I can find a well to get more water?"

Her mind suddenly flooded with more questions than she could voice. She did not know how to keep a home in this strange place!

Philip's face threatened to smile. He placed a gentle hand on her head and assured her, "Most of these rooming houses have water in them. There will be a spigot somewhere. You can find it in the daylight." He picked up the remaining cheese and one of the crackers. He was already wearing his hat and coat and now he stepped out the door, closing it tightly behind him.

Margaret was alone. Papa had trained his family well to plan their day in the morning's first hour. And Margaret now tried to plan her day. Realizing she would need it later, she blew out the tiny candle and lifted a stove eye to get a bit of light from the fire inside. The small room was warming nicely now and Margaret was feeling sleepy again. She sat down on the side of the bed and tried to look around the room. What would she do with her day? She was sure there was much she needed to do. Somehow she just couldn't make a plan. The warmth was seeping into her limbs; she was finally willing to take off her coat. She laid the coat across her legs and stretched out on the bed, just for a moment.

She awoke to weak sunlight pouring through the dusty windows. She smelled smoke and realized she had drifted to sleep with the eye open on the stove, allowing smoke to come into the room. There was no sign of fire from the stove now, but the room held warmth from the earlier blaze.

The morning now felt a little more like she was accustomed to. She swung her legs off the thin mattress and moved to tend the stove. There were still red coals atop too many ashes, so she needed to add more wood. The box contained both small bits of wood as well as black chunks of coal. Margaret had never seen coal inside a home. Papa used it in the forge when he was repairing wagon wheels or shoeing the horses. And she knew the heat it could produce. After the flames rekindled with the remaining wood, she placed a few chunks of coal on the fire. She watched for the blue flame as Papa had taught her.

With the smell of the coal and a memory of Papa's forge, she felt a pang of homesickness. *How are they all doing? she wondered. What do they think of me?* Shaking her head, she turned her thoughts to the room that would be her home, and then to the day before her.

Last night's supper of cheese and crackers no longer sustained her and she thought of the eggs in the basket. Pulling the small skillet from Philip's pack, she cracked two eggs atop the now warm stove. Why had she not thought of the frying pan before Philip left? She felt immense guilt that he had left for a day's work without a good breakfast. The room soon filled with the smell of the frying eggs. She added a small piece of the jerked deer hoping for a tiny amount of fat to cook from it. The eggs would not turn in the dry skillet, scrambling when she tried, but she cared little. As she prepared to eat, she was again reminded that she should be thanking God for providing this. She closed her eyes and could only feel shame and chose not to face her Lord. She ate the eggs and jerky directly from the skillet.

With a little bit of rest, warmth and food, she began to feel more human. She looked at her new home with fresh eyes now. Everything seemed to be covered with a thin layer of dust. She would clean, and then she could make a better plan for this home.

She thought that she must find water so she grabbed the pewter basin, opened the door and looked first right then left trying to decide her direction. The hallway loomed long. The stairs were near the end to her right so she started that way. She looked out the window at the end of the hall trying to see a well or cistern. There was none in sight so she turned and made her way down the stairs.

On the second floor, as she turned onto the larger staircase, another woman with pitcher in hand was making her way down as well. Margaret spoke to her with a big smile and holding the basin high greeted her, "Good morning. I'm looking for water too."

The lady was thin with her dark hair piled atop her head. She spoke, but Margaret did not understand her words. However, she sounded vaguely like Philip when she spoke. She was moving away from Margaret now and Margaret could only follow her. Surely this lady knew where to find the well, and she seemed to be motioning Margaret to follow.

Down the stairs, to the entry hall, then through a hallway toward the rear of the house she followed this lady. She could hear the noises from the street outside indicating that many people were in the full swing of their day's activities. Now they were on another, narrow staircase which ended in a rather bleak room. Margaret saw a large fireplace with iron hooks hanging in it as well as long wooden shelves and counters. She realized this could be a fine kitchen.

Her silent friend had moved to the opposite end of the room and now motioned for Margaret to join her with more words that Margaret could not understand. Margaret watched as she grasped a tiny handle that was attached to the wall, turning it. Water suddenly gushed out of the wall! The lady seemed unconcerned and simply placed her pitcher below the water flow. After filling her own pitcher, she reached for Margaret's basin and filled it as well then moved her hand again and the water ceased.

With more of the strange words, the lady handed Margaret her vessel, reclaimed her own pitcher and waved good-bye. Margaret could scarcely move. She looked from the wall to the woman and back to the wall. Was this some kind of sorcery? She remembered the Old Testament stories they told of magicians who could turn rods into snakes or make frogs appear. She looked back toward the doorway through which the strange woman had disappeared. Could she be one of these magicians? Margaret immediately prayed, Lord, protect me and Philip from any evil in this place.

Taking the water, Margaret rushed up the stairs. As she climbed, she realized that the stairs continued up beyond the first floor. She followed them to the top and realized she was on the third floor and in fact very near her own room. This place she was to live in would take some getting-used-to she realized.

She spent her day cleaning every surface in the small room. She filled Philip's mucket with water and placed it on the back of the stove then with a rag she found among Philip's things, she began wiping away the dust. She longed for the strong lye soap that Mama always had in abundance for cleaning. Shaking the curtains, she wished she had a clothes line where she could beat the dust from the fabric and let the sweet sunshine freshen them.

On the shelf by the stove, she assembled their meager provisions. At midday she ate the remaining crackers with some jerky and water. All that was left were a few eggs and some jerky. That would be their supper she supposed. The frying pan was cleaned and placed on the coolest part of the stove.

She stood in the middle of the room assessing it. This was as clean as she could get it with the tools available. Somehow, Margaret was not satisfied. It was far from a home and not how she wanted Philip greeted when he returned from a long workday. Going to the windows, she tried to assess the hour.

She decided their windows faced north so by looking as far left as possible, she could see the sun sinking toward the rooftops of the distant buildings. Her stomach hinted that it was near the supper hour. The farmers would be coming home from their fields about this time, but Margaret was unsure when Philip would return as she knew this work he sought was very different than she was accustomed to.

She made up her mind to wait until Philip got home before starting supper. The eggs would take only a minute to cook and they would taste so much better hot. Surely he wouldn't mind waiting just that long.

Chapter 9

Margaret looked in the basin at the dirty water. *If there's that much dirt in the pan then I must be doin' some good here. But I'm gonna need more water.*

With basin in her hand, she headed toward the back stairs. Throughout the day, she had heard movement in the hall from time to time. Once or twice she had started to speak to the people in the hallway. Remembering the strange woman from this morning, she feared the people she heard would also be involved in evil so she stayed safely in her room.

As she opened the door, she heard someone approaching. Looking up, she saw a woman with the reddest hair she'd ever seen. The woman's rosy cheeks were freckled and her eyes sparkled at Margaret.

"Hello there. Haven't seen ya' here before, have I?"

Margaret was thrilled that she at least knew the words this woman was using although the sound of them was still different to any Margaret had ever heard. She didn't sound like Mama or Mary or even Lou and yet neither did she sound like Philip and certainly not like the strange woman from the morning.

Margaret shook her head slightly, reminding herself to answer this woman who seemed so friendly, "No, we only came here yesterday. And it was real late when we got in."

"Well, I'm being glad to know ya'. Name's Cara and I'm living just two doors down the hall there."

"Oh Carrie, I'm so glad to know you" Margaret smiled. "Not CarrIE, it's CarA."

Margaret had never heard this name, but she would try to please. After all, this was the first smiling person she had met. "Cara, I'm sorry I'll try to get it right. I'm just so happy to meet you. I met a lady this morning and couldn't understand a word she said. I was just headin' out to dump my cleanin' water and find some fresh water."

Cara fell into step beside her, "I'm on the very same errand. We jes' dump it out the window here at the end of the hall. Then we'll be going downstairs together to get some more."

They had reached the end of the hallway and Cara proceeded to slide up the glass pane and unceremoniously dump her basin outside. Mama had allowed the girls to dump their water near the back porch, always cautioning them not to get it near the cellar door or on the path that would cause mud to be tracked into the kitchen. Margaret looked down to the ground where Cara's water had drained. There was a good sized mud puddle there – this was clearly not the first basin to be emptied out the window. So Margaret followed suit and dumped the water over the window sill.

Cara beckoned her into the stairwell and Margaret followed, happy to have met this cheerful lady. "There's water in the basement, now ain't that a grand thing? This building used to be a great house and the kitchens downstairs are mostly empty now it's used for roomin'. I been told a woman once cooked for folks who took rooms but that was a'fore my time."

Cara chatted away as they descended the narrow back stairs all the way to the bottom floor that Margaret had visited earlier. Upon entering the deserted kitchen, Margaret's unease from the morning returned. "Cara, this is the same room where that other lady brought me. She did some kind of sorcery to get the water. You ain't gonna do that, are ya?"

Cara chuckled causing her rosy cheeks to flush redder; her whole body seemed to laugh. "There'll be no sorcery from me!" And she moved her hand from her forehead and across her chest. Margaret wondered why she did this and remembered Philip making the same kind of move when he ate with her family. She must ask him to explain it. Oh, there was so much that needed explaining.

"There be a pipe that brings water to the building. I never saw anything like it before I came to Chicago. We were in New York for a time when we first got to America, but the tenements there din' have anything like this. In fact, getting good water was quite a chore for us there. Me boy Liam…"

Cara prattled on as she approached the wall. Margaret was so focused on what her new friend was doing that she didn't hear a word she said. There was dampness along the tile and when Cara placed her hand on it, the water appeared just as it had for the dark-haired lady. Margaret's sharp breath caused Cara to stop her rambling, "Now child, don' ya be letting this thing scare ya. Le'me show ya."

She took Margaret's hand in hers and placed it on the cold metal. Together, they turned the handle and the water stopped its flow. Cara turned Margaret's hand the other way and the water returned.

"See there, no magic to it. It's a new kind of invention. And the water's pretty good. Not like we had in Ireland a'course but after the putrid stuff we drank on that ship, and then the battle we had for good water in New York, I'll not be complaining about this."

Margaret had a thousand questions, yet before she could utter any, Cara had the vessels filled with water and was ushering her back toward the stairs. "Now, me Liam is off at war. He sends me back a good pay every month ya know. Our eldest son, Breandan, he works at the docks now. So I'm always a'tryin to have him a good hot meal ready when he gets home. He's kind of the man of the house right now so I mean to be treatin' him like a man."

Margaret smiled at finally hearing something vaguely familiar, "Oh, my husband was hoping to get work at the docks today, too. I didn't know when to expect him home."

"Well, they'll be workin' till there's no more light for them to see their work. Sometimes if there's no work to be had, they'll be coming in early. Ye'll be hearing the men coming. Most of the folks in the house work on the docks."

They had reached the third floor again and Cara's breathing was more labored. She carried both a pitcher and bucket now filled with water. Margaret wished she had another vessel to carry water. She remembered at home there was never a need for buckets for Papa spent many hours each winter tightly fitting wooden slats together in all kinds of sizes. She shook her head. There was no way to get one of Papa's buckets. She could make do with her basin.

It was quite dark outside when Philip finally returned. She was so excited to have him home to talk with that everything seemed to gush out, "How did you do today? Was there good work to be had? How do ya' feel? I'll make the eggs now. I didn't want them to be cold, but the stove is hot so it'll only take a minute."

"Whoa, Margaret, too many questions! Wait until I get inside the door." Philip was smiling too. He dropped his hat on a hook beside the door and pulled her to himself. "It is good to have you here when I come home."

Margaret blushed and tried to return his embrace. Mama had told the girls so many times how they must never let a man touch them before they were married; Margaret had to remind herself that she was indeed married to Philip and that she must return his affection. Certainly, she wanted to, yet somehow she felt guilty, as though it were wrong somehow. She kissed him lightly and tried to turn to the stove, "You must be hungry. Don't you want me to fix these eggs for you? It's all we've got to eat."

Shrugging, Philip released her and began unbuttoning his coat. "There was no trouble finding work today. And I will go back to the same place tomorrow. They paid me my wages but it was too late to go to the market. Can you do that tomorrow?" He dropped two silver coins on the table.

"Well, I've been to the general store in Crossville many times. Surely I can manage." She knew it was only a brave front for Philip's sake. She wasn't at all sure. Everything was so different here.

With the remaining eggs on the table along with several pieces of the jerked meat, Margaret sat down beside Philip. She immediately dropped her head to pray; instead of prayer, she heard Philip dipping out the eggs. Margaret suddenly realized that she had not thanked God for a bite of food since she left home. This had always been such a normal part of meals that she was shocked how quickly she slipped out of the habit. Silently, she asked God to bless the food and her home and family.

Philip ate with the gusto of a working man. Margaret took only a very small portion because she knew he would need his strength. Except for another small portion of jerky, all of the food they had in the house was on the table now. Philip must have been thinking the same thing for his conversation was about food.

"Try to get some coffee tomorrow. We usually had coffee in camp but I have not had a cup since I left Chattanooga. I think the market will have some. Word at the dock was that supplies are plentiful in town. I have been south of St. Louis for two years so I was not sure what we would find here."

With their meager meal completed, Margaret retrieved the warm water from the mucket standing at the back of the stove and cleaned the dishes. She carefully placed everything back on the sturdy shelf.

"There were just a few pieces of wood in the box and some coal. At home we used coal in the forge; I didn't expect it in the house."

Philip was concerned about their heating, "Is there enough coal for the night? I can get some at dawn tomorrow – they will be selling it on the street. Of course that will not leave very much money for our food. You can take one of the fifty cent pieces with you. Hopefully you can get enough for a couple of days with that. Since the war, prices are very high."

Margaret peered into the little box, "I can make it last through tomorrow. We'll close the dampers down tonight. And we could sleep in our coats."

Margaret blushed, suddenly realizing that she would be sharing the sagging bed with her husband tonight. She tried to count the days since they were married. Everything seemed a bit blurred when she thought back on their travels. And last night she'd fallen asleep at the table.

Philip was at her side, wrapping his arms around her. "Do not worry little Margie, I will keep you warm."

His beard tickled her neck and she searched for another topic for them to talk about. She began to chatter about her day and the cleaning and what she imagined she could do to make this tiny space more of a home. She wasn't even sure if Philip was listening for he continued undressing and got into the bed.

She crawled under the blanket and Philip drew his wife to himself.

In the morning, Margaret could not tell what really woke her; Philip was moving about the room and her face was cold and there was noise on the street. She mentally shrugged, realizing it mattered little why she was awake; it was time to start her day.

The floor greeted her feet with a harsh chill and she quickly pulled on her shoes. Philip had stirred the fire and she saw the mucket pulled to the front of the stove. She wondered why as she knew they had neither coffee nor chicory in the house.

Philip greeted her smiling brightly around the piece of jerky still in his mouth, "Good morning. I hope we can get some coffee today." He poured a small cup of the warm water and washed down the dried meat.

"What will you take for dinner today?"

Philip held up the remaining few pieces of jerky in their cotton wrapping and smiled. "I have to get down to the dock. I will see you tonight."

The door clicked behind him and the only noise in the room leaked in from the street.

Margaret looked around her home. She began to mentally order her daily routine. First, she would straighten the little room. She also began making a wish list. Right now she wished she had a broom. She thought, "I'll have to ask Cara where a dry goods store is. The market where Philip bought food didn't seem to have nearly as many things as the general store in Crossville had."

There was little enough to be done in the tiny room. She puttered around until the sun was well up and she estimated the hour near seven. She had peered down at the street several times and now began to see women with market baskets on their arms and felt it was a reasonable time to venture out to buy some food.

Closing the door to her room, she went down the front stairs and out the heavy wooden door. A cold wind hit her face, almost making her take a step back. She bent her head down and walked into the wind, turning down the street. She was not entirely confident she could walk directly to the market they had visited two days ago, so she was thrilled when she lifted her head upon reaching the intersection and saw the familiar building across the way. Careful not to hinder the many horses and carts travelling on the dusty street, she made her way to the market's door.

Inside, a rather gruff-looking little man greeted her briefly and called a young woman to help her. "Good morning I'm Ginger, how can I help you today?" she greeted Margaret.

Margaret smiled when she heard the accent that sounded a bit like her friend Cara. She mentally noted how many different languages seemed to exist in Chicago. At home, everyone had sounded pretty much the same – but no one sounded like home-folk here. She closed her eyes and in her mind she could hear Mama's sweet voice instructing her daughters as she worked and the chatter of the children at play.

It seemed like music to her now and she longed to hear those voices, even to hear that language of the mountains.

"Ahem," Ginger softly cleared her throat snapping Margaret back to the here and now.

"Oh, I'm so sorry, I am afraid I let my mind wander for a moment" she apologized.

Ginger smiled kindly, "That is perfectly fine, I am guilty of the same thing far too often. What were you needing today?"

Margaret had no paper to write a list, but since she had nothing to work with, she could surely remember what was necessary to make her husband a decent supper tonight. She just needed to remember their limited funds. She thought of what she'd learned as Papa taught Matthew how to trade and she looked deeply into Ginger's eyes wondering if she should try to haggle with her.

Deciding she had little choice, she would trust her. Margaret breathed a quick prayer and lay the silver half dollar on the counter. "I need to buy some food, and this is all I have."

In one move, Ginger's eyes darted around her and she gently pressed the coin back into Margaret's hand. "I will help you, but don't show your money in here until you have to pay. These are perilous times and it may not be safe."

Ginger took in a deep breath as though some danger had been scarcely avoided, "Tell me what you were wanting?"

"Coffee, can I get some coffee? And a little meat – whatever you have, maybe bacon or some soup beef. What about a few potatoes?" Margaret's list poured out.

Ginger looked more at ease now, "Yes, I think we can manage most of that. Let's see…"

On a little slate, she had been jotting down Margaret's

thoughts and now seemed to be tallying the cost, "We can get you a quarter pound of coffee, and some potatoes. Do you have salt?"

Margaret was so relieved that she could scarcely find her voice. "Yes, we have a little salt left. Could I afford any flour?"

"Yes, I think a half pound. It wouldn't make much bread it'll just get you started. That wouldn't leave any money for lard. Are you getting milk already?"

Margaret had been so accustomed to getting milk from the barn that she scarcely thought of asking for it. "No, can I get that here?"

Ginger smiled again, "No, you will have to get that from the milk man. He'll bring it each morning to your house. Ginger turned and began visiting bins all along the counter.

With a few parcels wrapped in heavy paper and tied neatly with string lying on the counter, Margaret again handed her the silver coin.

She returned a few coins to Margaret and said, "This should be enough to get a pound of soup beef from the butcher. There are so many slaughtering houses around that you should always be able to get meat so long as you don't want the best cuts."

"Where will I find the butcher?"

Lifting the counter gate, Ginger walked with Margaret out into the busy street. "I imagine you can follow your nose. Can you read the signs?"

"Oh yes," Margaret assured her. "I can read."

"Well, it's about 10 doors down, and there's a big sign that just says 'meat'. That's Mr. Brown and he's honest so it's worth the walk to his shop."

With that, Margaret started down the crowded sidewalk

with her basket over her arm. It was so flimsy that she tried to protect the precious contents with her left hand and ended up cradling the basket on her arms. Feeling like she had not breathed since leaving Ginger's side, she entered the door below a painted board announcing 'meat' was sold there.

After a brief wait as there were two ladies already placing their orders, a gentleman in a slightly bloodied white apron asked for her order.

"I'll take ten cents of soup beef." She ordered with as much confidence as she could muster but with none too loud a voice.

The butcher did not seem to notice that she had never ordered meat before and simply told her the current pricing. "I can give you a pound for twelve cents."

Margaret knew that she had received thirteen cents change. She had ordered low hoping that she could offer something back to Philip toward the coal. Now she was relieved that she would have enough for a full pound.

Margaret's errands had taken only a couple of hours from her morning. When she returned to her little room she felt more tired than she'd often felt after a full day of field work. This strange place, the people and the unfamiliar ways required her complete attention for even the most mundane tasks.

Knowing that she did not have the luxury of dwelling on her tiredness, she picked up the basin and the now empty mucket and made her way downstairs to retrieve the water she would need for her cooking. She planned as she made her way first down the three flights of stairs and then back up. She would put the soup beef on to cook slowly for the rest of the day and a nice stew would be waiting for Philip.

She carefully saved the peelings from the potatoes and

put them aside in water to begin a sponge that would allow her to make bread. It would take several days so they would have to eat their stew tonight without bread. She wondered how she might get some milk.

With supper on the stove and a small fire cooking it, she looked around her room wondering what needed to be done. She certainly found it simple to keep her little home tidy. With a smile, she admitted to herself that they had nothing to even pick up. Mama had always been directing her family to pick up shoes and papers and books.

A gentle knock at the door broke into her thoughts. She opened the door to find Cara holding a small bottle of milk high to indicate her reason for visiting.

Thrusting the bottle into her hand she said, "I din' see you at the milk cart this morning and thought maybe you could be using this."

"I was just wondering how I would go about getting milk."

Her new friend seemed happy to guide her, "Mr. Burk or his son bring their cart by every morning. You just have to go down to meet him. If you are wanting extra, tell him the day or two before and he will always have it waiting for you. They have cream and butter I think, of course I can never afford that."

Margaret looked almost lovingly at the small bottle of milk. She could see that there was good cream settled at the top and hoped she could make cream biscuits with the small amount of flour she'd gotten at the market. "I put aside potatoes for a bread sponge, but we'll have biscuits till it gets to workin' right - if I can get cream like this every day. I'm brand new to Chicago you know; how will I know when the man is down there?"

"You'll be gettin' used to the sounds soon enough. Until you do, I'll send one of my girls to knock on your door when I hear him coming."

As Margaret shut the door behind her, she realized she had not even offered her new friend any refreshment. Looking around, she scarcely knew what she would have given her. Perhaps that was why the visit was so brief. She must try to get enough provisions that she could offer something should anyone call.

Chapter 10

Margaret's days all ran together those first couple of months. Every day, Philip dropped two coins on the table for her to buy their meager food. She was able to save a few cents from each shopping trip and she began to visit the hardware store and bring home a bucket and a pitcher to accompany the chipped basin she'd found in their room. Slowly, her kitchen began to show the signs of a home. Each day she looked around the room to ensure everything was clean and tidy. And she never failed to compare it to her mother's home. Somehow she couldn't make this room feel like the home she wanted to make for her husband.

So too did they begin to settle into routines of marriage. Philip talked about the men on the dock and how he did not care for their sort. He reported that they were a coarse and ignorant people that would die in their poverty.

Philip dreamed of his fortune and planned continually for the making of it. Margaret tried to join in his dreaming but he didn't seem to want her there. So, she sat quietly and listened to him. His voice was still enchanting to her, and his dark hair and deep-set eyes drew her to him.

Not until she was alone did she long for the home and family that she had left.

"I must write to Mama," she told herself almost every day, yet she never did. What would she say? Would Mama even want her letter? Somehow she was certain that Mama did not understand why she'd left. Perhaps Mama even hated her now. Thinking of her parents brought a nearly overwhelming feeling of shame. She thought of laying her head on Mama's lap and pouring out all of her rebellious thoughts and deeds along with a million tears. She refused to allow the tears, and Mama's lap was not available. Each time the tears threatened to escape, she would shake her head, straighten her shoulders and turn to her next task.

And in this way the late autumn days turned into cold winter. Philip was sure to bring up coal every couple of days so the little room was warm enough. Margaret got some wool thread and Philip fashioned a pair of knitting needles from wood he brought home and with these Margaret began making heavy socks and hats for both of them.

Margaret knew that Christmas was approaching and she couldn't help remembering the wonder with which the holiday had always been celebrated. As she sat the bowl of stewed potatoes and fried pork on the table she tried to share her thoughts with her husband.

"It'll be Christmas soon you know."

Philip was pouring over an old newspaper he'd picked up and never lifted his eyes. "Uh huh."

Margaret drew in a deep breath, "It's a real special time a'year. The birth of Jesus Christ deserves a little thought."

Philip nodded; Margaret watched closely, was that really a nod?

"Mama would always cook a special meal. We'd have bread – light fluffy bread made from sifted flour, not cornbread like we eat most days. And there'd be a good piece of meat, maybe she'd make a roast or if Daddy or Matthew had killed a deer then we might have a deer ham. Either way it was a good meal. And since it's gettin' so cold there's not so many chores to be done so there's more rest to be had in the winter. Oh and we'd have a stack cake – always there was a stack cake."

Her head tilted up as though she studied the corner between wall and ceiling but her eyes were closed. "Don't guess we could have a stack cake, ain't dried no apples. All my life I've been workin' beside my Mama to put up for the winter months but that day we left Elmore I never even thought how we'd get by without all the stores that were waitin' in the cellar."

A light scratching drew her attention and she opened her eyes to see Philip jotting numbers down on a scrap of paper. *Did he hear a word I've been sayin'?*

"Well I've got your supper here. Let's don't let it get cold.

As he dropped a chunk of butter onto the steaming potatoes he answered as though he'd been a part of the conversation all along. "Fish. We are supposed to eat fish at Christmas you know."

"S'possed to? Where'd that rule come from?"

"It is not a rule but it is what everyone in my village eats for Christmas.

She smiled down at her plate, *At least I've learned something of his family, but surely I can do better than fish for Christmas.*

She scrimped the daily rations and had enough to buy a nice cut of beef and flour for a cake. At the butcher she considered for the briefest moment asking if she could get fish but decided it might sound absurd with all the beef and pork being slaughtered in Chicago.

It might not be just what he's used to, but I will make this day so special that he'll have to love it as much as I do.

On Christmas morning Philip left early saying that there

would be extra work to do at the dock and he couldn't give up the pay.

Margaret blinked away a tear as the door clicked closed leaving her in the murky light of dawn with only a single candle burning. With a deep breath she lifted her shoulders and turned to start her day.

The meal was waiting, along with candles tied with a bit of red ribbon when he returned.

He stopped short just inside the door taking in the sight and smell of their little home. Then he crossed the kitchen in two long strides to wrap his arm around her waist, "Margie, you have worked hard today."

Margaret beamed at him and nodded. She hadn't been sure he would even notice.

"Well there ain't no holly to be had round here and I spent the extra money on food rather than buyin' ribbon and extra candles."

He pulled her close to him whispering, "I thank you for this. The food smells very good."

Margaret had grown accustomed, even fond of Philip's touch and today she truly appreciated it. She melted into his embrace and looked up anticipating his kiss.

As they sat down to eat, Margaret wanted to ask him to pray over their meal. She had many times thought they ought to give thanks to God for his provisions; she just wasn't able to explain her conviction to her husband. She had to admit she hadn't tried very hard. Now, at Christmas, she remembered the family devotions the Elmores would share tonight and she felt a pang of regret that the Berai household would not do the same.

She snapped out of her reflecting when she realized Philip was speaking, "...guess there will not be much sleep tonight. The whole neighborhood will be in a drunken roar."

"What? That's a strange thing on Christmas. Why an uproar?"

He shook his head again and again, "Bo".

"What's that mean?"

A tiny smile crept across his face, "It is something we said back home and it means 'I do not know' because I do not know why they act like that except that maybe it is just a silly American thing. In Italy, we would go to Mass at midnight and it was very serious."

"What is Mass, will you tell me about it?"

Philip paused and for a moment, she thought he was about to really answer her. Then he resumed eating and simple said, "It would be better to show you. We will go one day."

Margaret might have had more questions, but she had learned to recognize when her husband was finished talking about something. And he was clearly finished now. They ate the rest of their meal in near silence and the evening progressed as any other evening. As Philip predicted, the streets grew louder and louder. They lay down but sleep was scarce that night.

When her calendar read March, Margaret imagined that spring must be near, although she was unable to see the signs of the springtime to which she was accustomed. She wasn't feeling well and wondered if the sunshine would heal both her body and soul. Then she realized the cause of her sickness and was troubled more deeply, wondering if Philip would welcome their child.

After days of dread, she knew she must tell him. Before she went to the market, she took down the tin from the kitchen shelf and looked at the coins she'd saved. Each day Philip gave her half a dollar and she frugally saved any coins she could bring home from her market trips. She didn't really have a purpose for them, although she knew she needed to have something put-by. Today, though, she would buy a roast and carrots and enough flour and sugar for a cake. It would be a celebration and a wonderful surprise for Philip.

After her market trip, and ample time to thaw her toes from the ever-present wind, she assembled their meal and began the cake. She had just finished the cake and was slicing fresh bread when she heard the men beginning to return to the boarding house. She made a quick check of her appearance, brushing away stray crumbs that were caught on her skirt. Then she heard footsteps stop at her doorway.

She was smiling when the door opened, ready to rush to her husband. She stopped short realizing this was not Philip that walked through the door. Instead, this man was older, thinner although he did greatly resemble Philip.

Philip entered behind him. "Joseph, this is Margaret. And what a smell! She's a good cook for sure. Is that a cake?"

Joseph smiled and reached for Margaret's hand. She was so shocked that she almost jerked it away. Philip had never brought home anyone from the docks. He seemed to dislike most of them. And while she welcomed the idea of company, she had planned a special night and there wasn't room in that plan for company.

She had little opportunity to mourn her thwarted plans. Philip was ready to eat and he was seating this strange man at her table and directing her to set a plate before him. She moved automatically.

Joseph greeted Margaret in the same English that she had grown accustomed to hearing from Philip. As the meal began, he turned to Philip and spoke strange words.

Philip raised a hand to stop him, "No, Joseph, we must speak English now. We are in America and that is the language that will make our fortunes."

More of the strange words came from their unexpected guest.

"Joseph, I see the immigrants who cling to their ways. They live only among themselves and mostly in poverty. We will speak English and we will sell to English speaking customers and buy from English speaking merchants and we will be Americans. And the Berai brothers will be wealthy, just as we planned before we left Italy."

Margaret's fork clattered against her plate, "Brothers? This is your brother?"

It was Joseph that answered, "Yes, Filippo has not told you of *Ju-zep-a* his older brother who came first to America and made the way for him?"

"*Fi-leepp-o?*" Margaret tried to work out the word but it felt strange on her tongue.

Philip turned to her to explain, "Margaret, I have told you about my brother. He was Giuseppe in Italy, but Americans understand English names, so he became Joseph in the army. I became Philip. It is best to be like the others." He turned before he finished, addressing his brother, "But we are not like the people around here because we will not always live in this tenement – we are here to make our fortunes."

The pair cheered their agreement.

Joseph complied with the English speaking and even though Margaret knew Philip had not asked it for her benefit, she was able to listen to them and to begin to understand more about her husband. They talked of their mother and fondly remembered how hard she'd worked to pay their passages to

America. They talked about the war they'd both entered more for the certainty of the Union paycheck than for any political leanings on the issues that drove the nation to war.

As their conversation turned to the battles they'd fought and where they had traveled with their units, Margaret cleared the table and cleaned their dishes. She looked around their tiny room and wondered what they'd do with Joseph tonight. She moved toward her knitting needles only to hear Philip declaring they must all sleep. He still had to be at the docks at dawn and Joseph would join him there to bring in another dollar each day. Philip dropped the coins on the table for her and looked at her, "Can you buy enough for a third mouth on the same amount?"

Margaret had learned a lot in the past months. She had listened to Cara and to Ginger and she now knew the prices and the days when the butcher sold cheaper. Yes, she could provide for the third mouth, Joseph was just not the one she had intended to be feeding. "Yeah, I can manage on the same amount."

Joseph picked up a pack he'd dropped just inside the door and began to unroll his bedding near the warm stove. Philip blew out the candle before he moved to the bed. Standing on the same side as Margaret, he reassured her, "Tomorrow we will hang a blanket to make you a sort of dressing room."

Margaret knew that Joseph was there to stay.

As Margaret lay in bed with her hand upon her stomach, she pondered how and when she would tell Philip her wonderful news. He seemed so happy to have his brother and they spoke so fondly of family. Surely he would want his own family. With the addition of Joseph to their tiny home, she began to wonder how they would manage so many people when a baby came. She grew more and more fretful, all the time trying desperately not to toss and turn in the bed. Philip turned in his sleep and wrapped his arm about her. For the first time in months, she began to pray.

Lord, I thank you for this new life growing within me, but I am scared. How I wish Mama was here to help me through this. She would know the answers to all these questions that are a'swirlin' in my head. Help me to find the right time to tell Philip and please Lord, prepare his heart for this news.

Having unburdened her heart, she fell into a peaceful sleep.

The day dawned as normally as each one had in the previous weeks. Margaret rose and prepared a simple breakfast by reheating yesterday's meat and frying eggs. With the oven quickly heated she slid in a pan of biscuits, making sure there was enough for Joseph as well.

They ate quickly then Philip and Joseph left together, talking as they went about getting work for Joseph at the docks alongside Philip. Philip gave Margaret the same quick kiss good-bye that he did every day wasting few words on her as was his custom. He seemed to see no difference in the addition of Joseph to their home.

With the room again empty, Margaret went through her day's routine. Everything seemed to make her stomach churn, yet she noted that she was not throwing up and she breathed a quick prayer of thanksgiving for that little blessing. She began to wonder what she would need to do to prepare over the coming months.

Maybe I should talk to Cara about it? She's had a passle of babies. Even as the thought crossed her mind, her hand moved protectively to her stomach and she shook her head dismissing the unspoken idea.

As the shadows grew in the room and she knew Philip would be home soon, she finished the stew that she'd prepared and sliced yesterday's bread. She had butter now because she was careful to skim cream from the milk she bought and save it over a few days. It had been difficult to improvise a churn for some weeks but she had now managed to buy a small one. At home there had always been a plentiful supply of milk so the butter was made with whole milk leaving buttermilk that Mama used for more things than Margaret could even count. Now, Margaret was simply making do without the precious buttermilk because she could not afford to buy the extra milk.

The door opened and Philip entered alone. Dropping his hat and gloves on the table, and with a warm smile he reached for Margaret, "Hello there. I am glad to be home. The warmth sure feels good. It was awfully cold down there today."

She tried to return his embrace while watching the door. "Where's Joseph?"

"He will have his supper with old friends tonight. Then he wanted to get a drink."

Margaret was pleased that Philip chose to come home to her rather than go with his brother. She gave him a sweet smile as she said, "I'm surprised you didn't go with him, but I'm glad. I have supper ready so I guess it's best that you weren't late or the food wouldn't have been any good."

Philip was removing the layers he wore each day to the docks. Weeks ago he had brought home an overcoat; even that was not nearly heavy enough. He wore it over his wool uniform blouse with a cotton shirt beneath. "I do not have money to throw away on liquor these days. There is a business for sale on Madison Street and I am hoping I can get the money together for a down payment and maybe I can talk the owner into taking payments. "

Margaret stopped between the stove and table, her hands full. "What, a business? How could we ever afford that? How much money have you saved?"

Margaret saw a hint of a grin that disturbed her. Why was saving money funny? "I saved some from my Army pay. We will count it as soon we have eaten. I am starving."

With that, Philip was tearing into the soft bread and watching eagerly as Margaret brought bowls of hot stew to the table. Between chewing the chunky vegetables, he talked eagerly about the business. So many nights she'd listened to him dreaming of owning a place and working for himself but now the dreams were more specific. Margaret tried to ask questions about the plans however he seemed to have little time to answer them. He was simply speaking aloud the plans that were forming in his head. So, she contented herself with watching him dream.

Philip talked about meeting with the building's owner and the details he hoped to work out with him. He dreamed they would somehow have enough money saved to pay the whole price, yet he felt that was only a dream. He was looking at her as he talked, but it was not a discussion. She smiled at him, genuinely happy to see his wishes coming true. Eventually he began talking about the time when their fortune was made and he took her hand in his and promised a life of ease for her.

When Philip's second bowl was empty, Margaret cleared the table and began cleaning the few dishes they'd used. She heard Philip working at the table. He'd now stopped sharing his plans and the silent work was comfortable to her. When she returned to the table, Philip was busily ripping the lining from his Army blouse.

"Philip, what…" she began to question him but stopped short when the lining peeled back to reveal rows and rows of greenbacks. She had seen such a small amount of Union paper money that she scarcely knew what she was looking at. Matthew had carried some Confederate bills. Papa never trusted them so what little money the Elmores had was kept in gold whenever possible. There were so many bills in Philip's coat that she was speechless.

Philip ran his hand over the neat rows of bills. They were stitched with coarse thread in long, uneven stitches which Margaret quickly assessed were done by Philip's own hand. He looked on them with distinct pride and Margaret knew it was a lot of money to him as well.

"Philip, how much is it? Where did it all come from?"

He did not look at her as he continued to finger the bills, "It is almost all of the pay I drew from the Army. When the other foolish men drew their pay, they bought liquor and tobacco; sometimes they would buy fresh bread or good meat. I ate my Army rations and took a chew from the other fellow's tobacco twist. I knew that I would have to save if I was going to have my own business. You do not make a fortune by spending."

He began to count aloud, "Ten, Twenty, Thirty…" Almost all of the bills were marked 'ten'. Philip finished with a deep breath, "Over three hundred dollars. I never counted it you know. Each month they paid me thirteen dollars. At first they were giving us gold, but that got pretty hard to carry and since I didn't have anywhere to send the money to hold it, I knew I would have to carry it with me. As soon as we started getting the greenbacks, I began trading my coins to the other soldiers. They were glad to trade because most of them did not understand the paper money."

Margaret could not even repeat the number. Three hundred dollars? There was not that much money in all of Elmore community and she had certainly never seen so much. Her mind flooded with thoughts, remembering how hungry she'd been as they traveled north and how she had not had so much as a water bucket to start their home. A moment of bitterness flashed through her mind but she immediately chased it away, telling herself this was Philip's money for his dream.

Philip had not even noticed her solemnity and continued making his plans, "Help me get the stitching out. I will take it to the man tomorrow. It is worth missing one day's work to settle the business. If Joseph could have saved enough to make up the rest of the price we could get started with almost no debt. Of course we will need a little more for furnishings so we will probably have to borrow that somehow."

"Is his coat lined with Greenbacks too?"

Philip laughed at her. "He sent his money to a family that he lived with before the war. He thought they would keep it safe and I hope he was right. That is where he has gone tonight."

Margaret wondered why he had not gone there before. Why was he sleeping on her floor if there was a family willing to keep him? She didn't dare ask the questions; Philip was passionate about family and Joseph was the only family he had in America.

As Philip worked to remove the stitching, he began to talk about the plans that would affect Margaret, "We will keep our rooms above the business. I will need your help and living there will save you walking it every day. It is a long walk. Plus we can save the price of this room."

"Yeah, we'll need more space I think," she gently added.

"There will be more space, and Joseph will have rooms of his own. You are feeling cramped in our cozy home here?" Philip's mood was perhaps lighter than she had ever known it.

"The baby would be underfoot in this little room."

He froze. "What baby?"

Margaret beamed as she tried to explain, "Our baby. I think we'll have one by wintertime. December, I'm guessing."

"A son! I will have a son."

Margaret moved to hug him as she chuckled, "Well, it might be a girl, you know."

Still seated, he wrapped his arms around her waist and rested his cheek against her stomach, "I am sure it will be a boy. And he will learn the business and he will grow with our fortune."

They did not even try to sleep until all of the bills were removed from their stitching, stacked on the table and wrapped in a handkerchief. Even then, as they lay in bed, both were too excited to sleep.

Margaret had just drifted off when the door burst open and a drunken Joseph stumbled into the room. She sat bolt upright and Philip loudly scolded Joseph. He spoke in Italian and that shocked her as much as his tone. Whatever he said, Joseph responded immediately, falling onto his rolled up blankets.

Chapter 11

The morning found Joseph still atop his bedroll. He had never even roused enough to properly make his bed. Margaret rose before either man to stir the fire. As she glanced at her brother-in-law, she thought how terribly uncomfortable he looked and wondered if he would even be able to walk after sleeping in that position.

As Philip rose to start his day, he prodded Joseph with more gentleness and respect than Margaret would have expected, given the greeting he offered his brother last night. The night's disturbance seemed forgotten as Philip helped Joseph to the table.

"Boil the coffee strong today Margie and bring the pot to the table. His head will be foggy and I will need him able to think today." She did as he asked and sat the pot and tin mugs on the table as gently as possible.

After allowing his brother a few moments to clear his head, and the steaming coffee to wake his mind, Philip turned to business. "Were you able to see the Mrs. Dorhn? Did she have your money?"

Joseph's head was mere inches from his coffee cup and Margaret was pretty glad his first words came out in Italian. Finally he ended in English asking, "Why are you asking me questions?"

Margaret saw a flash in Philip's eyes and expected his temper to flare, yet with a deep breath he responded coolly.

"Becausa we need to make a decision on that building today. How much money did you get?"

From the pocket of the coat he'd worn through the night, Joseph pulled a leather pouch and thrust it toward Philip. He still did not lift his head.

Ignoring his brother's attitude, Philip pulled open the pouch and dumped out a wad of bills and several coins. After counting it Philip glared at his brother, "There is not even a hundred dollars here. How much did you send her? Did the woman spend it?"

Joseph's speech was so thick Margaret could barely understand him. "You are making me sick. We will talk later."

Philip's anger did not subside so easily and he practically growled, "Oh, we will definitely talk later. I will not abandon our dreams because of your recklessness. I will see the man today by myself and try to get that building; you get to work. We must keep working at the docks."

Joseph seemed in no condition to do any work. "I cannot go to the dock today."

Philip leaned down, into his brother's face. "Yes, you will go to the dock. We will not lose our fortune to your lust and thirst before we have even earned it." Turning to Margaret, he directed her to pour strong coffee. "Do you have any meat to cook for him?"

Margaret quickly fixed the breakfast and tried to make herself scarce in the tiny space, as Philip ordered his brother to eat and get to work. Even after Joseph was out the door, Philip continued to rant under his breath.

Shortly after Joseph left, Philip carefully wrapped the additional money in the handkerchief with his own savings and secured it in the pocket of his overcoat. He brushed at the sleeve, "This does not look like a business man. I look like a common dock worker."

He reached into his pants pocket and pulled out the loose coins. He had wrapped only the whole dollars and kept both the fractional paper and the smaller coins in his pocket. Thumbing through the coins, he counted three dollars and the fractional bills added another two.

"It is half enough of what I need to buy a decent suit of clothes."

Margaret's eyes widened as she whispered, "Ten dollars for a single suit? I been knowin' you needed new pants since I've had to stitch up your uniform pants at least once a week."

Philip dug into Joseph's pack and pulled out a slightly soiled and very crumpled white shirt. "Can you get this clean?" he asked a slightly stunned Margaret.

"I think so."

Leaving the heavy uniform blouse, he pulled his coat over his cotton work shirt and headed for the door. "I will be back as quickly as I can."

Not entirely sure what he was doing, Margaret set about the work of cleaning Joseph's shirt. She put water on to boil and went down the stairs with her bucket for more water.

After much scrubbing on the sleeves, Margaret smoothed the white shirt over the table. She had just decided that she was satisfied with her work when Philip returned with a paper-wrapped parcel under his arm.

"I ca not expect to make a fortune looking like a field hand." He untied the wrapping and removed the paper. Inside was a beautiful pair of deep gray trousers and a dark coat. Margaret could see the work of a skilled tailor, but they were not new.

Having nodded his approval of the shirt he asked, "Can you work on my boots?" Philip was already changing his clothes as Margaret took the rag she used to clean her only lamp and used the coal oil that was soaked into it to buff out some of the scuffs on his boots.

"The army certainly gave you fine boots. My Papa never had such boots in all his life."

Philip's attention was solely on his dressing as he tossed back, "That is hardly what they issued to me. I took them off an officer on the field."

Margaret had stepped away from them, confident that she had done all she could to improve their appearance, before she realized they belonged to a dead man. Philip gave her no thought as he pulled on the soft leather and smoothed his trousers over them. After buttoning the coat, he inspected the sleeve and stood at his straightest before her. "Now do I look like a proper business man?"

She smiled, admiring her husband. "You look like a man of great wealth."

Satisfied, he secured the bundle of money inside his frock coat and without another word he was out the door again.

Feeling a bit bewildered, Margaret turned to the routine of her day. While she was home alone, the day was as normal as any other. She had no idea how drastically her life was about to change when Philip and Joseph returned home.

Having concluded his business late, Philip met Joseph at the dock and they walked home together. When they came into the room, Philip immediately walked to the table and laid a large ring of keys on it. Margaret froze, realizing what that meant. "You got the building?" she fairly screamed as she rushed into Philip's arms.

He returned her embrace, enjoying her excitement. "We have a lot of work to do. I am afraid that we have almost no money left to setup the business. So I will have to try to find work near the building. I think we should move right away. That will allow us to work on the building and it will save the price we pay for this room."

Philip turned to Joseph and they began making more plans while Margaret finished their supper. As she sat it on the table, Philip turned to ask for her input, "Margaret, do you think you will be able to work, at least for a few months?"

Thrilled to be included in this adventure in some small way, Margaret answered, "Of course. I was raised to work hard!"

"Good, you will run the kitchen. Then, when we have hired the girls, you will have to watch over them as well. By that time, we will have some help in the kitchen. Joseph, I wish you could resist the liquor. If we do not have control over the bar we will never make a profit."

Liquor? Margaret cocked her head trying to understand. She would be sure to ask Philip about it, the first time they had a moment alone. Surely, she thought, working would help Joseph resist liquor. And working in a fine eating establishment ought to be all the better – at least that's what it sounded like they were planning since there would be kitchen help and girls working for them.

Her imagination began developing a picture of this restaurant and she tried to join the conversation to share her vision. However, the men were so engrossed in their dreams and plans that they scarcely heard a thing she said. Finally, she got a simple question into the conversation, "When can I see it?"

Philip stopped. He suddenly realized that his wife would need to see this place that would become her home before he loaded up their meager possessions and moved her. "I guess we do need to go over there. We will go Sunday so I do not have to miss a day of work."

Joseph cocked his head back looking down his nose as he asked, "Do you not think we should leave the docks right away? A businessman should not be hauling bags and pushing carts should he?"

Phillip shook his head, "I have got to earn as much as I can. We will need quite a lot of money to get things started."

Margaret resisted questioning him any further.

Sunday morning after the morning's chores were completed, Margaret dressed for the trip to Madison Street. Sunday was the only day Philip didn't go to work at the docks and Margaret thought they should go to church, yet whenever she suggested it, Philip always had something to do and she soon found it was easier not to mention or even think about church.

She knew from hearing Philip and Joseph talking that it was a long way to this building where they would setup business; Philip said he could walk there in about thirty minutes. Today, he had promised to splurge on a horse-car because he did not feel like Margaret could walk so far.

"Philip," she called across she room as the pinned up the last strands of her hair, "I really think I could walk today. I'm feeling much stronger now you know."

Philip's head was buried in the newspaper he had brought in earlier that morning. Almost every day now she saw him pouring over these printed pages and Margaret read them after he finished, searching for news of the war and how the

Tennesseans fared. She longed to know that Matthew's unit was out of harm's way.

Occasionally Philip would read something and call for Joseph's attention. However, he rarely shared these things with Margaret. In fact, she found that whenever his brother was home he scarcely spoke to her, finding Joseph's company far more inviting than his wife's. He had promised her when they moved to their new home they would have rooms of their very own and she looked forward to the time when they'd be more like a family.

As they exited the apartment house, the April sun warmed Margaret's face immediately and she almost wished she could walk in it. By the time they reached the corner a horse car had answered Philip's whistle and there was no more chance to enjoy the sun on her face. Philip helped Margaret in, holding her hand firmly and steadying her back as she stepped up into the car. Philip's voice held an air of pride and authority as he advised the driver they would be riding to 410 Madison Street. Margaret had listened to him dream for months of walking in as the proprietor of a business. She knew both he and Joseph had shared this dream since before they even left Italy. They cared little the nature of the business; they just felt sure they could never earn their fortunes working for another man. Now, they had found a business that they felt they could open and begin living their American dream. She was very proud of her husband as she sat beside him en route to their own place of business.

She realized, however, that she didn't really understand the business. She had decided it must be a restaurant, but she had never visited a restaurant and really knew nothing about how to run one. When she turned to Philip about to suggest that they should go to such an establishment so that they might better understand the business, she found that he and Joseph were in deep conversation, speaking in hushed tones in deference of the other passengers. She could not hear what they were saying and decided to hold her suggestion for later. So, Margaret spent the ride looking out the dusty windows. She rarely strayed this far from their rooming house and the sights were all new to her. She felt the ride had only just begun when Joseph stood and, speaking to the driver, stopped the car while Philip helped her to her feet.

They exited the car and walked another half block before stopping in front of a building much larger than Margaret could have imagined. It appeared to be three stories tall, built sturdily of wood although it was in need of paint. The first floor windows were boarded yet Margaret could see there was glass in the upper windows, and it seemed intact.

Philip unlocked the massive entry door and stepped aside to let first Joseph then Margaret enter. "Try to look beyond the dust and cob webs and see what we can make here. Margaret, do you have the candles I asked you to bring?"

Indeed, they would need the candles. The boarded windows were allowing only slivers of sunlight to pass despite the brightness of the day. Even before the candles were lit, Margaret could see they had entered a very large room. There was a counter that stretched along one whole wall and behind it were huge mirrors. A few small tables stood about the room in various states of disrepair. At the far end, Margaret saw a piano and small stage. She turned to her right where she saw a broad staircase beside wide swinging doors.

While Philip and Joseph were walking about the large room, talking, Margaret couldn't resist looking behind the swinging doors. She found the largest kitchen she could imagine. The room was long and narrow with windows along one wall and a long counter running below them; a little cleaning would certainly allow more light in the room. There was a big iron stove that reminded her of Mama's but was much larger. Her first thought was how hard it would be to chop enough stove wood, but then she remembered that they would probably use coal. There were two large water reservoirs, one on each end. A long wooden table promised space to prepare all sorts of food, and a large sink stood before the water spigot she was now accustomed to using.

"It will need a good cleaning, but we can certainly feed a lot of people out of here", she said to the empty room.

As she moved about the kitchen, noting that there were some pots and pans on the shelves along the walls, she imagined what it would take to cook here. Philip had said they would eventually get help in the kitchen and she thought how it would be like working in Mama's kitchen when Mama would direct her along with Mary and Catherine to prepare the family's meals or preserve food for the winter.

That made Margaret wonder about the source of their food. She could never carry enough food back from the market as she had been carrying their food over the past months. Would Philip know about this? She would have to ask him.

"Margaret," Philip called, "Where have you gotten to? Let us go upstairs and see the rooms we will live in."

Margaret was eager to see her new home and hurried back out the swinging doors. Philip and Joseph were waiting at the foot of the staircase.

As they made their way upstairs, Philip continued to plan, "We will take our rooms on the top floor and leave the second floor for the customers."

Margaret didn't understand but was too focused on her new home to try to get any questions answered. It was a long climb to the top floor and they had barely glimpsed the wide, carpeted hallway on the second floor.

As they exited the stairway on the third floor, Margaret immediately began assessing it as a home. It reminded her a lot of the house they currently roomed in. The hallway was nondescript and uncarpeted. Just like downstairs, everything was covered with a layer of dust. This did not concern Margaret – she could certainly clean away dust.

They began opening doors. The first door opened to a good sized parlor with a few pieces of furniture. Tall windows looked down on Madison Street. Noise from the street filtered into the room that was dimly lit by dirty windows. Margaret saw an open doorway and through it could see additional rooms that completed this apartment. They moved to the next group of rooms.

These rooms faced the back of the building, overlooking a small, overgrown courtyard. These rooms were quieter without the bustling street below. Margaret thought the parlor was a little larger and she turned to look at the adjoining rooms. She passed through a room that must be used as a kitchen for there was a large round table placed near the windows. There was also a squat stove with a flat top. She imagined it would be tiring to cook over such a stove, but thought she could manage. Beyond, she found two large bedrooms.

Stepping back into the parlor she knew this was where she would want to make their home, "Philip, we can make a fine home here."

He smiled at her, "I think you are right. We will look in the other rooms on this floor and see what furniture we may be able to move in here. We certainly cannot buy furniture right now."

After seeing the rest of the top floor and taking a quick glimpse at the second floor, they returned to the large first floor room. This was Philip's primary concern.

As Philip and Joseph talked, there was more discussion of drinks and liquor. Margaret still could scarcely believe they would be selling liquor. A new pang of guilt washed over her and she was deeply convicted that they should avoid strong drink. Both Mama and Papa had often talked about its evils. Papa talked of many men in the community who had come to ruin after becoming too dependent on the stuff. While Mama kept a bottle on the top shelf for the most severe coughs and for treating deep wounds, she too had much to say about her neighbors who over indulged. Matthew often questioned why Jesus turned the water into wine, and Papa answered with enough other scripture warning away from alcohol that even Matthew chose to refrain and certainly Mama and Papa never touched the stuff.

Margaret couldn't help shuddering a bit when she wondered what her Mama would say about selling it.

Chapter 12

As they returned home from visiting the new building, Margaret's mind flooded with so many thoughts she could scarcely sort them. *I'm gonna have to find a way to tell Philip what's weighin' so heavy on my mind,* she thought.

Joseph exited the horse car well before Margaret recognized their block and she was glad. She knew it would be a lot easier to talk to Philip without his brother listening in. Somehow when Joseph was with them, she could never really talk to her husband, as though he felt like he had to pay attention to Joseph first and any response to Margaret was measured by Philip's anticipated response.

She smiled at Philip, trying to steel herself for what she feared would not be an easy talk.

Philip took her hand and squeezed it gently as he stood and pulled her to her feet. The horse car had stopped near the familiar building they had called home these past months. Margaret took a good look at it as she moved up the walkway. She felt just a little melancholy as she mentally prepared to leave it. She had learned a lot about city life and had really begun her married life here. She smiled as she shrugged off the unhappy feeling, reminding herself that they were embarking on Philip's dream as they started this business.

In their little room, Philip immediately sat down with a small pencil and the ledger book he used for planning. With a pot of coffee made, she sat at the table with him. "Philip, I've got s'many questions, and we never seem to get a chance for to talk."

Philip was beaming. He wanted to talk of nothing but this business, and he was uncommonly willing to answer her questions. He laid his hand on her arm as he reassured her, "We have the whole afternoon to talk dear Margie. What do you want to know?"

"Well," she began then faltered, wondering where she should start. "The rooms we chose over there will need some cleaning and there was furniture in other parts of the building that we can use so that will all have to be moved. When will we do that?"

He sat down the tin mug with his eyes closed as he measured his answer. "I am really torn about that. We have spent almost all of our money buying the building so I feel like I should spend at least another week at the docks. Of course, we are spending money to live here and the building will earn no profit so long as it is empty."

Philip continued sipping the hot coffee and Margaret knew by his distant stare in the general direction of the table's corner that he was weighing all the options. Finally, "Our room here is paid a week ahead. So I will give notice here tomorrow and we will move on Saturday. "

He looked around the room measuring their belongings. "I will hire a wagon. It is really too much to carry, isn't it?"

Margaret was thankful they wouldn't have to carry everything. She had been buying one or two household conveniences every week and had now accumulated several pots, pans, buckets, a churn, blankets and such. Still, they had very little. "I've never even been in a restaurant; if we're going to be runnin' one maybe we should go see what other folks are

135

doing with that kind of business."

Philip looked at his wife and wondered at her innocence. Somehow, it made her attractive to him and he wanted to protect it as long as possible. His smile seemed odd to her but he continued reassuringly, "Joseph is an expert on our business. He has seen every watering hole from here to Georgia so I think we will do just fine."

Margaret didn't understand "watering hole". She cocked her head as she tried to understand how Joseph would ever have either time or money to visit all of those places. Perhaps that was why he had saved so little from his army pay. "You and Joseph were talking about liquor. I really don't think we should get involved with that; God won't bless us if we're temptin' people to sin. And Mama always taught us that too much strong drink is definitely a sin."

Now Philip laughed out loud. "Your Mama will not be our customer, I assure you." And with that, he got up from the table and busied himself with the papers he had been accumulating over the past days.

Margaret knew he was finished with their talk. She thought, *Of course Mama won't come to our restaurant. We'll probably never even see my Mama again.* Holding back tears, Margaret left the table too and tried to find something to do in the little room.

The process of moving was long hours of hard work. Margaret was thankful that the morning sickness had eased somewhat and she seemed to have plenty of energy. She scrubbed every inch of the apartment in the new building, scavenging furniture from all of the rooms on the third floor. Philip forbid her to touch the rooms on the second floor saying they would need to be put in good order very soon. Margaret didn't really understand why, but told herself he must plan to rent rooms to supplement the restaurant business. She had little time to worry about either the restaurant or the budding business plans as she made a new home for her husband and expected child.

It was a blessing to have a little more space. Joseph slept somewhere else, Margaret scarcely knew where, and this was also a blessing although he was usually at their table for supper when he and Philip talked incessantly about their plans and dreams for the business. Margaret hardly even listened to them anymore. They didn't ask for her input and she did not care where they would buy their liquor or how many tables would be needed. She was, however, mildly interested in the entertainment as she'd understood they were hiring a piano player.

Frequently as Philip and Joseph planned and dreamed in front of her, Margaret would think she might ask Philip for more information after Joseph was gone. But Joseph was rarely gone and when he did leave Philip was either so tired he fell right to sleep or he was out the door to do more work downstairs. She was so thankful whenever Philip did spend time talking with her that she chose not question any of the dreams he shared.

Philip found work in a butcher's shop on their same block. He went there three days each week and she understood that Joseph had also found work within easy walking distance. Philip continued to give her half a dollar each day which she used to provide their meals. Just as in the rented room, she was able to save out a few cents each day and buy special things for their home. Now she looked toward homey touches like curtains on the windows and colorful quilts for their bed. She began thinking of making clothes for the baby but knew there was much work to be done while she was still able to move freely. I can sit and sew when I'm too big to for deep cleaning.

With their apartment made livable, Philip asked Margaret to begin work in the kitchen. She had been coming and going from the back staircase that was closest to their rooms so the day that she came down the big central stairs, she was shocked by the work Philip and Joseph had accomplished.

The boards had been removed from the windows allowing bright light into the room. She noticed there were heavy shutters at each window, all of which were open now. The big mirrors behind the counter were bright and clean and stools stood all along the counter. The broken tables and chairs had been repaired and some were painted. The floors were cleaner than before, although she felt a coat of wax was needed.

Margaret found herself in the middle of the room turning a circle. She heard someone enter and turned to see a beaming Philip. "What do you think? You have not been down here in several days, have you?"

"No," she answered. "I can hardly believe all you've accomplished."

He moved to an unpainted table and placed a large piece of oil cloth beneath it. "We have to get these tables painted, but I don't think there are enough of them. We'll probably have to buy some more. If you will start working on the kitchen, I'll help you when this room is in good order."

"Okay, I'm goin' to the kitchen now. I guess the place to start is to get everything cleaned?"

He'd picked up a brush and was painting while he talked to her. "We wi'll get it cleaned then you can take an inventory and see what you will need to cook in it."

"Well, all I need to clean is soap and water – I have that.

Before I can tell you what I need to cook, you'll have to tell me what sort of food I'll be cooking."

He didn't seem inclined to answer her question right away so she moved into the big kitchen.

Looking around her, she hardly knew where to begin. Philip had brought home a huge box of soap flakes which she'd used in the apartment carried it downstairs along with all of the cleaning rags she had. Moving to the water spigot, she thought how she'd need hot water to clean and she eyed the huge iron stove warily.

"Nothing to do but try to figure you out," she said aloud, speaking to the chunk of metal.

Without much trouble, she located the firebox in the center. Of course, it was stone cold. Peering inside, she saw only an abundance of ash. There was a coal bucket beside the stove which was completely empty. She would have to find something to start a fire here, even if she brought some of the coal from their apartment.

As she began looking for the coal or wood, she realized she probably needed to explore a bit anyway. Down a short flight of stairs, she found a larder with all sorts of cubbies. Many of them appeared to be recessed into the earth and the whole room was chilly, reminding her of Mama's root cellar and all of the produce they stored there each summer. Retracing her steps up the stairs, she saw the coal box with the tiniest bit of coal left. *Well, I guess I can heat the water with this. Buying coal has to be at the top of our list though.*

Margaret returned to the kitchen with the half-filled coal bucket and managed to get a fire burning. Looking around, she realized there was really a good supply of pots and pans. Not wanting to wait for the stove's big water reservoirs to heat she sat two large pots filled with water directly over the blaze and began sweeping while they warmed.

By the time Philip joined her, her stomach was telling her that it was nearing noon. The now-familiar nausea was returning and she knew she'd waited almost too long between meals. She felt good about her accomplishments though. The floors were now ready to be scrubbed and the big work table in the center of the room was thoroughly cleaned. The stove had been wiped and Margaret had taken a stock of the available cooking utensils.

Philip was thinking of food, too. "Do you want to go upstairs and eat?"

"Yeah, I need to. It sounds strange, but eating helps the sickness." She followed him up the two flights of stairs to their rooms where there was bread and cheese, as well as a bit of cold meat from last night's supper.

As she walked, with her hand unconsciously on her stomach, she wondered if she'd been sick too long. She had heard Mama talking to neighbors about pregnancies many times and now she tried to remember how long they said they'd been sick. Didn't Mrs. Padgett say she was sick the whole time she carried her fourth child? The thought of it terrified Margaret and she longed for Mama's trusted advice. Girls from all over the plateau would come to talk to her and now her own daughter was having to face this alone.

As they entered their third floor apartment Philip asked, "How do you find the kitchen?"

She uncovered the meat and handed him the plate of cold beef before turning to slice bread. "Well, I can have it cleaned in another day I think. There's plenty of pots and pans and such. You need to help me understand how many people you expect me to feed and we still need to talk about what kind of food you have in mind. Remember that Mama taught me to cook, we just never had anything fancy like you should eat in a restaurant."

Philip looked toward the ceiling as he counted potential customers, "We have room for fifty, but only tables for about twenty-five right now. I would not expect more than half of them to order food. We would need to be prepared for more, can you do that?"

Ignoring his comment that some people wouldn't order food, she responded to him, "Well, it depends on what I'm cooking."

"A hearty stew I think, we will keep bread and cheese and some meat cuts. Does that sound right to you?"

Margaret was a little surprised, "I guess I had expected finer foods. That's not even what we would have fed a party of field workers."

A smile danced at the corner of Philip's mouth as he replied, "It's not like anyone is coming for the food."

"Why else would they come to a restaurant?"

Philip rose and moved toward the door. As usual he'd quickly finished his noon meal and would be back at work downstairs for the rest of the afternoon. He clearly did not intend to answer her questions or to help her understand this very confusing business.

Margaret shrugged off the question and chose not to give it any further thought. She cleared and cleaned the luncheon dishes and was back in the kitchen just a few minutes behind Philip.

By the end of the second day, she felt that she was ready to cook in the big kitchen. Now, she would just need to get a supply of food and coal.

Stepping through the swinging doors, she looked for Philip in the main room. He was behind the counter, unpacking glasses from wooden crates.

"Philip, I need to talk to you about getting food and coal."

Philip looked up from his work. "You are right, we will be open for business by the week's end. We will need to have food to serve."

Margaret looked around. The glass shelves behind the long counter were now filled with all shapes and sizes of bottles. And, there was a wooden barrel at the counter's end. "Why are you putting the glasses behind this counter instead of the kitchen?"

"This is the bar, not a counter," he corrected.

"Oh, I washed some plates and bowls in the kitchen but you're right, I didn't notice any glasses. How did you know we needed them?"

Philip took a deep breath and closed his eyes as he said, "Margaret, you do understand that the bar here is the biggest part of the business?"

No, Margaret didn't really understand anything that had been happening in the past few weeks. And, she couldn't see why this long, wooden bar would be the center of anything. "I don't guess I do understand. I thought the restaurant was the main part."

"The food is just an extra that we will offer. It will be practically free. We just do not want the men to leave if they get hungry."

"Won't they be hungry when they come here? Ain't that why they're coming in the first place?"

Philip looked at her almost like a child, "No, they will come here for the liquor and the company." With that, Philip returned his attention to his work with the crates and glasses. He might as well have left the room, for Margaret knew from experience the conversation was ended. She stood for a moment watching her husband and somewhere deep within herself she felt unsettled. Was Philip hiding something from her? What 'company' was he talking about?

She shook her head and put the questions aside choosing to return to her cleaning and not thinking very deeply about Philip's plans.

Chapter 13

As she finished her work in the kitchen, Margaret was still pondering Philip's strange explanation of their customers when she heard voices coming through the front door. Philip and Joseph never used the front door so she thought she should check on who was there. As she swung open the kitchen door, she found Joseph standing in the center of the room with a woman holding onto his arm. A second girl stood apart from them and looked around as Joseph gestured while he described grand plans for the room.

While the young girl in the back was dressed plainly, Joseph's companion seemed almost gaudy to Margaret. In her hat, she wore the largest feathers Margaret had ever seen. They appeared to be dyed scarlet red and perfectly matched the close-fitting coat she wore. Her boots were highly polished and her skirt was just high enough to show them off.

Hearing her movements, Joseph turned, "Ah, Margie, come and meet the first of our girls."

Margaret bristled a bit, as Joseph used the familiar nickname that Philip had settled into.

Turning to face the lady on his arm he said, "This is Candy. She is just like a sweet from the sweets shop, no? And that is Daisy." He indicated the young girl behind him with a wave of his hand.

Smiling, Margaret offered her hand first to the lady in red, the handshake she received seemed somehow forced. It seemed clear this woman was not interested in knowing her so Margaret took a few steps to stand before Daisy and again extended her hand. The greeting she received from Daisy was warm, and the look in girl's eyes was sad and pleading. Margaret continued to smile but really she wanted to take this girl in her arms and cry with her. She was sure Daisy might break into tears at any moment.

Joseph had apparently concluded his tour of the business and turned to ask Margaret, "Do we have rooms ready for these girls on the second floor?"

Margaret still did not understand what they would use the second floor rooms for and she had scarcely given them a thought. Smiling at the newcomers Margaret answered, "I've only just finished in the kitchen. I'm sure the three of us could get two rooms in good order in no time."

Candy sniffed loudly and Joseph seemed to understand. "You take Daisy and fix up the rooms. Candy and I will have a drink and make some plans. She will come up in half an hour." His movement toward the bar told Margaret he intended to serve her the liquor the men had been unpacking and storing there.

Margaret started to protest as her mind flooded with thoughts. *Joseph Berai will not be giving me orders and I thought these girls were coming to work for us – why am I being sent to prepare rooms. What kind of lady would even drink liquor anyway, maybe we don't want her working for us.*

With a slight shake of her head she decided that she would rather be working on the second floor away from this pair, and she chose not to confront Joseph. Instead she motioned for Daisy to follow her and the two proceeded up the wide staircase. As they climbed, Margaret admired the polished wood as her hand slipped along the smooth hand rail. Philip had worked hard on the staircase and now it was beautiful.

Margaret was so consumed by her own thoughts that she had forgotten Daisy who moved quietly beside her. "Oh, Daisy, how rude I'm being. I'm sorry; my mind just ran away with me. I guess I've spent so much time alone lately that I've forgotten how to carry on a conversation. Please tell me about yourself."

Daisy's drooping head seemed to fall further. "There's nothin' to tell - nothin' anyone would want to know."

"Well that's silly. Of course I want to know, I asked ya' didn't I?"

"My mother died twenty-one days ago. Gerald, my step-father, sent me with Joseph. I think it was the only way he'd let him have Candy." She spit the words out and looked at the floor as though she could see them in all of their foulness.

"Is Candy your sister?"

Daisy blanched white, "Oh my no!" She answered with such force that Margaret swerved backward slightly. "She's one of Gerald's girls."

At the top of the stairs, Margaret moved to the first door, "I don't understand. Does he own a restaurant like ours?"

Daisy looked up for the first time, "Well, he has a dance hall on the south side of the stock yard. He said the men that work in the yards would have money to spend, that's why we went there. Mama was never happy there though; she had to work an awful lot. I think that's what killed her."

Margaret had frozen in the middle of the room. She didn't understand this Gerald-man. *Maybe without his wife he didn't feel up to finishing raising his step-daughter.*

Looking at Daisy, Margaret guessed she was fifteen or

sixteen. She was terribly thin and pale and Margaret felt an overwhelming need to care for her. All that she really understood from Daisy's breathless description was that the girl had lost an unhappy mother and her step-father turned her out.

Margaret had a guilty curiosity about this 'dance hall' that Daisy described. Papa had always taught them that dancing was wrong so Margaret wasn't sure she should ask about such a place. Her compassion for Daisy won out over her curiosity and she decided to wait for a better chance to ask her questions. She smiled at the young girl and tried to get her to focus on the work at hand.

"Well, we'd better get these two rooms in order. Then, you can come up to my rooms and we'll get some hot food in you. Have you been cooking for your step-father?" Daisy kind of shut down again and didn't seem inclined to answer many questions about her life with Gerald. Everything was met with a barely audible "Uh huh" or "Huh uh". Margaret kept up a steady chatter as she made quick work of cleaning the room.

Margaret had already swept out the worst of the dust from the first three rooms on this floor. The second floor rooms were scantily furnished, but there was a bed and wash stand in these three. She and Daisy fluffed the feather ticks and spread on clean linens, wiped down all the wood surfaces and gave the floor a final sweep. Looking at their work, Margaret declared it livable.

"Maybe one of the first things I'll ask the girls to do is give the rooms on this floor a thorough scrubbing; my husband Philip has said the girls will answer to me."

Daisy looked shocked. "Candy will not clean anything. Gerald even had a woman come to get her clothes to wash."

"Well, what did she do? Why would he keep anybody

on that wouldn't do the work she was given?"

Daisy just shrugged her shoulders and looked at the floor. "Gerald said she was the star of the hall. Mama didn't like her much, I know that."

Margaret was about to ask more questions when Candy breezed into the room ending all conversation. She looked around, pursing her lips as she assessed her quarters. She ran a gloved finger along the furniture and tested the bed with her hand. "It will be okay for the moment. Go, I'm tired."

Daisy took Margaret's hand and pulled her from the room. They were just about to turn to Daisy's room when Margaret heard Philip calling her as he came up the stairs.

"I'm here on the second floor, Philip," she called to him. "Daisy, come and meet my husband."

They met him at the top of the stairs. "Philip, Joseph brought two girls to help us. This is Daisy."

"I saw Joseph downstairs." He looked at Daisy from head to toe. Margaret couldn't help thinking he judged her like livestock he was thinkin' of buying. Without a word to Daisy, Philip looked to Margaret, "What are you doing now?"

Unsure how to counter the discourtesy she answered him without emotion, "We're just about to do up Daisy's room. The other one, Candy, is in her room already."

With a second appraising look, he turned toward the third flight of stairs. "Leave her to it; I am sure she can manage."

Unsure what would be the best thing, Margaret looked questioningly at Daisy.

"You go, I'll be fine." Daisy put her hand on the door across from Candy's as Margaret had indicated this would be hers.

Philip did not approve of the room assignment. "Choose a room further down the hall."

Margaret spoke up, "Well, I've not touched any of the rooms beyond the third door."

"Daisy, choose a room down the hall and get started cleaning it. Margaret will come back and help you after a while." With that, Philip disappeared up the stairs.

With a look of apology, Margaret followed him.

She couldn't have started more than ten steps behind him, but he was already in their room, pacing, when she got to the door.

"Philip, you were very unkind to Daisy. She's just lost her mother and her step-father has turned her out; she's sad and we've gotta' help her get through this time."

"I do not care if she is sad. What was Joseph thinking? She will never do. No man will ask for her."

Philip continued to rant, leaving little opportunity to hear what Margaret had learned about the girl. And he was still going on when Joseph came in a few minutes later, bumping into the doorway as he entered. Philip turned his attention to his brother.

"Are you drunk?"

Joseph fell into a chair. "I just had a couple with Candy. Wanted to make her feel welcome, you know. Maybe Margie will give me a cup of her strong coffee."

Margaret moved to the little stove and pulled the pot onto the hottest portion.

"Joseph, I met that girl Daisy. When you said you were going out to get some girls, I thought you of all people would be able to choose. No one is going to want her."

"I had to take her to get Candy. Did you meet Candy?

149

She is the very best that Gerald Moser had. And it took a fancy bit of work to make him part with her. Really it was just luck. We were both drunk and playing poker and he lost a lot of money. I had been trying to talk him out of Candy all evening. So, he thought he would rather part with her than his greenbacks. Only thing was that he would not send Candy without Daisy."

Philip seemed more shocked. "Daisy was working for Gerald?"

Now Margaret certainly had something to add, "No, Gerald had married her mother; I think Daisy kind of grew up in his house. I tried to tell you that her mother died just a few weeks ago."

Philip still addressed Joseph, "Has she even been working?"

"Bo - It was not a question I asked him. Did you meet Candy? When men learn she is here, she will really pack the house."

"Well it is something you should know, if she does not pull her weight, we will not keep her around. I do not care to put her on the street if she does not make us any money."

Chapter 14

Opening day rolled around almost before anyone realized. Philip and Joseph said everything was ready. Margaret had ordered more food than she could ever imagine cooking. The larders were stocked and she knew what she would prepare each day. Despite Philip's idea of a simple soup, she planned to do the best that she could. In fact, Philip had to caution her from ordering too much food.

Both of the men had been working away as much as possible to have the necessary funds to get started. However, as opening day drew closer, Margaret sensed that they were running short. Philip had now decided that he would continue working at the butcher's shop even after the opening. He believed he could work a few hours each morning and planned to open the new business only in the evenings.

Now there were five of 'the girls' occupying rooms on the second floor. Each time Joseph brought another one in, Margaret was more shocked. Margaret would only have deemed Daisy a "girl". All of the others were certainly women, and of a class Margaret had seldom encountered.

Candy continued to be haughty and distant. She acted as though this business belonged to her instead of Margaret's husband. Anytime Margaret asked her to help, she would sniff loudly and go to her room. In fact, only Daisy ever did anything that Margaret asked.

Margaret confronted Philip on this matter,

asking why they were not working if they were hired to work for the Berai family. Philip hum-hawed a bit and managed to leave the room without adequately answering.

Daisy had been in the kitchen with Margaret all afternoon on opening day. The stove was crowded with pots and pans. There was in fact a very good stew simmering and loaves of hot bread were cooling on the tables along the side wall. There were strawberry pies in the cooling larders downstairs. The June heat in the kitchen was stifling and Margaret knew those pies would be no good if they were too warm. Huge pots of coffee were ready to be boiled as their customers arrived, although Philip insisted no one would want coffee.

Margaret heard Philip calling from the small room they had converted into a staff dining area. "Margaret, the girls will need to eat before opening. Do you have their dinner ready? Where is Daisy, everyone is here but her."

Margaret looked apologetically at Daisy. Philip had been gruff with everyone in the past week and she didn't want Daisy to receive the tongue lashing she'd been subjected to on several occasions. "She's here with me," she called. Both ladies grabbed bowls of food that were standing ready to feed the staff and headed through the door.

As they entered the small room, Margaret nearly dropped the heavy stew she carried. She was facing the familiar round table where sat her husband, Joseph, and the four other girls they had hired. Today, each girl was dressed – if you could call it 'dressed' in the brightest colors imaginable. Their shoulders were bare, necklines dipped low, and none of their skirts reached their ankles.

Trying not to look at their indecency, Margaret fastened

her eyes on their faces as she served the stew, only to be again shocked by rouged cheeks and painted lips. With a gasp, she fled to the kitchen.

Behind the kitchen door, Margaret buried her face in her hands. The reality that she had carefully ignored during the past weeks came crashing down upon her. All of the unasked questions about the nature of their business were suddenly answered by the appearance of these 'girls'. She heard Philip opening the kitchen door and a second flood of emotion washed over her. She wanted to throw herself into his arms for the only comfort she knew in this strange place but at the same time she knew that he was responsible for what she had just seen in the next room. She knew that Philip and Joseph had carefully planned for these women and had purposely established a business that would require such staff. With that realization, she wanted to flee from Philip or maybe to pour her wrath out on him.

Philip followed her into the kitchen, "Bring in some water, do you have coffee made for them?"

Initially, he either missed or ignored Margaret's sobbing. Harshly he demanded, "What is this? Why are you crying? You know we do not have time for this."

She refused to look at him – refused to acknowledge her new understanding. "Have you seen what your 'girls' look like? They do not look like decent women! What will people think about us?"

"You are going to have to get your head out of the clouds, Margaret. This is a dance hall – do you know what that is? The girls are here to keep the men drinking and dancing and spending their money. And they will do whatever it takes to keep them here." He turned as though he would leave the room.

"What men?" The words escaped from Margaret in a whisper; she had not intended to ask the question. They froze Philip in his tracks and he pivoted to face her again.

Philip's voice was rising now; rarely did he get angry with her and she was frightened to see it now. "What men? What men, you ask? Our customers!"

The door continued swinging after Philip crashed through it in his haste to leave the room.

Margaret could not breathe. She could not move. She had never been so utterly shocked in all of her life. This business that she had convinced herself would be a respectable restaurant was in fact a dance hall! She had never even heard of such a place until she met Daisy. And when Daisy mentioned living in one, the very name of it made her ashamed for Daisy and Margaret did not ask for an explanation. Now, after seeing the appearance of the girls in their dining room and hearing her husband's explanation, the picture was becoming pretty clear. Her mind began to imagine what he meant when he said the girls would do 'whatever it takes' to keep the men there. She could no longer imagine respectability in this place.

What am I to do? she wondered.

Oh how she longed to run to Mama and Papa and have them tell her what was the right thing to do. In the same thought, she was glad she had not managed to find the time to write them. She had intended to write for she was so proud of Philip and wanted them to be proud too. All that pride was long gone now and she wasn't quite sure what the emotion was that had taken its place.

How much timed passed while she stood unmoving in the kitchen, Margaret could never tell. When she could move, she could only fall to her knees.

She prayed. For long minutes she could only beg, *O Lord, forgive me.* Eventually she was able to talk to her Savior as she had when she was newly saved. *Father, what have I gotten myself into? I have rebelled against your word and the precious parents that you gave to me. I have sinned against YOU! Please forgive me, forgive my rebellion. I don't know what to do now and I have no one to turn to but you. Your word says flee from sin. How do I flee from my husband?*

Her hand went unconsciously to her stomach and the new life growing there. *Is this what my child will grow up in? Lord, how do I raise a baby in this?*

Margaret felt like she could have, in fact probably should have, remained on her knees the whole night through. However, the growing activity and noise in the bar room crept into her consciousness and she knew that she would not long be permitted the solitude her prayers required. So, she rose and numbly continued the kitchen work for which she had been preparing these last weeks.

Well before midnight, Margaret was so exhausted that she could not stand without supporting herself against the kitchen work table. She could not count the bowls of stew she'd ladled, plates of bread and cheese she'd assembled, and all of the strawberry pies had been served. She had managed to keep the kitchen reasonably cleaned in the process but the stack of dirty dishes seemed to continue to grow larger.

Philip came in with a coffee cup in hand and went straight to the pot she'd kept hot through the evening. He had been right and scarcely a single customer had called for a cup of the strong brew. However, Philip and each of the girls had drunk numerous cups.

On this trip into the kitchen, Philip looked at his wife

and seemed to realize that she was nearing exhaustion, "Margie, you look terrible. You will not faint, will you? Maybe you should go upstairs now."

"Thank you, I believe I will go up. I don't know why I'm so tired."

He smiled and stepped close enough to place a hand gently around her waist and she bristled a bit at his touch, "You have been going non-stop for weeks. And you are carrying our child, remember."

The smell of stale coffee hung on his breath and cigar smoke was upon his coat. She looked at her husband and wondered how he could be so kind now after the harsh words he'd spoken just a few hours earlier. Had he forgotten them? Had he completely dismissed her breakdown? Did he have no pangs of conscience for what was going on just through that door?

Margaret's hand went unconsciously to her stomach as she nodded to him, and she moved toward the back stairs. As she climbed, her hand gently stroked the home of her unborn child and she began to pray again. The reality of the home her child would know grew heavier and heavier until she began to silently weep for him.

As she reached the second floor door, the oil lamp she carried to light the stairway caught a heavy shadow that might have spooked her had she not been so caught up in her own thoughts. She stopped and peered closely to realize that it was Daisy. She had folded herself so small that Margaret first thought it was only a pile of clothing. While she made almost no sound, her frame shook with sobs.

"Daisy, is that you?" Margaret stopped, her own cares forgotten for the moment.

With a gasp of breath, Daisy acknowledged her.

"Honey, whatever is the matter with you?"

Daisy turned and fell into Margaret's arms nearly pushing her off her feet on the narrow stair tread. She did not speak, just sobbed even harder.

Margaret shushed and patted her, wrapping her up as Mama had so often wrapped Margaret after hurt feelings or bruised knees. As the sobbing quieted, Margaret tried again to find the reason. "Daisy, can you tell me why you're crying?"

"I can't say it," her voice was so weak Margaret strained in the darkness to make out the words. "I'm so ashamed."

"Whatever do you have to be ashamed of Daisy?"

"Oh, Mrs. Margaret, Candy painted me and stood me in the bar room. Then when a customer bought a ticket, she made me dance with him. He put his hands all over me and I couldn't get away. When he started talking about going upstairs with me, I ran away and I've been hiding in the stairway here ever since."

With her story finished, the sobs again threatened to escalate. Margaret shushed them away. "Hush now, you don't have to do that. Let me think. Does your room have a lock on it?"

"Yeah, I think it does."

"Then you go to your room, I'll make sure the hallway is clear before you go out the door. Then you lock yourself in your room and put a chair under the doorknob. No one will bother you tonight. Tomorrow, I'll talk to Mr. Berai and we'll sort this all out. Do you have any water in your room?"

"Yes, I always fill the pitcher in the mornings."

"Good. You can wash your face and get a good night's rest. We're going to get through this, I promise you."

Margaret eased the door open a bit and immediately

heard footsteps. Peeking through the tiny crack, she saw a man coming from Pearl's room and she controlled the gasp that wanted to escape. He staggered a bit as he reached the main staircase and held tightly to the banister as he made his way downstairs. With the hallway cleared, Margaret opened the door and ushered Daisy out.

Daisy hurried down to her room and was safely behind the door before Margaret continued on to the top floor. She scarcely knew where she had found the energy to comfort the young girl for she now doubted she could make it all the way to her own bed. She prayed as she walked, *Lord, I know I need to spend time with you. It's been so very long since I have. Can I ever stay awake tonight?*

She unlaced her boots as she sat on the side of her bed, telling herself that she had to pray.

Chapter 15

When Margaret awoke to bright sunlight streaming in the windows she knew God had answered her question. For the first time since leaving home, she awoke with a prayer on her lips and a song in her heart. "Thank you Lord, for giving me this new day."

She was almost surprised by Philip's sleepy voice, "What did you say, Margie?"

"Shh, you go back to sleep; I din' mean to wake you," she whispered.

Margaret looked down at her sleeping husband as last night's events and emotions unfolded in her head. For a brief moment she was furious with Philip but somehow the emotion quickly passed. After eight months of marriage, she finally faced the fact that she really knew nothing about this man. More and more she was realizing she hardly knew herself.

As she made her way into the parlor and poured a glass of water, she felt the baby give a little fluttery kick and gently rubbed that area of her stomach. The room was quiet and she had no idea how long Philip would sleep. He had not planned to go to the butcher's today and she didn't know how late he'd worked in the hall.

The hall, she thought, *it's a dance hall!* For just a moment she thought she would cry again. "What good will tears do?" she questioned aloud and quickly put her hand to her mouth. *I don't want to wake him*, she told herself, silently this time.

She remembered that she had every intention of writing to Mama today. She almost spoke again, but caught herself in time, *I could never write her now. What would I ever say? I couldn't lie to her; she would see through that right away.* Her heart ached with the now-familiar pang of homesickness. Each time she felt it, she pushed it back down deeper within herself yet somehow it always found a way out.

She sat down beside the window and glanced at the scruffy lot below. She had thought a dozen times that she must plant flowers down there. There had simply been no time for flowers in the weeks that had passed. Now, as she looked down on it, her own soul felt as unkempt as that little piece of ground. *Oh Mama, what can I do? she wondered.*

Even as she asked the question that her mother could not hear, she heard Mama's voice in her heart, *Pray child, pray.*

Lord, help me, she breathed quietly.

She remembered praying on the kitchen floor last night. Had that really happened, or did she dream it? No, it was not a dream, for that would mean the whole of the evening's memories were dark nightmares.

Somehow she knew she needed to read her Bible, but that was left in Tennessee. She had missed it a few times over the months - never so sharply as she missed it today. *I will have to get one. Surely I can get one in this big town.*

The more she thought about her world, the heavier her heart felt. The peace she woke with seemed to be fading. A part of Margaret wanted to curl up and never move again, never leave this room. Part of her wanted to run as far away from this place as she could. She looked around her at all of her efforts to create a home here for her husband and their family; she saw evidence of Philip everywhere. *There's no running now Margie!*

Wallowing in either self-pity or circumstances had never been permitted in the Elmore home. Margaret knew if she were in Tennessee now, Mama would be pulling her up by her hand and telling her that God had work for her today, she'd better get after it. With a weak smile, she began moving quietly about the room trying to begin her day.

She heard Philip beginning to stir and knew that her quiet meditation was coming to an end. There were countless dishes waiting for her downstairs and he would expect everything to be cared for and ready for tonight's business.

After putting on the coffee pot, she stepped into the bedroom. "I'm making your coffee now. Do you want some breakfast or do you want to wait and eat with the girls?" The title given to their hired women tasted sour in her mouth this morning.

Finishing dressing, Philip nodded a thank you for the offer. "I will just take the coffee now. Go ahead and make some eggs and pork downstairs, just do not expect anyone in the dining room to eat. They will just get it whenever they come downstairs. We have to try to find Daisy. She ran off last night. I am going to give her a beating when I find her. She did not bring in a penny last night."

Margaret had hoped for a chance to talk to him about the poor girl. "She will be in her room. I found her cryin' on the back stairs last night."

"What in the world was she doing there? I know no one got rough with her, I saw her dancing with one man then she just ran away. I thought she would come back yet she never did."

Margaret stepped aside to allow Philip through the doorway into the parlor. "Philip, she said the man had his hands all over her and he expected to come upstairs with her. She didn't know what to do besides run away. I don't blame her. I would have done the same thing."

Philip huffed in disgust muttering something in Italian under his breath, "That Joseph, what was he thinking when he brought her in here? She knows what her job is. She is to keep the men in the bar and drinking – keep them happy."

A part of Margaret wanted to cower away from this discussion, but she knew she had to help at least this one girl. With a flash of wisdom she asked Philip, "I really need help in the kitchen and you said we would be hirin' a girl for that. Why don't you let me use Daisy for the kitchen work?"

Philip just shrugged his shoulders and turned to a ledger he'd pulled out. "That is fine," would be his only answer and Margaret was going to take it.

"I'm headed to the kitchen now. I'm afraid I left it in a poor state last night."

She was out the door with a lighter step than she could have imagined a few minutes earlier and her first stop was Daisy's room. She lightly tapped the door and spoke softly, "Daisy, it's Margaret. Are you awake?"

The door opened immediately. She wondered if Daisy had been posted just inside waiting for someone to call. Daisy was cautious in her greeting, "Good morning."

Margaret's bright smile lifted her caution quickly. "Daisy, you are going to work in the kitchen. Can you cook?"

Her words spilled out without a breath in between, "Well, a little I guess. I will certainly try. And you know I'm a hard worker. Does that mean that I won't have to talk to the men?"

Margaret reached to squeeze her hand, "Yes. That's

exactly what it means. How long till you can come downstairs?"

"Now," Daisy was out the door before Margaret had finished her question.

Margaret and Daisy worked long days together and their friendship grew. Margaret began to feel a spark of the camaraderie she had enjoyed with Mama and her sisters. The dark cloud that hung above her heart seemed to be thinning. She began to find quiet times every day when she could pray and pour her heart out to God.

As the days drew nearer that she would have the baby, her time in the kitchen had to be shortened. One morning she knew that she had to break this news to Philip.

"Philip, I don't think I can spend much more time in the kitchen. I'm there fewer and fewer hours every day, and I can hardly walk after just a short time because my legs are so swollen. I think Daisy is ready to handle it by herself, don't you?"

Philip had brought a newspaper up to their rooms and seemed much more interested in reading than talking. Still he was very anxious to protect his unborn son and the mention that Margaret's health might be in danger snapped him away from the news.

"Oh Margie, you have been so strong that I sometimes forget you are with child. Of course you need to rest more. You do not need to go down at all until time to cook for the customers."

Margaret smiled at his insensitivity. "Philip, because you were the last child your mother carried, you don't realize all that's involved. Even Mama had to rest in the last months she carried Jesse. And the baby will be here in no more than two more months."

"You do not think Daisy will run away again like she did the first night?"

"Philip, she has never run away from work, even really hard work. No, I think she will do just fine. It really is a lot for just one person. Do you think that we are able yet to hire someone else?"

Philip leaned forward to reach the now familiar ledger book. He spent endless hours buried in that book. Now, he sought an answer to Margaret's request there. "We are doing really quite well. You know I have all but stopped the work at the butcher shop. There are more customers every night. I was thinking we needed to add another girl. I will see if I can find someone for the kitchen instead."

Margaret was pleased to tell Daisy that there would be more help coming. And she was even more thankful that the new addition would not be another of the painted girls who worked in the bar.

It was just two weeks later that Philip entered the kitchen while both Margaret and Daisy were working and announced their new helper would be arriving the next morning. Mrs. Walsh had been recommended by the greengrocer. Philip explained she was a widow and directed Margaret to find her rooms.

"We can put her on the second floor, close to the back stairs. We do not want her in the way of the girls when they are working."

Margaret closed her eyes as the comment hit her, but began thinking of the rooms available. Allowing Philip a moment to leave the room, she turned to Daisy, "You know you might prefer to move down the hallway a bit too. It would keep you away from the other girls and out of the traffic when there are customers in the hall."

Daisy's eyes glistened at the idea. Even when she was serving the meals in the staff dining room, she gave the girls a wide berth.

"Oh yes, I would like to move. Thank you so much. Would you like for me to clean two rooms later today?"

While Margaret had looked in all of the second floor rooms shortly after moving into the building, she had not revisited them in several weeks. And she knew the girls had scavenged furnishings from the empty rooms. "Let's go up together as soon as we get the vegetables ready for the stew. We'll see what's available in the rooms and what we'll need to do to make them livable."

By the next morning, Margaret and Daisy had Mrs. Walsh's room ready and they were eagerly awaiting her arrival. Margaret wondered how old she would be. Since the war, widows came in all ages so Margaret tried hard not to have any expectations at all. *I'll just be happy for the help,* she thought.

When Eileen Walsh arrived mid-morning, Margaret realized she could never have anticipated her. The short, round woman had a plump face that looked like it was created to smile. Mrs. Walsh did not smile. In fact, everything about her looked almost angry.

Mrs. Walsh entered through the back door and quickly found her way to the kitchen. She asked to speak to Mr. Berai. Margaret explained that she would be in charge of her work and she would be happy to talk with her. This answer didn't seem to sit well with Mrs. Walsh; at least Margaret assumed that's why her answers seemed to all be, "hmmff". She looked around the kitchen, assessing it.

"Would you like me to show you to your room before

we talk about the work?" Margaret asked while indicating the way to the back stairs.

Mrs. Walsh had one small carpet bag which she stowed in the corner near the back door. She returned to the kitchen tying on a clean white apron which amazingly encompassed her hearty girth. Margaret couldn't help smiling as that thought flitted through her head. She looked directly at Mrs. Walsh and hoped the older woman would believe it was simply a friendly smile.

Understanding that she was ready to work right away, Margaret began a simple tour of the way she had organized the large kitchen and the foods that were stored in the various larders. "We have some good roasts today so I am cooking them for tonight. Daisy and I have the vegetables cleaned and ready to be cooked. Of course we can't start them until much later. We will also have to prepare a light lunch for the staff."

Mrs. Walsh's eyebrow rose slightly at Margaret's description of their employees as 'staff', but she said nothing. In fact, Margaret began to wonder if this woman could talk. She decided to continue the day as she and Daisy had begun and returned to her work, pointing Mrs. Walsh to work of her own.

Margaret and Daisy began to chatter as they had grown accustomed to doing while they worked with Daisy doing most of the talking. More and more, Margaret thought about the coming baby and what her life might be like with the child and the serious thoughts kept her quiet.

She remembered dreaming of having her own family as she'd grown into young womanhood. Somehow she couldn't make those dreams fit into this business and living among all of these people. She didn't share these thoughts with the two ladies who worked alongside her.

Margaret's Faith

Margaret began leaving the kitchen each evening just as the noise in the barroom was growing. Mrs. Walsh and Daisy were well able to handle the meals and to keep up with any demands Philip, Joseph or the girls brought to them. Margaret didn't like leaving Daisy with Mrs. Walsh. Daisy enjoyed chattering to Margaret while they worked and she knew that Mrs. Walsh would not pay attention to her. However, she had no choice. As the time for the baby drew nearer, her body was demanding more rest.

Chapter 16

The day that she had been eagerly waiting for and slightly fearing arrived with little warning. Margaret woke in the overly warm room before daylight. Her first thought was that her back had a terrible ache in it. She turned and writhed in the bed, seeking a comfortable position. Finding none she moved to the window and peered past the drawn drapes looking for a hint of the hour from the sky.

The total darkness made her wonder if it were very early or very late. Stepping into the parlor, she saw Philip's boots by the door and her question of time was quickly answered. He had slept in the smaller room for a few weeks as Margaret grew more restless each night and his late nights in the dance hall caused him to disturb her when he finally came to their rooms.

She crept to the pitcher with one hand knotted in the small of her back. She was thinking that maybe some water would help and she was certainly parched. She had never grown accustomed to standing as far back from the table as her bulging belly required and she was clumsy with the water. Before she could begin to drink the water, she felt the first of the telltale pains spreading across her stomach and joining the ache in her back. Although she had heard Mama describe them many times, the feeling was foreign and threatened to take her breath.

"Oh Mama, how I need you now," she spoke aloud as she maneuvered her way into a comfortable chair in the parlor.

She knew that now she was playing a waiting game.

The gray dawn seemed to reach through the windows and prod Margaret awake with another pressing pain. This one brought an uncontrolled gasp from her lips. She adjusted her position seeking elusive comfort. She heard Philip stirring in the next room and dreaded his waking. She was trying so hard to be quiet yet she was sure her movements were disturbing him.

Thinking that she should try to return to the bedroom, she began hoisting herself from the chair, only to be forced right back down by another pain. That was too soon, she thought. Only once had she been present when Mama helped a neighbor in labor and now she tried to remember how quickly the pains should come. Mama had comforted the lady for hours saying that these things take a long, long time. When the pains came close together, she knew the time was near. Knowing she was going to need help, she wondered if she should wake Philip. When she had talked to him about this day he'd gone straight out to find a doctor that would come to her aid.

"Philip," she called as gently as she could. When no answer came from the closed door, she called a bit louder and louder until she heard his feet on the wooden floor.

When he appeared in the doorway disheveled and scowling, she announced, "It's time, the baby's comin' soon."

His face relaxed immediately, replacing the grimace with a small smile. He took one step toward Margaret with arms outstretch before checking himself and turning back to his little bedroom. He was out the door with hardly a word to his laboring wife.

Margaret had never felt as alone as she did when the door clicked behind him. She thought of the births that Mama had attended on the mountain and knew the family and neighbors who always gathered. A tear slipped from her eye as she longed for the comfort even of a stranger. Then she realized it was indeed a stranger who would comfort her for she had never even met the doctor that Philip would bring to her. She was about to slip into self-pity when another pain stopped her pouting.

By noon, Margaret had indeed brought forth a Berai baby. The doctor stepped from the bedroom to congratulate Philip as his wife served as nurse and attended to both baby and mother.

Margaret was exhausted but could not close her eyes to sleep for looking at the baby. She could clearly hear the conversation in the next room as Philip greeted the doctor, "Doctor is he here?"

"He? No, your daughter is here and in fine shape. That's quite a little Mama you've got yourself. I don't know when I've seen a mother birth her first child so quickly and with such little trouble."

Philip seemed to have missed entirely the compliment the man offered about Margaret, "Daughter? Are you sure? I was certain it would be a boy."

The doctor chuckled as he cleaned and stored his instruments in the tattered leather bag. "Yes, son, I'm sure. I've been delivering boy and girl babies for a lot of years. It's a girl. You can see her and your wife now."

Philip stepped into the bedroom where Margaret was holding their newborn daughter. She looked at her husband, beaming with pride in the baby. "Philip, come and see her. I think we should name her Grace because I can't stop thinking about the grace God has shown by giving her to us."

She was so mesmerized by the tiny new life that

she ddn't immediately look at her husband for a response. When he said nothing, she looked up to ask again about the name.

Philip straightened from his close inspection of the baby, "Grace is fine, I suppose. I have to get to work now. The business does not stop for babies." With that he was gone.

Margaret's only visitor was Daisy. She tapped ever so gently on the door shortly after Philip's abrupt departure. The doctor had left directly behind Philip leaving his wife, resting in a corner of the bedroom and periodically checking on Margaret. With the baby fed her brief first meal, Margaret fell asleep until she heard Daisy's knock.

Daisy was beaming and her steps practically bounced. She announced that Philip had sent her to sit with Margaret and to see to her needs. This was the dismissal that the doctor's wife had been waiting for. With a few instructions to Daisy, the stranger was gone.

Daisy looked closely at the bundle lain at Margaret's head. She reached a hand toward her but did not touch. Margaret wanted to reassure her friend, "Daisy, this is Grace. Isn't she beautiful? Would you like to hold her?"

Daisy's mouth formed an 'Oh' yet no sound followed. Her hands moved up to the bundle but she still did not touch it. With a smile, Margaret lifted the baby into Daisy's arms, guiding her hand to cup the tiny head.

After long minutes staring at the precious bundle in her arms, Daisy looked to Margaret with tear dampened eyes, "She's perfect, ain't she? I had no idea how precious a baby could be."

"Daisy, I never asked you, do you have any brothers or sisters at all?"

As Daisy slowly shook her head from left to right,

Margaret was reminded how blessed she was to have grown up with her loving family. And that reminder brought a fresh pain to her heart as she thought those siblings might never know her little Grace.

Throughout the day, as Margaret would wake from napping, she found Daisy either holding or simply admiring the baby. She felt Daisy would have never left her bedside had not Philip come to fetch her to the kitchen as the evening business hours drew near.

"Daisy, what are you still doing here?" Philip called from just inside the bedroom doorway.

"Well sir, you told me to take care of Mrs. Margaret. So I've been here doing everything that I could."

"Mrs. Walsh needs you in the kitchen. We can hear her grumbling and dropping pans all the way to the bar and that isn't what our customers want to hear."

Margaret doubted the customers could hear much of anything above the din of the piano, loud men and coarsely laughing women. She smiled genuine thanks at Daisy as the young girl gently patted Grace. Reaching to her with her free hand, Margaret thanked her friend, "Daisy, you have been so precious to me today. Thank you. You will come back to visit Grace tomorrow?"

A quick smile filled her whole face as Daisy eagerly answered, "You know I will. Just as soon as the house is awake tomorrow, I'll be here." Daisy nearly skipped out of the room and Margaret heard her quick step down the hallway, toward the back stairs.

Margaret turned her eyes and attention to her husband, assuming he had come to get better acquainted with their daughter. "Oh Philip, I can already tell that she is a very sweet baby. I've slept a lot today, and I hardly heard her cry at all."

Philip only nodded. She realized he had come to their rooms to change his clothes before the customers began arriving. He had little to say and scarcely looked at Grace.

The September evening was warm, yet Philip had brought a chill into the room. Margaret pulled the baby closer to herself as though to protect her from her father's inattention.

Philip seemed to have completely dismissed the life-changing event Margaret had passed through during this day. "There was a fire last night at one of the houses down the street. We should be overrun with business tonight. I hope that Mrs. Walsh has plenty of hearty food. She is not as good of a cook as you are Margie, but she does get the job done. I have told the girls to expect plenty of men tonight; this would be a good time to have a couple more girls. I wonder if I should try to hire some from Maude. Lula used to work for her and she says she is a hard woman. Still, with the fire damage, her girls may need a place."

Margaret began to silently cry. Philip never noticed.

Philip left the room, tossing his Italian good-bye, "Ciao", over his shoulder. With that, Margaret was alone with her baby.

Replaying Philip's monologue in her head, she became overwhelmed by the realization that Grace would grow up in this house, this dancing saloon. Instead of her aunts and uncles, she would know only 'the girls' and from the way Philip was talking there would be even more girls to come. Margaret would put her to sleep with sweet lullabies then risk her being awakened by the raucous music from the hall downstairs. Margaret looked at her sleeping baby and asked aloud, "How can I raise you like that?"

With no answer to her question, Margaret fell back into a fitful sleep, knowing she would be awake through the night whenever Grace needed feeding.

A few days after giving birth, with Philip off to his morning's duties, Margaret moved to his desk and took a sheet of paper from a slot then picked up Philip's steel pen. She rolled the pen in her fingers as she rolled words in her head. She had thought so many times in the last year of writing to her family, had even composed letters in her head as she thought of dozens of things she wanted to share with them, somehow she could just never quite put the words on paper.

The pen felt strange to her. Papa knew the value of reading and writing and pushed his children to practice their writing even when schooling was finished. Papa would sit by the fire and watch as they practiced letters on their slates. In later years Margaret realized he watched them with pride in his children but also with a longing for the knowledge that each was gaining as they learned their letters. Lawrence Elmore's father had not realized his son would need any book-knowledge. In fact, the elder Elmore held little regard for academics of any kind. The children always believed that Mama's love of books and her own mother's commitment to literacy was one of Papa's first attractions to her. And he'd insisted that each of his children learn to read and practice reading. In response to Papa's urging, Margaret had read every printed word she could find. She realized now that it was from books she learned to dream of a life of excitement far away from the family's farm.

Now, it had been so long since Margaret had held either a quill or slate pencil that it felt strange to her fingers. She wondered if she could write a legible letter. She dearly wanted to share the news of their first grandchild with her parents. Still she found great difficulty in composing the letter. Dipping the pen in the ink well, she began:

Dear Papa and Mama,

I am sorry my letter is so long in coming to you. I fear you've believed me dead and I never intended to worry you. I trust this letter will find you and all of the family doing well. I wish I could know what news you have of Matthew as I hear the war is not going well for the Rebs. I have so many questions I want to ask you, but I must limit the letter to news for you I think.

Philip Berai and I have been married since leaving Elmore Community and we are living in Chicago. He has started a business and he is pleased with the success. I have just birthed our first child, a daughter and I have named her Grace Ann. All has gone well and my health is good. Grace is beautiful. I believe she looks like Grandma Elmore with her dark eyes and hair. Of course, I know the color may change still the likeness is there nonetheless.

The hardships of the war are not so keen here. There are a lot of people and there is good work. Philip says he can make his fortune here. The work has been hard but it's nothing worse than you taught me to endure.

I miss you all terribly. Please give my love to Mary, Catherine, Paul and Jesse. Has Lou returned to you from her folks' farm yet? If so, please greet her for me as well. I will send more news soon.

Your Loving Daughter, Margaret Berai

Margaret looked at the slightly wavy letters her shaking hand formed. She re-read the words and wondered why they sounded so hollow, even stilted. Her mind wandered back to the farm and she could hear the chatter of her siblings and Papa teasing them and Mama laughing with the girls as they worked over some household project. She stopped herself with a shake of her head.

That won't do you any good. You are here and you have to stop longing for something you cannot get back.

Giving the ink another puff of air, she folded the paper carefully and slid it into a ready-made envelope carefully addressing it to Lawrence Elmore. She held the wax stick over the open stove and applied it to the envelope's flap. The seal seemed to have the opposite effect on her heart; somehow her heart opened a bit with the completion of this first letter home.

Margaret had helped a great deal both with her younger siblings and neighbors' babies still she had never had sole care of a newborn and she found herself with many questions. However, with neither her mother nor any other experienced women available to her, she pressed on with each new task.

Margaret was thankful that Philip did not press her to return to her work in the dance hall. She found she could really do nothing more than what was necessary to care for little Gracie, as she'd begun calling her. She withdrew within herself and tried to wish away the awful business downstairs.

She loved this baby as she'd never imagined loving anything. And the baby made her smile, but the smiles lasted only moments… then the heavy veil of gloom settled back over Margaret. She knew she should be praying through these feelings of despair, she just seemed unable to do so. She still did not have a Bible and was barely leaving her apartment so the prospect of getting one seemed very small.

Philip returned to their shared room commenting, "If the baby wakes you every two hours anyway, I will not disturb you too much when I come in at three in the morning."

Just as Margaret thought in the first days, Gracie was indeed a very good baby. Within a few weeks, she was sleeping several hours every night. Margaret was hopeful that she would be the rare infant that slept the night long from an early age. Philip did not complain about the noise or disturbance, although Margaret cringed at every peep in the early morning hours after Philip's long nights in the bar.

Spending hour after hour alone with only baby Gracie, Margaret began to see the third floor rooms more like a prison. She had completely forgotten her excitement when Philip first brought her to their new home and what initially felt like a spacious home now seemed to close in on her. The curtains and pillows she had carefully sewn to bring color and cheer to their surroundings threatened to smother her.

She cried almost every time she looked at her precious child. Margaret remembered the bitter tears she'd shed a few months ago in the big kitchen when she had seen the reality of this business for which Philip had worked and longed. And she remembered reaching out to the Lord in prayer that night. God had seemed so near then; she had been sure she could overcome this situation with His help.

Now, as she sat holding Gracie for hours at a time, she tried again to pray. Every time she turned her heart toward God, she was flooded with the memory of what was going on downstairs. She reminded herself that she had willingly come away with Philip and married him. And she decided she deserved this fate.

She began to talk to the baby, almost expecting her to respond and was greatly saddened when all her daughter offered were little coos and whimpers.

Philip took note of his wife's declining state but scarcely knew how to handle it. He put no demands on her time thinking that she would recover and return to her part in their booming business.

And yet, Margaret did not recover, not for many months. She withdrew even from Daisy's company. The girl continued to visit her only real friend but she no longer felt wholly welcome in the third floor apartment.

The warm temperatures steadily fell and soon Margaret was watching snow fall from her windows. The first sight brought a girlhood thrill and she held tiny Gracie up to see the white flakes outside the window. Just moments later she was again blue, thinking only of the dark winter days she faced.

The room that had seemed so warm and comfortable during last spring's cool days now felt damp and chilly. Margaret feared for Gracie's health and spent even more time holding the baby close to her body for warmth. She remembered Mama's stories of her own childhood, growing up in drafty cabins and often sweeping snow from the bedroom floors after a particularly windy night. "How did all of her ten siblings survive, I wonder?"

She thought again, as she did almost every day now, *How would Mama handle this?*

As much as she longed to talk with her mother and to pour out her burdens to this sage woman of God, she was ashamed to even imagine that conversation. Even if she could see her, she knew she could not tell Mama the truth of their business here.

The business was making money. Both Philip and Joseph had long since stopped working for other men to bring in cash and Philip was even spending some of his share of the money. Of course, Joseph had always spent every cent Philip would give him.

Philip was very careful and still gave Margaret just what

he thought would be needed for her necessary purchases. It mattered little to Margaret since she scarcely left the apartment except to go to the dining room when Daisy failed to bring cold meat or bread on her regular visits. Philip knew that something was not quite right in her spirit. Trying to cheer her, he had brought her several yards of a beautiful, heavy silk for a new skirt and even asked if she wanted to buy new boots.

Despite his obvious disappointment that Gracie had not been the anticipated son, he also sought to provide for her. There was a little cradle at the bedside and he'd also brought home some soft pink flannel and a length of white ribbon.

Caring very little about her own appearance, Margaret sat down with scissors and needle to make a long gown for Gracie. The child seemed to grow longer from morning to evening. The clothes that Margaret had prepared before she was born were no longer able to keep her little ankles warm, and she always seemed to kick free of the blankets.

It took Margaret only a short time to complete the seams in the gown and turning it right side out she wondered if Mama would have approved of the work.

As she pondered the tiny garment and remembered the hours she'd spent in the little mountain cabin learning to sew, she seemed to be able to hear her mother's voice, *Margie, why do you keep turning to me? You need to turn to God.*

Margaret dropped her head and the ever-ready tears instantly spilled down her cheeks. *God isn't here either.*

The eyes of the Lord are in every place, was the answer her heart heard.

"If he can see me then he is ashamed of me." Now Margaret spoke aloud.

Margaret heard the phrase, no condemnation. She asked

herself, What does that mean?

As her mind began to toy with the phrase, she heard Philip's steps at the door. Somehow, she almost felt guilty and looked around for any physical sign of her meditations. The finished gown was on her lap and Gracie still slept peacefully in her cradle near the stove.

As he walked through the room, Philip threw his ledger book on the desk and began unbuttoning his coat. She knew something had not gone exactly right but wasn't entirely sure she wanted to ask about it. She didn't have to.

"That Walsh woman is going to break me," Philip ranted. He paced back and forth so close to the cradle that Margaret moved to shelter Gracie. "Margie, you just have to get back down to the kitchen. She is either ordering way too much food or we are paying too much for it. I do not know where any extra is going – we are not serving that much more food. Can you go and check the larders?"

"Oh, I had not thought of going back to the kitchen." Margaret caught herself before she said, ever.

"You have got to. The baby is three months old now; surely you can come back downstairs and help me. Our profits are really down this month. I do not even know what I said to the grocer's boy when I got his bill." With that, Philip stepped into the adjoining room and she knew the conversation was over. Philip had decided what she would do and he would not further discuss the matter. Margaret had grown accustomed to the nature of these decisions so, she would go to the kitchen.

Looking out the window at the gray day, she judged it was too late to go down today. She would plan to go first thing tomorrow and began to move about her apartment preparing for the work before her. Gracie awoke about the time Philip headed down the stairs. Margaret noticed that he wore new clothes; she thought he looked like a dandy man in his bright red vest. Taking a second look, she realized his coat was made of velvet. She'd never seen a man in a velvet coat and started to question the choice then thought better of it.

Margaret tried to affectionately bid him good night but wasn't sure whether she seemed affectionate or formal. She found they talked less and less. In fact, all Philip ever talked about was this awful business and the money he either was or wasn't making, depending on the day.

Chapter 17

Margaret woke at dawn and laid expecting Gracie's cry. In the silence she rolled to the side of the bed and reached down to the little cradle to find her baby, warm and sleeping peacefully. Rolling onto her back, Margaret stared at the ceiling contemplating the day before her. As the darkness to which she had grown accustomed began to settle over her, she was reminded of yesterday's meditations.

Lord, are you there? She paused, knowing that he would not audibly answer her. Yet somewhere in her heart she knew He was indeed with her. She continued to pray, *I have got to find my way back to you. Gracie needs you so she's going to need me to walk with you. I guess all I can ask for is help. Please help me today.*

Margaret got out of the bed as quietly as possible and took Gracie into the parlor to change and nurse her. She wanted to get the day started for she feared if she waited she might lose her battle with that dark feeling. With a few morning preparations completed, she carried Gracie down the back stairs with as many quilts as she could carry. She planned to lay her on the quilts in a quiet corner of the kitchen. She hoped that maybe she could go out later today and find a basket for her. If Margaret was to be in the kitchen regularly, she'd have to find a way to care for her daughter there.

In the quiet kitchen, Margaret put Gracie down and made her way, with a lamp in her hand, to the storage room. Setting the lamp on the work table, she began opening each of the larder doors. There were some food stores, but it wasn't altogether well stocked. She couldn't see that anything was spoiling; although some of the meat seemed a little older than she preferred and she wished it had been salted. There were not enough potatoes or carrots for the stews that they routinely served, and there were no cabbages or turnips.

With a mental note of what was needed, she returned to the kitchen. After checking that Gracie was still sleeping, she stirred the fire in the big stove and set water to boil. She had not found enough eggs to feed the household although she had found pork and oats, so that would be their breakfast.

By the time the big pot of coffee was boiling, Daisy joined her in the kitchen.

"Mrs. Margaret, whatever are you doing here?" Daisy seemed torn in her question; her eyes were alight at the sight of her friend, while she looked all around the room and over her shoulder as though she feared who else she might see.

"Daisy, what's wrong with you? Did I scare you? Philip asked me to check on the food stores. Since I was down here, I made the coffee and was about to start some oats for breakfast. There don't seem to be enough eggs to feed ever-body."

Daisy continued to look nervously over her shoulder. "Mrs. Walsh...she don't..."

Daisy stopped short when she heard heavy steps on the back stairway. She stared at the doorway as Mrs. Walsh arrived. The woman looked disheveled and just a little grumpy. Margaret was shocked by her appearance and had to control a gasp that she knew would be rude to express.

Mrs. Walsh did not immediately see Margaret as she stood shielded by the iron stove. "Daisy, do you have the fire going? Hmmff, smells like you made coffee too. Weak stuff, it won't be fit to drink." Mrs. Walsh continued to grumble as she moved around the stove, only to encounter Margaret watching her. Shocked, she stopped short, "What're you doin' here?"

"Good morning Mrs. Walsh. I've made the coffee good and strong and I've started some water boiling for oats. Shall we slice up the salt pork to have with them?"

Mrs. Walsh looked as though she had more to say. Margaret smiled kindly at the older woman and moved away, checking the condition of the rest of the kitchen. She was not altogether pleased with the cleanliness and set Daisy to work with hot soapy water and made a plan to scrub the floors after breakfast.

Between helping and directing Daisy and caring for Gracie, Margaret was able to stay out of Mrs. Walsh's way most of the morning. When the light breakfast was cooked and served in the staff room, Margaret spoke to the two ladies, "Let's turn to scrubbin' the floors. If we do it right away, they'll get dry before we have to start workin' on the evening meal."

Daisy faced the hard work with a cheerful attitude, while Mrs. Walsh grumbled with every move that she made. "I'm too old to be down scrubbing. I'm here to cook and not clean. I don't know why you'd want to clean in the middle of the winter time; that will make everyone in the house sick for sure." The tirade continued as she scrubbed.

When Philip opened the door, the floor was nearly cleaned. "Margie, this looks great!"

Margaret smiled, appreciating the compliment. She had missed that since he rarely said he appreciated anything she did for him personally. She got to her feet and moved to pick up the waking baby and follow her husband to the adjoining dining room.

Finding the room empty, she tried to report to her husband about his concerns. "Philip, I've looked at the food stores. There's not a whole lot of waste, but neither is there much food on hand. I'll put together an order for the grocerman today."

Philip was not pleased with the report. "I had hoped you would put my concerns to rest. We will have to get rid of one of them. I think Mrs. Walsh, what do you think? Daisy is too simple to be stealing from us."

Margaret didn't like his description of dear Daisy. Neither did she want to put Mrs. Walsh out on the street. "I don't think we should let either of them go right away. Let me get the larders filled and see how things go."

"Okay, only if you can be here regularly with the child." He indicated their daughter as though she were a piece of furniture.

Margaret held Gracie a little closer, wanting to protect her from her father's harsh words. "Gracie will be fine. She's an awful good baby." Margaret would have further explained that she compared their baby to her own younger siblings as well as numerous babies born in the Elmore community through the years but Philip didn't want to hear anything about Gracie. He sat at the table and seemed to dismiss both of them.

With the floors properly scrubbed, and Gracie bundled for a walk outdoors, Margaret headed out to place her food orders. It was nearing noon as she turned down West Madison Street. The wind bit at her exposed cheeks, but she turned her face up to the sunshine. The brightness seeped into her soul and lightened her step.

Lord, she prayed silently, Thank you for the sunshine. Somehow it proves that you are still here.

As she walked she continued to pray, occasionally speaking words of comfort to Gracie. She quickly walked the two blocks to Clinton Street and turned the corner to the grocer Philip had chosen to use months before when they first moved into the new business. The street bustled with people. Margaret had been secluded in her apartment for so many weeks that she seemed to have forgotten how many people surrounded her in this big city.

Entering the grocer's building, she greeted the man at the counter and asked to speak with Mr. Fitzgerald. The middle aged gentleman stepped through a curtained doorway, wiping his hands on his heavy apron. He offered a genuine smile and greeted her in the Irish brogue she had grown accustomed to, "Well, good morning to ya, if it's not Mrs. Berai I'm seeing! It's been so long since I been hearin' from ya' that I thought ya must'a left the town."

"Good day Mr. Fitzgerald. I've had someone else ordering for me. Have you been making the deliveries to us?"

Mr. Fitzgerald closed his eyes as though searching orders written on the lids. He began shaking his head before he reopened them, "No, we've not had an order from the Berais in four or five months. I met your Mrs. Walsh on one of me last deliveries. She been doing the ordering for ya'?"

Margaret thought to herself that this might explain some of the high costs that Philip was so concerned about. She would have to try to find out what grocer Mrs. Walsh had chosen to use. She recalled that Philip had spent some considerable time choosing the grocer and had talked with a number of men who could supply the foods necessary to run their kitchen.

"Yes, she has," Margaret answered him.

"Well, she'll not be caring too much for me; too Irish, I

s'pose."

Margaret cocked her head as she tried to understand the kind man. He saw her confusion and explained further, "A lot of me Irish brothers – and sisters – resent that I own this business and that I've prospered in America. Many of them have not fared so well. Maybe Mrs. Walsh has struggled and she din' want to see me succeeding." He shrugged his shoulders with raised hands. "There is nothing I can be doin' about it."

"Well, I'm sorry about that." Margaret made her apologies without really understanding. Mrs. Walsh had the same accent that her friend Cara from the boarding house did. Cara had been Margaret's first exposure to an Irish immigrant and Cara's jovial, friendly nature made Margaret try all the harder to befriend Mrs. Walsh, but the two ladies were as different as could be. If Mrs. Walsh didn't care for her own countrymen, Margaret wasn't sure that a southern girl had any chance of befriending the cook.

Turning her attention back to Mr. Fitzgerald she said, "I do have an order for you today. There are several things I will need as soon as possible, and then I'd like to put together a weekly order again, if that will be possible?"

The man smiled and nodded, "Sure, be happy to do it for you. Let's see what you'll be needin' now and I'll be tryin' to get it to you afore the day is out."

As he picked up a bit of a pencil and paper, Margaret listed those items she'd found lacking in the larders this morning. Next, she asked what he had in season as she knew that some of the outlying farms might already be bringing in field greens. She was pleasantly surprised to learn that some early cabbages had come in on the train from the south end of the state. The heads were small, but she felt that the customers would enjoy the many things they could do with cabbage and ordered several heads to be delivered.

With her shopping completed, she adjusted Gracie's weight in her arms and headed out the door. As she walked, she became distracted by her own thoughts and walked straight past West Madison Street. She didn't realize her error until the clanging of bells interrupted her thoughts. The sound was familiar, it was just much louder than normal and looking around, she stopped in her tracks.

Just ahead on the same side of the street was a big old stone church and it was obvious the chiming noise emanated from this building. She watched as a woman came out of the big wooden doors leading a little boy and descended the stairs. She wondered if they were finishing a service and tried to remember what day it was. Surely it wasn't Sunday. No, the grocer would not have been there to take her order and anyway, it was much too late for Sunday services to be letting out. Her curiosity drove her feet and almost before she knew it, she was walking through those enormous doors.

This church did not look like the Clear Creek Baptist Church. She wasn't surprised if big city churches might be a little different, but she was shocked when a gentleman dressed in a long black robe with a white collar about his neck approached her.

"Good afternoon, I am Father Michael. I don't believe I've seen you in our congregation before." He spoke so softly, she leaned forward to make out the words. And, he approached with both of his hands reached out to her.

"No Sir, I haven't been here before. To tell you the truth, I'm not quite sure how I even got here today."

He continued to smile kindly at her, "Perhaps the Lord

has led you. Can I help you in some way?" He looked at the baby bundle as though this might be her reason for entering the church.

"I, uh, I'm not sure," she stammered for just a moment. Then she remembered the phrase that had come to her last evening and had continued to bounce around in her head through the day, no condemnation. She knew that she could readily find that if she only had her Bible. Surely this man could help her to get one.

"Well yes, as a matter of fact, you can help me." Margaret was encouraged that his demeanor did not change with this announcement. "I don't know this city very well and when I came here, I'm afraid I left my Bible at home. Can you tell me where I might get one?"

His smile broadened as he answered her, "That is certainly not a need that I often hear when strangers come through that door. It is a need I can certainly help with though."

Turning, he motioned Margaret to follow him. She hesitated only a second before following him. She easily kept pace with him as he moved down a narrow hallway and turned into a small office with many books, a tiny desk and several chairs. He went directly to a shelf and pulled down a brown book that clearly had been used many times. "This copy should serve you well. It belonged to an aged parishioner who left many books to the church when he passed away. Please enjoy it."

Margaret reached out her free hand to take the Bible. "I had thought that you would tell me where I could buy one."

"Well, I have this one and I'm happy to give it to you. I would enjoy seeing you at Mass someday."

Margaret smiled, not entirely sure where he wanted to

see her. She turned to leave the room still looking at the precious volume in her hands. "Thank you ever so much."

Chapter 18

As she came down the stone church steps, Margaret had to force her eyes up to watch where she was going. Gracie began to stir and she realized that she had completely lost track of time and now would have to get home quickly to feed the baby. She looked both ways and saw no landmarks that were familiar to her. For the briefest moment she was frightened that she may have become lost. The fear passed quickly as she reached out in prayer, thanking her Lord for directing her steps this day. *Lord God, I know that you have brought me down this strange road because you knew I needed this Bible. Thank you for sending this preacher into my way and for giving me Your Word. Please bless him for showing such kindness to a stranger. Now I just have to find my way home and I'm gonna' need your help.*

The way home very quickly presented itself as she saw the grocer's building and the familiar landmarks marking her turn onto West Madison Street. The baby would wait no longer as she entered the back door of the saloon. Gracie was growing louder by the minute as Margaret hurried up the stairs to change and feed her precious daughter.

Whil tending to the baby's needs, Margaret talked in soft tones to Gracie telling her of the events that the baby had mostly slept through.

When she had Gracie settled again, Margaret sat down for a moment with her new treasure before her and bowed her head to give proper thanks for this little miracle. She was still

praying when Philip opened the door. She heard the door and
Joseph's voice all at once.

Philip saw Margaret right away but did not understand
her position. "Margie, what are you doing there? Are you asleep
in the middle of the afternoon?"

Smiling, Margaret looked up to her husband and
brother-in-law. "No, not sleeping, I'm praying."

Joseph's eyes glinted mischievously and he snorted
before speaking. She knew from experiance that he was going
to tease her unkindly but Philip didn't allow him the
opportunity when he spoke before Joseph could get beyond the
snort, "We often found our mother praying. Remember that
Joseph?," it almost had the ring of a warning to his brother.
"When have you written her Joseph? I have not written for a
long, long time. When I left for the war, I never got a response
to my last letter. It would have saddened her that we joined the
Army after she worked so hard to get us away from the
territorial wars in Italy." Philip said no more on the subject as
he turned to the stove to pull the coffeepot forward to warm.

After Joseph left for his own rooms and while Philip
was dressing for the evening's work, Margaret stepped into the
bedroom to share the afternoon's events with her husband.

"Philip, I took a wrong turn when I left the grocer's
today and you'll never believe what I stumbled into."

Philip was preoccupied with dressing, choosing a
brightly colored vest and inspecting his white shirt for stains,
"What is that?"

Margaret refused to allow her feelings to be hurt by his
lack of attention. Her heart was full and she desperately wanted
to share it with her husband. "It was a church. You know the
bells that we're always hearing? Well, I found the church where

that comes from. And I met the preacher there. Only, I don't know what kind of church it is 'cause the preacher was wearing what looked like a long black dress. The church was really pretty inside though."

"What street was it on, do you remember?"

"Umm, I think State Street, but I'm not really sure since I was actually lost when I found it," Margaret almost giggled as she realized how silly she must sound.

Philip had traveled around the city both before the war and since returning with Margaret. He knew the area much better than she did. "Yes, I know that church. It's a Catholic church. The priest you met was wearing a cassock."

"Cassock? I never heard of such a thing? And I never saw a man dressed like that before. He was very kind though, and he gave me a Bible!"

This piqued Philip's attention and he paused in his dressing, "He gave you a Bible? Why ever would he do that?"

"Well, I left my Bible in Tennessee and I asked him where I might buy one. So he led me down this little hallway to a room with lots of books and he gave me this one." Margaret was holding the precious volume in her hands. "He seemed to apologize because it had some use. Don't you think a Bible is even better if it's been used some? I've never even seen a new one anyway."

Philip was growing more confused by the moment and frankly becoming a little agitated. He wanted to finish preparing for the evening in the saloon and he found his wife's story confusing. "I do not understand. What were you doing at the church and why did you ask him for a Bible?"

Margaret sat taller and straightened her shoulders as though preparing for battle, "Philip, we have a child now and I want her to grow up knowing the Lord and knowing his word. She won't know unless we teach her."

"Well, we will enroll her in catechism classes when she is old enough. That will not be for a few years."

"Catechism? What's that?"

"Oh Margie, I do not have time to teach you all the tenements of Catholicism tonight. I have to get to work." This he said as he buttoned his coat, then he left without another word. He cast only a glance toward the sleeping baby.

Margaret was left feeling dejected. She had hoped that Philip would embrace the plan to raise their daughter in the way of the Bible. She wanted to know that she had a partner in this parenting endeavor. He wanted to train Gracie in something called 'catechism' which Margaret had never even heard of. She was pretty sure that wasn't in the Bible and she thought she'd have to ask someone what that word meant. In the meantime, she began praying and resolved with the Lord that she would continue to pray, even as she worked in this awful business her husband had gotten their family mixed up with.

She so greatly enjoyed her Lord's fellowship that she didn't want to leave the little room. Still she knew she would have to return to the kitchen before the evening's business began. So, with a deep breath to brace herself and with Gracie in her arms, she started down the back stairs. Still praying as she walked, she asked God to bless Gracie's upbringing and she promised to read his word every day.

She found the kitchen empty, but the stew simmering and bread rising. Either Daisy or Mrs. Walsh had been hard at work during the afternoon and they had done just as Margaret had instructed them. With a smile, Margaret began putting the finishing touches on the evening meal and setting the table for the staff to eat first.

As she worked, she continued to contemplate her discussion with Philip. If her mind wandered at all, Gracie would coo or cough and remind her of her greatest responsibility. She resolved within herself that this child would indeed receive a godly upbringing and biblical teaching even if she had to do it all by herself.

As she made these plans for Gracie, she began to wonder why this wasn't more important to Philip. She remembered Papa always urging the children to learn their letters so they would be able to read God's word. Despite the fact he had to depend on Mama to read the scriptures to him, still he taught his children from the Bible every day. Even when they worked in the fields, Lawrence Elmore taught them about his Lord, using the creation that surrounded him. Margaret thought this was the way of all men and fathers.

Then a single fact hit Margaret and she froze in her work. Philip did not know The Lord, her husband was not saved.

Margaret felt renewed shame and conviction as she realized that she had never asked this man about his relationship with God. She had never even contemplated it and they had now been married over a year. Mama had taught her that this was the most important thing to consider when choosing a husband and she had neglected it all these months. Lord forgive me, she prayed.

"That seems to be my only prayer," Margaret whispered.

"Pardon me, Ma'am?" Daisy had slipped into the kitchen during Margaret's musings and Margaret had been so distracted that she never even heard the girl.

With a bit of a start Margaret turned to her friend, "Oh, Daisy, I didn't hear you come in. I'm afraid I was talking to myself."

Daisy smiled, "Don't worry, I talk to myself all the time, only I try to only say it out loud when I am alone."

Now it was Margaret's turn to smile. "I've missed our work together Daisy. And you know what? I wasn't talking to myself, I was praying and it just spilled out my mouth."

"Praying?" Daisy questioned.

Margaret wanted to share everything that was in her heart with her friend. And, in this moment, she began to feel a longing to see Daisy come to know the savior. However, just as she began to share her day's adventure, Candy burst into the room demanding her supper and complaining about something that Margaret neither understood nor cared to understand. Then the moment was gone. Margaret resolved to find a way and a time to finish this conversation. She also knew that she must start praying for her husband.

Margaret's time alone with her baby had come to an end. She now was in the kitchen almost every day and resumed the role directing all the operations in there. Mrs. Walsh was content to cook what Margaret planned with the ingredients ordered for her. She wasn't really happy with anything, but she accepted Margaret's leadership. What she found harder to accept was Margaret's improving attitude and spirit of kindness.

Margaret had never thought of herself as especially sweet or kind, for her treatment of others came naturally after years of training at her mother's knee. She did know that she was feeling more like her old self. She continued to have moments when an overwhelming sadness threatened to overtake her; times when she looked around at her circumstances and Gracie's surroundings and it all seemed too much to bear. Thankfully, those times were less and less frequent.

Always needing a routine to follow, Margaret established her days starting with time in the Bible. She quickly realized that the Bible she had been given was slightly different than the one Mama read so often to the family. When she turned to read the story of Esther to her now toddling daughter, the book was not in its place. With a little searching, she found the familiar story amid unfamiliar books, and there seemed to be parts of the story of Esther that she did not remember. She reminded herself that she had been long away from reading the Bible and she thanked God once again for leading her to the church and the priest who had given this book to her.

And she prayed for her husband. Every day she prayed for him. He showed no desire to leave this evil business and he enjoyed the profits he was making. However, he did not hinder Margaret's time in the scriptures, nor her prayers. He even took his small family to church occasionally. It was the same church that Margaret had found accidentally and the service was very strange to her. She didn't understand anything the priest said. Even though she had many questions, she held her silence in hopes that Philip would continue to attend.

With the kitchen running smoothly, and Mrs. Walsh and Daisy doing all of the cooking, Margaret began to join the staff for their meals. While she had never been exactly unkind to the girls Joseph hired and brought to work in the saloon, neither had she ever gone out of her way to befriend them. She still bristled at the thought of Gracie's role models being these painted ladies, but somehow she was drawn to spend more time with them and to show them some kindness. And Gracie was such a joy to all of them that Margaret felt unable to deny them her company.

As she spent more time with the girls, she began to feel a burden for them. She had spent months mourning the condition of her own life and the upbringing it would offer her baby. Now she began to look at the kind of life the girls led. It was easy to allow herself to judge them for choosing this and yet, the more she thought about them, she found herself judging less and pitying more. And she found their names on her lips as she prayed each day. She prayed for each of them daily and she felt a sort of love growing for them.

Many of the girls did not make it down for breakfast, so this meal was the smallest. Philip and Joseph often used the time to discuss the previous night's business and whatever girls were present joined that conversation. Margaret gracefully bowed out of the dining room, quickly removing Gracie from talk that centered on liquor, drinking men and the company those men sought.

Pearl was the only true morning person among the girls and she was always at breakfast. Margaret began to build a friendship with Pearl. She was careful not to pry into the woman's past and this kindness was not lost on Pearl. Initially, Pearl was guarded, not allowing Margaret to see any humanity in her. Each day Margaret asked how Pearl was doing, whether she had rested well and what she thought about today's weather or breakfast or some other trivial question. And when Pearl answered, she really listened to her. Eventually, Pearl began to talk a little longer, asking about Margaret and Gracie. This allowed Margaret opportunities to share a little of her heart with the girl.

When Lula and Babe saw Pearl's companionship with

Margaret, they too opened up to her. And again, Gracie naturally drew all of the girls to herself.

Except Candy. Since the first day Joseph brought Candy into the building, she held an air of contempt for Margaret. Even little Gracie could not melt her icy heart. The little girl somehow sensed Candy's distance and tried to befriend her in her own little ways. Finding a bit of cookie, she carried it to Candy one day instead of quickly eating it herself. Candy gave Gracie her usual sniff and head toss as she walked away.

Margaret could not understand the woman's attitude, and it was hurtful to her. Still, she continued to be as kind and as friendly as possible to Candy.

And Margaret sensed a growing coldness from another member of their household. Mrs. Walsh was always a little grumpy and could be very heartless with poor Daisy. More and more she was distant from Margaret as well. She followed Margaret's directions well enough, but refused to be drawn into conversation about even the most trivial matters. Margaret saw a hint of the reason when Pearl entered the kitchen one day to seek out her new friend.

"Mrs. Berai, I took a walk this morning while it was still a little cool – don't you think this is going to be the hottest summer ever? Well, anyway, I happened upon a confectioner's and could not resist a bit of a sweet treat. So, I brought both you and Gracie some candy."

Margaret was thrilled, "Thank you, Pearl; what a treat – for both of us!"

Pearl moved toward Gracie where her dress-tail was firmly planted under a table leg to keep her safely in place. Before Pearl could pull out the candy, Margaret stopped her. "Let's take it upstairs and we'll enjoy it all together."

As Margaret lifted the edge of the table to free her daughter, her eye caught Mrs. Walsh. Margaret nearly gasped when she saw the harsh look the old woman gave her. She turned toward the older woman to question her as Mrs. Walsh turned her back squarely to Margaret and resumed her work.

Refusing to let the grouch's attitude affect this rare moment, she mentally planned to work through this later and headed up the back stairs with Pearl in the lead.

The women moved up the staircase chatting. "I've been noticing that you're not eating very well lately. So when I saw that confectioner, I thought maybe a treat would get your eating back on track. I got penny candy for Gracie, and really that's what I planned for us as well, but they had these French Creams that I just couldn't resist. So I got me and you a few to enjoy."

Margaret was honored that Pearl had noticed the change in her appetite. And, she was right. For several weeks now nothing had tasted quite right and her stomach never really felt settled. Usually, when one member of the household got sick, everyone would have a turn at it. So far this time, only Margaret had been affected by this ailment, so she said nothing and managed to continue her work as normal.

By this time, they had reached the third floor and Margaret opened the door for Pearl. Sitting Gracie on a low stool, Margaret reminded her of the treat, "Gracie, look at what Miss Pearl has brought you".

Pearl opened a little sack she held in her gloved hand to reveal a dozen brightly colored bits shaped like shoes and hats and boats. Gracie's eyes were alight and fixed on Pearl as she reached a pudgy hand into the bag and pulled out two pieces which were immediately in her mouth.

"Now, be careful not to choke," her mother warned.

"And you have to sit right here until it's all gone in your mouth, okay?"

Gracie nodded enthusiastically, her lips clamped tightly shut as though the boat shapes might sail away from her.

Pearl was eager to share the treat with Margaret and opened a small paper box to reveal several chocolate rounds. "Don't these look wonderful?"

Margaret felt as excited as her toddler as she reached for the proffered indulgence. As it melted in her mouth, Margaret marveled at the thoughtfulness of this woman. When she was able to speak, she tried to express her thanks, "Pearl, it was so precious for you to think of me and Gracie and to share this with us."

Pearl dropped her head slightly, embarrassed, "Mrs. Margaret, you treat me just like a friend and I don't know why you would do that. I wanted to do something real nice for you."

"Well Pearl, you are my friend."

"Ah, Ma'am, women like you are not friends with women like me. Most women like you won't even look at my kind."

"Your...kind? What do you mean?"

Pearl's head dipped even further, now feeling shame. "You know, women what work."

"Pearl, don't I work here too? Do you remember before Mrs. Walsh came, how Daisy and I did everything in the kitchen?"

Now Pearl was able to raise her eyes to peek at Margaret without raising her head very much while her voice was still nearly a whisper, "That's not what I mean. You don't keep company with the men. You really shouldn't be my friend."

"Pearl, I don't ever want to hear you say anything like

that again. Do you know that Jesus Christ's ancestors included a 'working' woman? Her name was Rahab and she was a friend to the spies from the Children of Israel. Anyway, you must be my friend for I pray for you every day, the same as I pray for Philip and Gracie and my family in Tennessee. Do you know what happens when you pray for someone regularly?"

Pearl's eyes widened to resemble saucers. "No! Does it happen to you, or to the one you prayed for?"

Margaret smiled, realizing that Pearl expected some supernatural occurrence. "Pearl, when I pray for you every day, God grows a love in my heart for you. I don't understand it, but he tells me in his word to even pray for people who use and persecute me. Now, you've never done either of those, have you?"

"I don't think so, but I don't know what *persecute* means. If it's bad, I wouldn't ever want to do it to you."

Margaret wasn't sure she could explain the word, "Hmmm, persecute is like causing trouble for somebody again and again. You've not caused me trouble, so therefore you have not persecuted me."

Pearl seemed to let out her breath. "Why do you pray?"

Margaret reached for another candy because she needed a moment to answer that question.

"My Mama taught me to pray. She taught me and my brothers and sisters to always do what God commands us to do and prayin' is a big part of that. Well, it took me a while but now I understand that I have to obey God not just because my folks taught me that way. I have to obey because he loves me and he has saved me from my sins."

"How do you know that?"

Margaret said a quick, silent prayer as she tried to

answer Pearl. "Well, I know it because that's what the Bible tells me. Would you like me to show you?"

When Margaret reached toward the table where her Bible was always waiting, Pearl started to rise suddenly appearing nervous. "Not now, Mrs. Margaret. It's getting late, so I'd better get a little nap. Otherwise, I won't be any good to Mr. Philip tonight." Margaret smiled at Pearl's reference to her husband. Most of the girls were far too familiar with both Berai men, but Pearl always called them 'mister'.

Pearl was out the door before Margaret could even stand. Looking back to Gracie she said softly, "Honey, I sure hope we didn't spook her." Knowing this visit had been an answer to her prayers for Pearl, she prayed, *Lord, I hope I didn't do that wrong.*

Margaret thought about when she would again be needed in the kitchen and decided she would not go back today. Gracie needed her bath and a nap; Margaret felt she'd left everything in good order for Daisy and Mrs. Walsh to complete the evening's meal. She knew she would have to return eventually to confront Mrs. Walsh because the woman was growing more difficult by the day and Margaret felt she'd tried to knock her down with her eyes today.

Chapter 19

By the time Margaret made her way downstairs the next morning, she found Mrs. Walsh already chopping vegetables at the big worktable in the kitchen. "Mrs. Walsh, we need to have a talk, don't we?" Margaret quickly surveyed the kitchen to ensure they were alone. This conversation needed to be private.

Mrs. Walsh answered in her customary, "Hmmf".

"Yesterday, you seemed upset when I left the kitchen with Pearl. Did you think I was leavin' the work all on you?"

The sharp knife never stopped its steady chop-chopping, "No Ma'am. I reckon I have to do what you tell me to do."

"Then why were you upset? You looked downright mad at me."

Mrs. Walsh chopped with new vigor. She didn't answer for a long moment and Margaret almost wondered if she had not heard the question. Eventually, she stopped the knife and looked up at this woman who was younger than her by two decades and yet was her boss in this work. "You ain't got no business runnin' around with them girls. Now I know you're a Christian woman. What do you reckon that little one will ever become if you act like they are your regular friends?"

Margaret saw a flash of red but slowly blinked her eyes before she opened her mouth. "I'm honored that you believe me to be a Christian – in fact it shames me that I don't believe I've ever actually told you how I trust Jesus Christ as my Savior.

But surely you know that it's because of my faith that I must be kind to Pearl and to all of the women working here. How can we ever hope for them to know Christ if they don't see him in us?"

Mrs. Walsh clearly decided this conversation was not worth her time and she resumed her chopping, "I'll say my Rosary and let the Priest befriend the sinner."

Margaret didn't really understand what she meant. Joseph had brought Gracie a Rosary chain and Philip had explained the prayers that he wanted Margaret to teach Gracie. At the time, she had been thrilled that Philip even had an opinion about Gracie's spiritual upbringing, and she faithfully said the 'Our Father' and 'Hail Mary' prayers to her little daughter every day. In fact, she spent much of the time they were alone together praying aloud. Her earliest memories of her own mama were prayers and she hoped this would be Gracie's first memories as well. This was the first time she'd ever heard Mrs. Walsh speak of praying in any form.

"Didn't Jesus tell all of us to be witnesses for him to the whole world?"

It was useless to try to continue the conversation, for Mrs. Walsh's only answer now was, "Hmmf".

Margaret was troubled with this woman's words and her attitude. Once again, she longed for her mother's advice. She remembered how many times she'd had small disagreements with her friends and ran to Mama who always seemed to have the answer. Just like so many times before, something seemed to whisper to her heart, *Pray child, pray.*

As she turned to her morning's work, she did pray and she resolved to pray for Mrs. Walsh. She realized that she must pray for this household as her mother had prayed for the household where Margaret grew up. And she smiled at the irony that Mama prayed for her own children while Margaret's household was grown women and two men who seemed to care nothing for spiritual matters. She remembered the model woman Mama had encouraged all of her daughters to study in Proverbs. Margaret pondered whether that ancient household King Lemuel's mother described would have been anything like her own.

With the meal planned, all the supplies ordered and her kitchen staff instructed, Margaret and Gracie climbed back up to the third floor apartment for lunch and Gracie's nap. Margaret treasured this short time in the afternoon despite the rising temperatures as the early summer sun heated the city. The rooms were quiet and she could usually get enough breeze from the tall windows that the temperature cooled enough to allow Gracie to sleep.

This was Margaret's best time to spend reading her Bible. She tried to pray first thing in the mornings. However, all too often the mornings did not go according to plan. On those days, the time for her to get down to the kitchen, or perhaps even to the staff breakfast, were upon her before she spent her time with the Lord. Today she simply felt she needed more dedicated prayer time.

Margaret sat by the open window with her Bible in her hand and tried to pour out to her Lord a heart filled with emotion. Nothing came out. In fact, she felt her head dropping to sleep. With a snap of her head, she chided herself aloud, "What are you thinking? Little Gracie sleeps during the day, not you."

She thought perhaps a cup of tea would help. Looking at the squat little stove she didn't dare stir up even enough heat for the water. Thinking, *There's no sense in heating up another room, the kitchen is hot enough,* she grabbed her teapot and quietly opened the door.

She made her way down the narrow back stairs as she had so many times. Accustomed now to carrying Gracie's weight on these trips, she marveled at the ease of movement with only the teapot in hand. The kitchen was quiet and she quickly poured from the big kettle that was always full of near boiling water.

With the hot water added and the tea steeping, she faced the return climb to the third floor and wondered if she had enough strength. She was suddenly weak, even faint. Remembering that Gracie was alone in the apartment, she put her foot on the first step and made her body move up each tread by sheer will.

Margaret stumbled into the apartment, relieved that she did not hear a peep from her sleeping baby. After a quick glance in the cradle, ensuring Gracie still slept peacefully, Margaret fell into her chair and propped her head on her hand. As the teapot cooled nearby, she promptly fell asleep. And in that same position, Philip found her.

The creak of the opening door jolted Margaret awake. Immediately aware of the growing shadows in the room, she calculated how long she must have slept and wondered why Gracie didn't wake her. She saw immediately that Gracie was safe in her cradle. Having awakened from her nap, she had found a little stuffed doll in the cradle and contented herself in play.

Philip stood just inside the door, watching this scene play out. "Were you asleep Margie? That's not like you."

She tried to shake her head to clear it and thought again

of having a cup of tea. Reaching to the pot, she realized it was quite cold. "I must have slept almost two hours," Margaret talked as she lifted Gracie to change a sopping diaper.

Philip was satisfied all was reasonably well with his family and he moved into the bedroom to pull his evening clothes from the pegs where Margaret kept their wardrobe in good order. With Gracie cared for and again playing in the parlor, Margaret stepped into the bedroom, as was her custom, to spend a few moments with her husband before his busy night.

"You received a post and I put it on my desk in the parlor," he mentioned as casually as though it happened every day.

"What?" Margaret practically screamed. "A post?" She hadn't received any letters in all of her time in the north. "What is it? Who sent it?" She threw questions at him even as she covered the floor to retrieve the sealed paper.

Immediately, she recognized her mother's hand and froze. Months had passed and Margaret had almost given up hope that her mother would write her after she sent that first letter home after Gracie's birth.

Whether they did not write because they no longer cared for Margaret or due to the burdens of war, she didn't know, but she assumed the former. Then, after Lee's surrender in April, she hoped anew that mail into and out of the south would move freely. She even wondered if her letter had arrived in Tennessee, although Philip had rationalized that since that state was firmly under Union control the mail would be delivered with reasonable speed.

While Margaret had grown in her walk with the Lord during intervening months, she still longed for the comfort and advice of her mother.

Stepping into the parlor as he tied his white necktie, Philip asked, "You've been waiting so long for that letter and now I wonder if you are even going to read it."

Margaret smiled at him, seeming to return from another world. She broke the wax seal and unfolded the paper. There was only one sheet, with no outer paper covering the actual letter. Mama had written very small, much smaller print than Margaret was accustomed to from her mother's hand. Still, the neat script was unmistakable and the warm words wound themselves around Margaret as she read. She read the letter through twice, scarcely taking a breath the whole time.

Fully dressed in his evening attire now, Philip returned to the parlor, "Well?" Still receiving no report from his wife, Philip prompted again, "Is all well with your family?"

"Oh, yes, they seem to be healthy. Matthew has returned to them. He was injured, although she doesn't say where or how. He is home and she believes he will fully recover. She sounds so weary though."

By writing to her and addressing her as her beloved daughter, Bessie Elmore seemed to grant a full forgiveness of Margaret and that was what she truly needed to read. Characteristically, she had been sweet but honest with her daughter. Things were hard in Tennessee. The war was over yet there was a home battle to be fought now. The lean years of war had not yet given way to abundance. They no longer particularly feared raiders from either army stealing away their crops or livestock and for that Bessie was thankful. And she was thankful that Margaret was not suffering with them, but was living in abundance in the north.

Margaret glanced around her apartment and wondered

at her mother's idea of abundance. Philip had left to go to the
bar for his evening's work. The heat of the day lessened a bit,
and the open windows allowed dust to constantly invade the
rooms. Gracie played on a worn carpet.

Margaret breathed a prayer of thanks that she was
healthy and happy. Still, Margaret worried about her daughter's
future in this place. And for the first time, she wondered about
the rest of her children.

Where did that come from? she asked herself. Then, her
hand went to her stomach as understanding dawned on her.
There would be more children and soon. No wonder no one
else in the house was getting sick when Margaret had been
feeling ill for weeks.

Margaret felt a little foolish as she tried to understand
when the baby would come. Toward the end of the year, she
estimated, and it made her smile. "Christmas," she whispered.
She kept smiling as she moved through her evening's routine
preparing Gracie for bed and doing a bit of housework in the
apartment. She kept looking at the big clock on the mantle as
she longed to see Philip and share this blessed news. However,
as the minutes ticked past, she knew that it would not be wise
to try to stay up for him.

She thought how far away her husband seemed even
though he was only two floors below her. She mentally
descended the stairs and thought how it was like going into
another world. Looking around the apartment again, her
mother's words echoing in her mind, she could see the wealth
her Mama had referred to. Here she had been able to create a
sanctuary for her family. She thought how she carried little
Gracie in here early in the afternoon, long before the loud
music began and before the girls' raucous laughter echoed up

the stairs.

Margaret moved to Gracie's little bed and looked down at the precious child. Again, she unconsciously placed her hand over the new life that she carried. And she prayed. She prayed for Gracie's rest and safety through the night. She prayed for the new baby that he or she would grow strong and healthy within her womb. She prayed for Philip. She prayed for the whole household to come to know Jesus.

She wondered whether Philip appreciated the sanctuary he had in these rooms? Did he long for the quiet that she sought here? She longed for him to be here with her now and to share the joy she felt. It would be hours before the men would leave the bar and Philip would come to bed. Margaret no longer even knew when he came home for she was always either asleep or so tired the time did not register if she woke and talked with him. She realized she could not stay awake waiting for him tonight and he would probably not receive the news as well as he would when he was fresh in the morning anyway.

Hours later, Margaret awoke with Philip's arm around her. She lay still for a moment, first listening for Gracie's movements and then to her husband's steady breathing. Her first thoughts were of telling him about the new baby, but she decided to let him sleep. She slipped out of the bed and their room to wake Gracie and get their day started.

Purposely, she was a little later than normal heading down to attend to the staff's breakfast. She heard Philip begin to stir. She had made coffee on the little parlor stove and she poured a cup to take to him.

"Good morning dear," she greeted him as she slipped to the bedside.

"Is that coffee I smell? What a treat." He scooted the

pillows behind him and sat up to take the hot cup. "You are not usually in our rooms when I wake."

She giggled as she kissed him lightly on the forehead before settling the cup in his hand. "I wanted to be sure to talk with you before we went down."

"Well I am glad you waited. You look very happy. What has brought you this joy?"

Margaret took a deep breath. Last night she'd tried to rehearse what she would say to him but now the words seemed to leave her. As she opened her mouth it just seemed to gush out, "A baby Philip, we're going to have a baby."

He coughed suddenly, choking on the coffee. "A what? We have a baby."

Laughing, she answered him, "Well, we will have another one by Christmas. It's just the best Christmas present anyone could hope for, don't you think so?"

Philip rose from the bed and began dressing in the clothes that hung on the open wardrobe door. He didn't say a word.

The silence in the room was thick, Margaret seemed to feel it on her skin. The smile, that moments earlier had threatened to split her face, now fell and her chin slightly quivered. Without a single word, Margaret knew that Philip did not share her excitement for the baby. She could not understand why, but she knew it would be pointless to try to ask.

As quietly as possible, she slipped from the bedroom and took Gracie down the stairs. As she refused to cry, she bit her lip until she tasted blood. Gracie squirmed in her arms and she realized she was squeezing her too tightly.

Margaret made her way to the kitchen and retreated into

the routine she had established for herself and the household.

As the months passed, Margaret remembered Mama discussing pregnancy with Mrs. McCormick. The two mothers had faced eighteen pregnancies between them, delivered sixteen babies and raised fourteen children. How she wished she could sit between these two wise women now.

She knew that no two pregnancies are ever quite the same, but about six months into her second pregnancy, Margaret was getting sicker and weaker. She still dragged herself and her little daughter to the kitchen each day, yet she found she could spend less and less time there and she could turn off less work with every passing day. The queasy feeling that had been her first clue to the condition quickly matured into full-blown morning sickness. And she wondered who decided it was a plague of the morning hours, for it accompanied Margaret from daylight until dark.

Philip did not understand. The first day that she wasn't downstairs before noon, he came charging up to their apartment demanding to know what she was doing. "Do you not remember what happened to the kitchen accounts when you left their oversight for the first child?"

Margaret winced a bit whenever he referred to her beloved Gracie as 'the child' or 'the first one'. He had never gotten over his initial disappointment that Gracie had not been the son he expected. He was the only one in their household who could not see what a treasure his child was. He could not see it largely because he hardly looked at Gracie.

Perhaps Gracie realized even in her little mind that he would not be accepting and encouraging, for she took every new discovery to someone else. When Margaret was either busy or simply not within Gracie's sight, the little girl quickly found someone else with whom to share her accomplishments and discoveries. This was often Daisy, since she was always as close to Gracie as her work allowed. In fact, she often positioned Gracie just beside her and would carry on a running conversation describing everything she was doing, and making grand plans for adventures they would have together. If Daisy wasn't available, Gracie readily turned to one of the girls.

Probably in appreciation for the mother's kindness, each of the girls went out of their way to be gentle with Gracie; everyone except Candy.

Pearl often returned from her constitutional walks and dropped a few pieces of penny candy into Gracie's pudgy palm. Babe and Lula, who spent a great deal of time downstairs even when the saloon was closed, found boundless fun in trying to decipher Gracie's babbled stories. Polly and Maggie had joined the household later, when Philip and Joseph believed the business had grown sufficiently to benefit from more hospitality each evening. Gracie quickly accepted these new friends and went to them as readily as she did any member of this extended family.

As Margaret struggled through her second pregnancy, she relinquished Gracie to the girls for longer periods of time. After months of steady prayer both for God's protection of her daughter's character as well as prayer for the salvation of each soul under her roof, Margaret scarcely paused when one of the girls beckoned Gracie or when Gracie ran to greet one of them.

Each day, Margaret managed to find some time to teach her daughter. She told her the Bible stories she'd learned from her own mother. She told her about her surroundings. She began to teach her to pray. Nearing her second birthday, Gracie would sometimes listen attentively to her mother but was more often distracted by the smallest things. Margaret persevered, often praying aloud and reading from her Bible aloud even as Gracie played nearby.

"Philip, we need to talk about delivery," Margaret began one morning early in November.

Always working at his ledger books, Philip's pen paused briefly, "Delivery of what?"

"Of what?" Margaret questioned. "Try who. We need to talk about what we'll do when the baby comes. I will need some help, you know."

"Oh." Philip carefully placed his steel pen near the inkwell and stared at the pigeon holes of his desk. With the official end to the war, the business had grown more than ever and required even more of Philip's time. He was growing accustomed to the idea of a second child but he had found little time to show his wife how concerned he was for her. Now he wanted to find a solution to the question she presented him. "Mrs. Walsh ought to know what needs to be done."

Margaret was nearly speechless. Without even asking her, he had brought in a doctor and nurse when Gracie was born. Two years later, Margaret still had few contacts in the city and there was no one in her household that she felt could properly help her through this. Although Mrs. Walsh may have been in her shoes several times, Margaret had no faith the grouchy woman would be of any help.

"No, Philip, I'm afraid that won't do. Surely there is a midwife in this part of the city, don't you think?"

Philip looked at his wife, seeming to see her for the first time in months. She was thin and pale. She had gotten little sun through the summer months and now as snow returned to the city, she prematurely carried winter's pallor. "Well, we will figure something out when the time comes." Philip reached for his pen, dismissing the subject.

Margaret could not let it pass. She knew that things were not going quite as well this time and needed to be prepared for an early delivery. "Philip, we can't wait, we really must talk about this very soon. The baby would normally come by the end of December, but I'm afraid it may be earlier."

"Afraid? Why? And surely you are mistaken; it must come at the end of December."

Margaret smiled and spoke gently, "Babies come when they're ready."

She saw concern in her husband's eyes. Although Margaret always modestly layered her skirts to hide as much of her condition as possible from the public, he knew that she was not large enough to be this near delivery. He had not dared hope again for a son. And he knew the dangers of childbirth for his wife. "I will see the doctor today," he promised.

She thanked him with a gentle squeeze to his shoulder and moved on with her morning, coaxing Gracie to join her in her bedroom to dress for the day.

Margaret knew that once he promised, Philip would see the doctor. However, she did not know the doctor would arrive at her door the very next day. She wondered what Philip must have said to him to prompt this visit.

"Good morning. I'm Doctor Brown, we only met briefly when your daughter was born, but maybe you remember me. I understand you have another child on the way; your husband tells me that you may be anticipating some trouble." All of this he said as he stepped efficiently into the parlor with black bag in hand.

"Good morning Doctor. I'm sorry; I didn't know you

were coming. Could I get you a cup of coffee?"

"No, child, I don't need a thing. Now, let me look at you. When is this baby coming?" He stood at arm's length from Margaret and looked her over from head to toe.

Feeling quite uncomfortable, Margaret looked at the floor as she answered him, "The end of December, I think."

"No, that can't be. You have enough to eat, don't you?"

"Oh yes, we have plenty here. I've not been able to keep much down though."

"What can you eat?" he asked.

"Well, all of the folks here think it's strange, but buttermilk and bread stay down better than anything."

Doctor Brown pursed his lips as though tasting the sour meal. No one in Chicago appreciated buttermilk as Margaret did. In fact, the milk man brought much of the butter the house used which saved a great deal of time in the kitchen but cheated the family of the by-product of churning their own butter. Since she had been feeling so sick, Margaret had been either making butter herself or asking Daisy to help so she would have some of the valuable drink.

The doctor was shaking his head, as Margaret explained the medicinal value of buttermilk on a weak stomach. She would be polite to this man of medicine, but she knew she would continue with the meal that had proven most reliable for the past months.

The doctor left after a brief visit that involved poking Margaret's stomach, listening to her heart and looking into her eyes. He left orders for more rest and to call him at the first signs of labor, which he believed she would know well during this second pregnancy.

The doctor was right. Margaret knew exactly what was

happening the day labor started. After passing a particularly restless night, she rose to start her day as usual. She tried to stretch and bend every direction seeking relief from her aching back. No relief could be found.

Snow had been falling at last light and Margaret didn't even have to go to the window to see the snow piled in every corner. As she woke Gracie, she enticed the little girl to get up with a promise that snow was waiting for her. She loved to look out the window at the white world. And since the apartment windows faced the rear lot, the snow there remained unaltered most of the time. Margaret was glad Gracie didn't have to look down on the messy sight that West Madison Street became as the traffic of both horses and men dirtied the white wonder.

As she dressed Gracie, the ache in her back wrapped itself around her body stealing her breath for a moment. Her hands froze buttoning Gracie's dress. As Gracie turned to see what caused the delay, Margaret made herself smile, not wanting to scare the sweet little girl.

Philip appeared in the doorway of the small bedroom where he had been sleeping for several weeks. He had moved into the smaller room as Margaret had grown increasingly restless at night. He was dressed for his morning and came out with his pocket watch in hand. Seeing the morning routine not yet completed, he snapped the watch shut with a bit of a sniff.

Margaret expected him to chastise her for being slow so she spoke first. "Gracie, how would you like to go help Miss Daisy today? Mommy has work to do and I'll bet Miss Daisy would sure appreciate your help. You can go downstairs with your father." She finished while looking at Philip, trying to make him understand without words.

Whether Philip understood or not, Margaret was

unsure. He rarely took Gracie out of the apartment alone but seemed willing to escort her to the kitchen this morning. He actually seemed more concerned with whether Margaret was planning on appearing for work at all. "Will you be down soon?" he asked her.

"I'm not sure yet. I may need to do some things for Gracie's new brother or sister." Still reassuring her daughter, she tried to smile at Philip even as another pain wrapped itself around her mid-section.

"Shall I go for the doctor?" Philip was now in tune with Margaret's thoughts.

"Go ahead and get Gracie down to Daisy and I'll let you know if I need help."

After Philip and Gracie left, Margaret made preparations for her labor as well as she could. She had been planning for this day, so many things were already set for the event. Now the pains were coming fast and she felt weak-kneed and unable to move about the room very effectively.

As she heard the door opening, she breathed a prayer of thanks that Philip had come back. However, it was Daisy that greeted her instead of Philip. Seeing the girl, she forgot her own suffering and immediately asked about Gracie.

"Mr. Philip has left Babe and Lula to handle Lil' Gracie and sent me up to you. Is it time for this one to come?"

"Daisy, thank you for coming. Yes, I'm sure the baby is coming; I'm just so weak, I can hardly stand."

"Well Miz Margaret, I don't guess you ought to be standing at all. Let's get you into bed. I think Mr. Philip has gone to get the doctor and we'll be just fine till they get back."

Daisy gave Margaret the sweetest and gentlest care possible as they waited for Philip to return with the doctor.

Margaret was able to sleep when the pains were not on her. She woke as she heard Philip enter the room and knew from the window's light that several hours had passed.

He moved directly to her bedside, "It took forever to find the doctor. There has been a wreck of a horse car and he is working with the wounded. He promises he will be here just as soon as he's free. He thinks there will be plenty of time. He says that these things take hours and hours."

Margaret squeezed Philip's hand and closed her eyes to try to sleep again. Although she knew that Daisy had no experience with birth, she was comforted that her friend stayed with her; she knew Daisy would not leave her side until the doctor ordered her away. Each time Margaret woke, Daisy offered cool water and mopped her brow.

As the hours passed, Margaret grew more exhausted but was unable to sleep any longer. The pains now came more and more frequently until she felt they were constant. More than once Margaret announced to Daisy that the baby was coming NOW. However, despite pushing with everything she had in her, the baby still did not arrive.

Chapter 20

It was dark before Doctor Brown arrived. He looked haggard in his slightly soiled shirt as he moved efficiently about the room. Setting the ever-present black bag on the bedside table, he took charge of the labor room. He gave curt directions to Daisy which included sending for his wife to assist and effectively removed the girl from the room. Then, after checking Margaret, he announced that they were nowhere near delivery.

"Do you know when it started?" he asked her.

Breathlessly, Margaret tried to answer, "It must have been around seven this morning. My back was hurting all night and I din' get much sleep."

The old doctor nodded his head. He had done this many times and felt he knew all of the indications associated with childbirth. "You won't have this baby before mid-day tomorrow. I will ask my wife to stay with you, if you like. And I will return tomorrow morning."

With stethoscope stored, he snapped the bag shut and was out the door before Margaret could utter a word.

As soon as the doctor was gone, she heard Daisy slip back into the room and knew she had been hiding either in the hallway or even in the parlor. Daisy stayed by Margaret's side until the doctor's wife and nurse arrived a short time later and left only when Mrs. Brown absolutely insisted.

Throughout the night, Margaret labored. She grew

weaker and weaker. The nurse coached and comforted her, assuring her that sometimes labor could last for many, many hours. Shortly after daybreak, as Margaret slept between bouts of pain and straining to deliver the precious life within her, the doctor arrived and greeted his own wife. Margaret heard the report that she gave him through a near delirious fog.

"She's working hard at it, but somehow she doesn't have the strength she had with the last one. Do you remember how easily she delivered? And that was her first one."

Then Margaret was jerked wide awake by another wave of pain that seemed to start deep within her and expand to squeeze her whole body. Try though she may, she could not push the baby free.

By noon, with Doctor Brown's help and Mrs. Brown's encouragement, Charlotte Berai was born.

Margaret was barely conscious. She saw people moving around the room, felt someone lay the little bundle at her breast and blissfully she slept.

Margaret awoke to bright daylight streaming in windows whose curtains were drawn completely open. Her first awareness was of crying. "Ah, she remembered, the baby is born." Then she realized this was not a newborn's cry. It was Gracie. She had been kept from her mother for three days and she could no longer be comforted by anything or anyone.

Margaret lifted the blankets to go to her daughter, but the moment she swung her legs over the bed's edge, the room began to spin. Immediately, strange hands grasped her shoulders and moved her back to the pillows. Looking up, she vaguely recognized Mrs. Brown and she wondered why she was there.

Sensing questions that Margaret was unable to voice,

Mrs. Brown began to explain, "Good morning Mrs. Berai. It is certainly good to see you waking. Your little girls are wanting your attention."

The nurse placed a tiny bundle of blankets in Margaret's arms and she looked down upon her precious daughter.

"You named her Charlotte the moment you saw her, but I'm not sure you were exactly in your right mind. Is that the name you wanted?"

Margaret was smiling. She was gazing at the little pink face. "Yes, that's the name. We'll call her 'Lottie', I see now that name fits her best. She's too little to carry a name like 'Charlotte'. Oh, what about Gracie? I hear her crying. I have to go to her."

Mrs. Brown's hands were much faster than Margaret could move. "Whoa, you aren't going anywhere. I will bring the child in here."

When the door opened, Gracie was inside in an instant. "Mama," she gasped, "Cry an' cry," Margaret couldn't help but smile as she listened to the little language that no one else understood.

As Gracie clamored to get to her mother while Mrs. Brown held her off the bed, Margaret reached to stroke her face. "I heard you crying. Are you okay now?"

After a significant sniff, Gracie answered by snugging in as close as she could to her mama. "Mama," she whispered.

"Well, you are here now. And look what else we have," Margaret held up the newborn so Gracie could see her face. "This is your baby sister, Lottie. You're going to have to help me love her and care for her, okay?"

Gracie's face lit up at the promise of mothering the little baby. As Margaret looked at her, she remembered Mama saying the same thing to her when Paul was born. She had been just three years old, but the event was so significant the memory stayed with her. She wondered if this moment would be with Gracie in years to come.

Mrs. Brown shooed Gracie out of the room and began trying to answer Margaret's questions. Lottie was three days old and Margaret could scarcely remember the birth or anything from the last days. Apparently, she had been strong enough to wake and feed the baby. That was the only thing she could do.

Mrs. Brown came in each day and when she wasn't there, the other women in the house took turns to ensure Lottie had the care she needed. Mrs. Brown spoke with some disdain; it was clear she did not approve of the other women. Her professional nurse's demeanor returned immediately as she explained that Margaret had utterly exhausted herself during the labor.

Margaret would need to stay in bed for at least another week. Mrs. Brown concluded her explanations declaring she would go to the kitchen to get some strong broth that Margaret would have to eat if she intended to regain her strength.

Her strength was very slow to return despite daily doses of the strong broth, hearty stews, and every kind of baked delicacy that Daisy knew how to make or could cajole Mrs. Walsh into creating. Still, Margaret remained weak and wisely stayed in bed with Lottie beside her and Gracie climbing up to join them early each morning.

By Christmas, Margaret was able to move about the apartment and care for her little family. Philip was clearly anxious for her to return to her role in the business but he was also concerned for Margaret's welfare. He pondered aloud whether she might maintain ordering their supplies from within the apartment, then dismissed the idea knowing that someone needed to keep an eye on the inventory. As he mulled the possible solutions, Margaret told herself that she would have to get back to work soon. She felt she had spent too much time on this recovery and it must be finished.

With her mind set, shortly after the first of the year, Margaret carefully wrapped Lottie in her blanket and instructed Gracie to walk just behind and hold tightly to Mommy's skirt as they carefully descended to the kitchen. The staff had not yet had their breakfast, although Philip left the apartment over an hour earlier. Mrs. Walsh was scrambling eggs and froze in mid-stir as she saw the mistress enter with her children in tow.

"Good mornin' Mrs. Walsh," Margaret greeted the cook as though she'd only seen her yesterday. "Gracie, it smells like Mrs. Walsh is makin' eggs for your breakfast. Now you sit down here with your dolly and I'll put little Lottie near you in her basket. You keep an eye on her while I go down to the larder."

Somewhere during her instructions, Margaret heard the spoon resume its stirring and she smiled a bit to herself.

Returning from her inventory-work, Margaret moved to speak with Mrs. Walsh. "Mrs. Walsh, what're you planning for the evening meal tonight?"

But Mrs. Walsh only stared at her. Finally, she responded, "You are white as a sheep girl."

Margaret did feel a bit lightheaded after the climb up from the larders but didn't want Mrs. Walsh thinking she was unable to manage the kitchen. "I guess I've not had much fresh air lately."

"Hmmf. You look like death itself."

Margaret took a deep breath and silently whispered a prayer before she responded, "Thank you Mrs. Walsh, I think

I'm on the mend now."

In her customary way, Mrs. Walsh answered Margaret's questions and mostly followed her directions. Every time they talked, she voiced concerns over Margaret's health. This no longer annoyed Margaret, for she came to understand that Mrs. Walsh really cared and this was her only way to show it.

The days began to blur together. Margaret cared for her daughters almost automatically. Little Gracie quietly played while Margaret gave tiny Lottie the extra care a newborn required. Gracie turned to the other members of the household for attention. Just as she accepted her father's aloofness, she bore her mother's distraction without complaint.

Margaret stood at the closed window peering into the heavy clouds of the March sky. She longed for spring and strained to see any sign of buds on the few trees that stood in the empty lot below. *Surely spring will be the pick-me-up that I'm needing,* she thought.

But for the moment, she chose to move away from the window because she was always cold these days and the drafty glass made it all the worse. As she stirred the fire, she heard Philip waking. It was well into the morning, but his nights were longer and later all the time. Each morning, Margaret would slip from bed as quietly as possible when Lottie woke for her morning feeding and leave her husband sleeping.

Philip walked into the room looking decidedly sour, "Why is it so hot in here?"

"I was just thinkin that it is cold. We can't let the little ones catch cold right here at springtime."

"Well they are more likely to take a fever in this room. It was hot when I came in last night. How much coal are you using?" He moved to the heavy coal bucket that was filled each week and kicked it to estimate the contents. The hollow ring from the bin produced a frown on Philip's face.

"Well I don't know why I'm cold when you are hot." She turned from him to busy herself with folding diapers and sorting tiny clothes that had been laundered the day before. She tried to look unconcerned, but her mind was spinning as she remembered that Daisy too had thought the apartment overly warm. And Mrs. Walsh had mentioned how flush Margaret looked yesterday. She thought to herself, *Surely I'm not pregnant again so soon?*

She wasn't sure whether she should smile at the thought. She certainly loved her daughters and dearly longed to give Philip the much anticipated son. She just felt so weak after Lottie's birth. Now four months after the delivery, the stairs still winded her and she fell asleep every afternoon when she returned from a few hours in the kitchen.

After Gracie was born, she'd felt sad and alone. She recalled those weeks and months when she scarcely left the apartment. She now knew that her struggle had been largely spiritual and she had been living under a dark cloud of gloom. Although she had prayed an earnest prayer of repentance even before the delivery, in Gracie's first months of life, Margaret had to face the many consequences of her rebellion. She knew what she was facing now was totally physical for she continued to make the time to read God's word each day and her spirit felt alive and vibrant as she prayed over her entire household. After Gracie's birth, she had plenty of energy; now she could hardly make a cup of tea without taking a break.

As springtime finally blossomed around the city, Daisy drew Margaret out of doors with the children in tow. Margaret made herself go out mostly because she knew Gracie could not

227

grow up entirely in the saloon and truly needed the sunshine and whatever fresh air could be had in Chicago. Philip had brought home a baby carriage for Lottie and Margaret did want to try it out.

As the ever-present wind brought a gust from the stockyards with the stench of decay that surrounded that vast part of the city, Margaret was taken with a fit of coughing. She covered her face with her handkerchief and bent low to see if Gracie was affected. She was not. The little girl was fascinated with a butterfly and seemed to take no notice at all of the vile smell.

Between coughs, she tried to excuse herself to her friend, "Daisy, I don't think I can stand to be out here with the wind coming from that direction."

Daisy scowled slightly and lifted her nose to the wind. "Is it the slaughtering houses? I guess I don't notice it since my time at Gerald's house. It was so close to the stockyard you could hear the cattle and hogs all night long. The men that worked in the yards were Gerald's best customers I guess." Her shoulders gave a quick shudder and she regretted allowing the memories to emerge.

Despite her discomfort, Margaret wanted to console her friend, "No matter, it doesn't seem to bother Gracie either and I'll be fine." She tucked Lottie's blanket a bit closer in her carriage and they continued down the street. Margaret stifled the coughs as much as possible until Daisy urged her to turn around and end their outing.

"We'd better make you some strong tea to clear up that cough before it sets up something much worse," Daisy was instructing Margaret as they pulled the baby carriage up the low steps to the front door. Candy overheard them as she descended the main staircase. She never used the service stairs as everyone else did during the daytime.

"Who is coughing? We don't want something to start here. You know how disease runs through a house. Mrs. Berai, you must take a shot of straight whiskey. That will knock it right out of you."

Margaret had rarely known Candy to be concerned about her welfare, or anyone's for that matter save Candy herself. She was not about to start sharing spirits with her but she smiled warmly, thankful that Candy would show any human kindness. "Thank you Candy, I'm sure some of Mrs. Walsh's mint tea will help me. You know she will want to tie the mint around my neck – or tie it somewhere! Still I think it works best in tea, don't you?" Patting Candy's hand as it lay on the bannister, Margaret lifted Lottie from the carriage and moved through the big door to the kitchen.

As Daisy helped Gracie out of her coat and bonnet, she chatted with her about everything they had seen on their outing. From a butterfly to a lonely flower or a lady's bright hat, everything was an adventure to Gracie and Daisy thrilled at the chance to recount the details with her. The pair moved toward the third floor apartment as Margaret picked up a bunch of dried mint from Mrs. Walsh's herb basket and followed with Lottie in her arms.

While the tea steeped, Margaret listened to Daisy and Gracie and took the opportunity to remind Daisy that with springtime's arrival, they would be celebrating the Easter holiday.

Daisy remembered last year's celebration. "You made a really nice meal that day. Are we going to go back to that church again? I didn't actually understand what they were saying you know, but it was a beautiful place."

Margaret smiled at the memory of Easter at church with Philip, Gracie, Joseph and Daisy. She had asked Philip many times for the family, including anyone in the household who was willing to participate, to go to church. He always insisted they go to the stone church where Margaret had met Father Michael. While they had attended several times, Margaret could never quite make out what the minister was teaching. She worried that Daisy, who always attended with them, would not learn anything that would lead her to salvation.

Margaret knew she must teach Daisy all that she knew about this precious holiday and began to tell her the story of Jesus' death, burial and resurrection. "If Mr. Berai wants, we may go back to church on Sunday. The most important thing though is that we understand why we celebrate the holiday."

Sensing story time, Gracie climbed into her mother's lap. "We are celebrating that Jesus Christ died in order to save us from our sins." She looked down at Gracie wagging a finger back and forth, "But he did not stay dead. He rose again after three days in a tomb." She looked back at Daisy, "Easter was always my favorite holiday in Tennessee."

Daisy smiled, "I love it when you talk about your home. You get a faraway look in your eyes and I think that, in your mind, you travel back there."

"I guess you're right in a way. A part of my heart is…" Margaret's coughing interrupted her thought. She poured the mint tea, offering a cup to Daisy who gently shook her head.

The tea did seem to help and Margaret resumed her story. She watched Daisy closely as she explained that Jesus had tried to tell his disciples he would die then he would rise again. Daisy seemed to not understand this part so Margaret gave her a chance to ask about it.

"Daisy, does that make sense to you?"

With eyes as wide as saucers, Daisy shook her head. "He knew he was going to die?"

"Yes Daisy, God knows everything and Jesus is God. I've always thought that was a hard thing to understand, but it's true. He allowed the men to arrest him in the garden and he willingly went with them."

"That just doesn't make any sense. If the Confederates had gotten into Chicago, I wouldn't have let them take me captive. I would have kicked and scratched and done anything I could to get away."

Margaret appreciated Daisy's thought for she well remembered whispered conversations with her sister Mary about what they would do if either army came and tried to take them from their home. "But Daisy, this was different. If Jesus had not allowed the soldiers to take him and crucify him then he wouldn't have been able to save us from our sins."

This thing was not getting any clearer for Daisy. "How can a dead man save me from anything?"

Margaret smiled at her friend, remembering that Daisy was only a couple of years younger than she was, yet there were childlike moments with Daisy. Now, Daisy's questions were quickly getting out the realm of teaching with which Margaret was comfortable. She knew the stories, but when it came to the questions she longed to run to Mama or Papa for the answers. Again something prompted her heart that her heavenly Father was just waiting for her to run to Him for all of the answers.

More coughing allowed her a moment to breathe a prayer, asking for wisdom.

Gracie slipped from Margaret's lap, ready to play with

her dolly instead of listen to the adults talking. Lottie was stirring and Margaret knew she would need to eat soon. Margaret felt almost desperate. She wanted to make this clear to Daisy for she wanted her friend to come to believe in Jesus as her savior. *Lord, help*, she cried within herself.

Margaret's face was alight as she explained, "Ah! That's the most amazing part. Jesus did die on the cross. And we know that he's not dead now; he's alive in heaven with God. Do you remember the verse I've read to you so many times that says whoever believes in Jesus 'should not perish, but have everlasting life'?"

Daisy nodded her head vigorously.

"Well, that's how Jesus saves us.

Daisy looked puzzled. The words were clearly foreign to her despite having heard them many times from Margaret's lips. John 3:16 was one of Margaret's favorite verses so she applied it to many situations and spoke it regularly even without quoting it specifically by chapter and verse. "You always say that, but I don't really know what you mean."

Margaret felt the power of the Lord upon her as she began to explain that 'everlasting life' would come in heaven and that the only way to get to heaven was to believe in Jesus. It seemed that Daisy was still confused.

"You have to die before you can go to heaven and I don't want to die," Daisy declared.

Margaret smiled kindly. "Now Daisy, we'll all die someday, won't we? And if you know that you'll go to heaven then you don't have to be afraid of dying."

Daisy's eyes were growing larger by the minute. "Well don't expect me to be looking forward to it!"

Now Margaret couldn't help laughing out loud. The

moment was lost, but she knew that her words were not wasted. She remembered hearing a preacher back home saying how God's word is never wasted – in fact, wasn't that in the Bible? *I should try to find that,* she thought.

Daisy had risen to leave the room and Margaret walked her to the door, giving her a quick hug before she left. Margaret leaned against the closed door and prayed for her dear friend. *Lord, thank you for giving me Daisy. I'm afraid I would have gone mad in this place without one sweet soul near me. I do so want her to come to know you. Please give me the words, and another chance to share them.*

By now, Margaret was accustomed to lifting up to God every little thing that she could not readily handle. So she had to pour all of her heart out to the Lord on Daisy's behalf before she was able to move through the remainder of her day unburdened.

Chapter 21

The summer months always saw farmers driving into town with wagons loaded full of luscious green vegetables. Mrs. Walsh's bland menus came alive with early spring greens, broccoli and cabbage. Last year, these flavors gave Margaret new life. Mrs. Walsh seemed to be hoping this year would be the same.

As Margaret returned to the kitchen after feeding the girls and getting them down for a nap, Mrs. Walsh was pulling vegetables from a pan of water. "Mrs. Berai, look what good greens Mr. Fitzgerald sent over. You'll enjoy them with some bacon and potatoes? He says we'll have new potatoes in a couple of weeks. Maybe then Daisy will stop complaining about peeling the wrinkly ones."

Mrs. Walsh was so consistently grumpy that Margaret found it somewhat disconcerting that she was being kind lately. Margaret couldn't even remember greens tasting good. "Thank you, Mrs. Walsh, I'll try to eat some. Will they be ready for supper tonight?"

Mrs. Walsh pursed her lips and tilted her head back as though she were inspecting Margaret. "What's wrong with you that you can't eat nothin' I cook up? You work when you look like death itself. If you don't pick up some, you're going to die down there among the larders and we'll have to haul your body up the stairs."

Margaret's breath escaped in a tiny squeak and she

turned to continue her work, trying hard not to react to the old woman's harsh words.

But Mrs. Walsh's words hit her hard. She knew she had no appetite, but she was not throwing up as she had when she was pregnant with Lottie. And she certainly wasn't gaining weight as she had so quickly with Gracie. In fact, her skirts hung so loosely over her frame that she was considering altering them. Philip would not hear of her abandoning the oversight of the kitchen; he insisted that any profit they were planning from the food would be completely lost if Mrs. Walsh were given free reign.

Periodically, Margaret dashed back up the two flights of stairs to check on her sleeping daughters. It was no longer practical to try to put both down for naps in the busy first floor of the house. Throughout the afternoon, she made multiple trips up the stairs to ensure they were still sleeping and Gracie wasn't up and getting into anything dangerous. She thought it was no wonder with all this climbing up and down the stairs that her chest hurt. She completely dismissed the pain until she happened to meet Pearl on the back stairs. Margaret was patting her chest, as though encouraging her lungs to take in enough air to propel her body the rest of the way up.

Pearl was coming down and stopped to give Margaret room. "Good afternoon, Mrs. Berai. Why ever are you patting your chest that way?"

Letting out a breath, Margaret stopped one step below Pearl. "It's my second trip up, I'm just going up to check on Gracie and Lottie."

"Well, you shouldn't be climbing these stairs so much. Stairs and corsets are an unhealthy combination."

Margaret nodded and continued climbing the stairs,

smiling. Pearl laced herself very tightly, as many of the girls did. Margaret, however, could never shake her mother's practical advice that fashion shouldn't get in the way of the work to be done. "And that was never more true, Mama," Margaret said aloud as she entered the third floor and received a sharp, stabbing pain in her chest. Pearl's concern remained in the back of Margaret's mind; *Why is my chest hurting?* she wondered.

The staff dining room was nearly full as Margaret entered late for breakfast the next morning. Philip looked up as the door opened and in his eyes she read clearly his thought, You are always late! Margaret begged the household to forgive her tardiness, offering no excuse. She tried very hard to make breakfast each morning for this was the best chance for her to interact with the girls. Since she was praying faithfully for them, she wanted any chance possible to speak a kind word or offer gentle encouragement to one of them.

Daisy already had the food on the sideboard and immediately began filling Gracie's special plate so Margaret put a little on her own plate and took her seat beside Philip. "Good morning Philip, I didn't see you before you left the apartment this morning."

Philip was looking at a newspaper and hardly raised his eyes, "You were busy with the baby I think."

Margaret nodded and smiled down at Gracie and Lottie acknowledging with a slight nod of her head that they filled her mornings. Looking around the room, she did a mental roll call, confirming that all the girls who usually came down to eat were already present. Turning to Polly, Margaret began to ask, "How are you feeling…" when she was interrupted with a bout of coughing. This had become so regular that the girls simply adjusted their conversation to the coughs.

Margaret's Faith

Polly turned to Margaret, waiting for her to finish coughing and lower the white napkin she held at her mouth, but Margaret did not continue her question. Polly was about to answer anyway, explaining the headache she'd suffered yesterday was much better, when she realized that Margaret had blanched ghost-white. "Mrs. Berai, are you okay?"

Margaret quickly tucked her napkin in her lap, jerking her head up. "Oh, well, uh, y-yes." The pause somehow drew the attention of everyone sitting around her. Margaret realized they were staring, "Oh, I am fine. You know, I think I'll go," she rose from the table, still clutching her napkin, "And, uh, uh, get some hot water for a cup of tea. Tea sounds good this morning, doesn't it?"

She left Lottie in her basket and Gracie sitting on Lula's lap as she stumbled hurriedly into the kitchen and through to the back door. Outside, in the sunlight, she finally released the death-grip she held on the napkin.

In the wrinkled folds was a splatter of bright red.

Unexpectedly, painfully, terrifyingly, the facts all began to sort themselves into a bleak picture. Margaret knew these symptoms. She had known people in Tennessee, had certainly seen neighbors in the rooming house, whose persistent cough led to loss of weight and fever - then the blood.

Her eyes darted all around the empty lot. The thought again flitted through her mind that she really ought to plant something out here. *What am I thinking about, planting? What am I going to do about this?* She held up the napkin as though showing herself what she must concentrate on.

A thousand thoughts swept over her. What would happen to her children? How long would it be? How sick was she going to get? What was Philip going to say?

Margaret was nearing a panic. Her eyes widened but she no longer saw the empty lot around her; her heart beat wildly in her chest and her breath came in short gasps. She was considering screaming or running or...

Suddenly, even miraculously, a calmness settled upon her. She closed her eyes and took a deep breath. The air was no longer stiflingly hot; there was no hint of the stockyards' stench. As she slowly opened her eyes, she almost expected to be in a beautiful garden and she couldn't help but smile at the dirt lot.

Then she prayed. She was ashamed of herself for not immediately turning to God. "When will you ever learn?" she asked herself aloud. And yet, God had come to her, had in fact tuned her heart to the sweet song of the Holy Comforter residing in her soul. Margaret turned to God to thank him for his faithfulness even when she was weakest. She thanked him for the sure knowledge that he had a plan for every day of her life, and every day of her children's lives.

As she turned back to the door she didn't have all of the answers. In fact, she had no answers. What she had was a sure confidence that God was sovereign over Consumption just as he was sovereign over every other element of her life.

When Philip came into the apartment to rest and dress for the evening, Margaret was ready to talk with him.

"Philip, I think I need to see a doctor about this cough. It just won't go away, you know. Do you think Doctor Brown would be the best choice?"

Philip was preoccupied with his dressing, "Cough? Oh, well you have been coughing a lot? Yes, Doctor Brown – I will see him tomorrow."

"Well, he came here when I had the children, but I know people could go to see the doctor in Crossville at his home. Should I go there?"

Margaret was sure she could see her reflection in Philip's boots, yet he continued to buff them. He didn't even look up as he answered, "I will ask him to come round."

Margaret was not completely satisfied with this plan. She left him and the subject alone for the moment hoping he would speak to the doctor quickly.

The staff was still in the dining room with their breakfast when Doctor Brown arrived the next morning. Knowing the front doors would not be answered early in the day, he entered through the rear door and the kitchen. Mrs. Walsh had already given him a cup of hot coffee when he made his way into the dining room and greeted those assembled there.

"Good morning, good morning. Is everyone healthy here this morning?" He grinned as he sat the big black bag on the corner of the table.

Margaret was surprised that all of the girls seemed to know the old doctor. She had only seen him during visits associated with the births of her daughters and she did not realize any of the girls had required his help.

After the briefest of greetings to the breakfast group, the doctor was ready to be about the purpose of his visit. "Mrs. Berai, would you have time to talk with me for a few minutes?"

Margaret was still a little shocked by his appearance first thing this morning, but with a quick glance assuring that Daisy had charge of her daughters, she obediently rose from her chair to lead him up to the apartment.

As Doctor Brown entered the familiar front room, he immediately opened his bag and withdrew the little wooden instrument he used for listening to the inside of the body. He flicked his wrist, motioning for her to turn her back to him. "Philip says you have a bit of a cough?"

It was hard for Margaret to talk to him without facing him, "Yes, I've had a cough for weeks and just can't seem to be rid of it."

The doctor reached around and placed his hand on her forehead. A moment later, with a soft, "Hmm," he placed the stethoscope on her back. For what seemed long minutes, Margaret felt the soft wood moving from place to place on her back. Periodically, Doctor Brown would ask her to take a deep breath or cough gently. She felt unable to cough gently, and as she feared, that started a coughing fit, which ended the examination.

As Doctor Brown moved to face Margaret, she managed to quell the cough. "Well Sir, what do you make of it?"

He looked very directly into her eyes. "Has there been any blood?"

Margaret's head dropped. "I was hoping you wouldn't ask about that. Yes, yesterday for the first time."

"You know that it's consumption, don't you?"

Nodding her head and unable to look at the doctor, Margaret answered, "Yes, I know. I didn't put the symptoms together until I saw the blood yesterday. That's when I told Philip I needed to see you. Thank you for coming so quickly."

As he repacked the familiar black bag he explained things Margaret already knew far too well, "You know that there really isn't anything I can do? You are awfully weak, much weaker than I would have expected."

"Well, you know I had a hard time with the last baby. I didn't have any strength the whole time I carried her. Do you think it was already on me, even then?"

"I would expect so. You are young and seem quite strong, so it should have taken a couple of years before you started coughing blood. Is your family consumptive?'

"Oh no, they are all very healthy. My Grandfather lived into his seventies."

The doctor was looking at the floor as he put the information together in his mind, "Well, there must be something about your constitution that has brought this on. Perhaps it is psychological. We know for sure that consumption is hereditary; that's the only way you can get it."

Margaret didn't know what that meant. It did not matter to her. She knew that her family was very healthy and strong and she longed for them to surround her now and lend her their strength. "What about Lottie?"

Doctor Brown raised his head with the unspoken question; he did not know who Lottie was.

"The last baby. Will she have it?"

Shrugging, Doctor Brown lifted his bag as he answered her, "Likely. We really see families having the disease. If you could get her, actually both of your daughters, to the country and preferably at higher altitudes, they might have a better chance. None of you will improve any so long as you are in this dance hall with the smoke and noise. I've read that in Europe patients are being treated at special houses built in mountains where the air is better for the disease." He moved toward the door, "I'll check back on you in a week or more. You will need to get plenty of rest."

As the door clicked shut behind him, Margaret closed her eyes and believed she could smell the fresh air of her father's farm. She mentally calculated what would be happening there now; the hay would be ready to bring in from the tall haystacks and forked into the barn. All of the children would be squealing as they stomped and packed it tightly in the loft to allow maximum storage. Mama's garden would be ripening fast and she would have beans strung all along the porch to dry. Margaret unconsciously licked her lips as she remembered summer meals at home. The vegetables would be bursting with flavor and seemingly endless in both supply and variety. Soon the blackberries would be ready and Mama would use precious flour to make pies that were worth their weight in gold

As a single tear trickled down her cheek, Margaret wondered, Maybe I should never have left. Deep within herself however, Margaret knew that she had been determined to leave the farm and the surrounding rural, mountain community. For the first time she realized that her rebellion began long before she rode Mr. McCormick's horse frantically after the Union soldier who wandered onto the farm and changed her whole world. Rebellion had lived in her heart. *Thank you Lord God for creating in me a clean heart and for renewing a right spirit. Now what?*

Only a moment longer did Margaret sit pondering her situation and her future. She needed to move, to act, to plan. Even as she adjusted her shirtwaist and smoothed her skirts, she was again taken with a bout of coughing. The coughing prevented her hearing the door open again and Philip surprised her as he slipped into the room.

"I talked to the doctor." He had rather a blank look about him. "He says that you definitely need to get out of the dance hall - says neither the noise nor the air is good for you."

She nodded her head, feeling that she had somehow let her husband down. "The winter will be the worst part. Consumption is worse in winter. So we will work hard to make a profit this summer and figure out what we do by summer's end. How does that sound?"

Philip was momentarily amazed that she was sounding so positive in light of the death sentence she had just received from Doctor Brown. Then he realized she was planning for him to leave his business that he had dreamed of, worked for, and succeeded with. The doctor had said she had to get out of the dance hall; why would Philip have to leave his business? He would certainly not abandon it when he'd just now begun to make real profit. His fortune seemed within his grasp. He would have to figure out another way. For the moment, he gave a slight nod of his head and left the room.

For the remaining summer months, Margaret worked as hard as she was able to do. She worked both for Philip and for the Lord. She spent endless hours ensuring the kitchen was stocked for many weeks in advance. Any supplies that were not perishable were carefully stored and inventoried.

She was teaching Daisy how to manage the inventories and, without telling her, preparing the girl to take her place in the business. She grew fatigued very quickly, but pushed herself on even when everyone around her urged her to rest. Beyond the hours in the storeroom and with Daisy, Margaret found time to talk at length with each of the girls, even Candy.

For the first time, Candy seemed open to talking with Margaret. She had always tried to ask Candy how she was doing or whether she liked the food, anything to get her talking. Usually the answers were very short and Candy left no opportunity for further discussion. One day, however, she was almost friendly to Margaret.

Margaret greeted Candy as she entered the dining room for lunch, "Good afternoon, Candy. How are you doing today?

It's awfully hot, isn't it?"

Taking the seat across from Margaret, Candy answered, "It is miserably hot. I'll bet it's even a little worse in your apartment since it's on the top floor."

Margaret was so accustomed to Candy's unwillingness to talk that she faltered for a moment. Margaret prayed fervently for a chance to share her faith with this woman. "Well, I don't know that it's any worse than anywhere else in the city. Fall will be here soon and we'll have a break." She searched for something deeper than the weather to talk about.

Candy provided the opportunity, "How are you feeling? You aren't coughing as much today."

Everyone in the household knew that Margaret was ill, although she had not told anyone of the doctor's diagnosis. No family had been spared completely from this dark plague so the symptoms told all that they needed to know.

"The coughing is a little better today, although I'm afraid I still don't have much energy."

"I don't know how you have any energy at all since you chase after and care for two babies. And you aren't eating, are you? I can see that you are falling off."

Margaret smiled, it was always easy to talk about her children. "They are such good girls that they don't take much out of me at all. I am very blessed to have them." There! She had found a way to count her blessings to Candy. Maybe that would open a door, just a crack.

Candy looked a little shocked. "How can you talk of blessings as sick as you are?"

"God's blessings are not dependent on my health, Candy."

Candy shrugged, "It just seems like …"

Margaret finished for her, "Like I may not live to raise the children?" A tear welled in her eye, "Certainly, that makes me very sad, but God can care for them far better than I can."

Candy looked shocked, "How can you have so much faith when God has let you get so sick?"

Margaret took a deep breath and began to tell her life story, "Candy, I was raised reading and hearing The Bible. I believed in Jesus as a child and asked him to be my savior. Then I grew a rebellious spirit. I thought that I needed a different life than what my parents provided and hoped for my adult life. When I met Philip, he seemed to be everything I'd been dreaming of. I love him and I am happy to be married to him but when I came here to be with him, I ran away from my home and from my faith and I realize now that was wrong. It just wasn't the right way to start our life together. Thankfully, God didn't run away from me. He has seen me through a lot of trouble and he will see me through this latest trouble too. I have come to understand that there is no glamour or excitement in this world that compares to heaven. So now I'm dreaming of that land."

"Why do you think it was God who saw you through the trouble?"

Margaret was smiling now because this was the triumphant part of the story. "When I realized how I had run from God and rebelled against his commandments, I admitted my sins to him and asked for forgiveness. From that moment on I have been turning to him and trying to follow his direction. I can't explain the peace you feel when you know you are forgiven."

"How can you believe God is directing anything here? You have these precious daughters and a husband who wants only wealth. And on top of that, you are getting sicker every day."

Taking a deep breath and an opportunity for another quick prayer because she was fast running out of answers Margaret said, "Candy, I can certainly understand why you would ask that. Let me ask you this, if God loved me enough to give his son for me, how could I not trust him with every part of my life, especially with my own daughters?"

"What do you mean, 'give his son'? You don't have a son."

Margaret smiled, happy that the conversation had turned back to where she might be able to offer some answers. "The Bible says that God loved the world so much that he gave his only son so we would not have to perish. The way that he gave his son was that Jesus died for our sins on the cross."

"Well, that doesn't make any sense at all. I think you may be feverish. Let me help you up to your room."

"That's a great idea, Candy. Let's go up to my rooms and I will show this to you in The Bible. It doesn't make sense to us because it's a supernatural thing."

Candy was moving toward the back stairs with Margaret. Margaret wasn't sure if she was listening now or only helping a sick woman; she was going to keep talking anyway. She had had opportunities to witness to everyone in the household except Candy, so she was going to count this as an answer to prayer. She no longer had enough breath to both talk and climb the stairs, so she used the time on the stairs to pray.

After Margaret had a moment to catch her breath, seated comfortably on the sofa, she tried to continue talking with Candy. However, as they moved upstairs, Candy had become belligerent.

"Mrs. Margaret, I know you are a very religious woman. You don't act haughty like most church women do when they see one of us girls, but you know this church stuff is not for our type."

Margaret smiled as she answered her. "Candy, Jesus Christ is everyone's savior, no matter what they've done."

"You could almost persuade me to believe in this." Candy said as she quickly left the apartment.

Margaret smiled as she recalled reading a very similar response to the Apostle Paul's witnessing. *Well, that must mean I got it as close to right as Paul did!*

Chapter 22

The summer months were winding down now. Margaret kept thinking of Doctor Brown's suggestion that she get her daughters out of the dance hall. She believed that winter would be the worst time for the disease, for that's what she had seen in other people suffering from consumption.

Philip refused to make any kind of plan for the winter; he refused to discuss Margaret's disease at all. Anytime Margaret carefully mentioned selling or leaving the dance hall, he immediately closed the subject. She began to realize that he had no intention of leaving Chicago. Despite the preparations she had been making with Daisy and the girls, she began to resolve herself to wintering here and to watching her health quickly deteriorate.

She cared little for her own well-being, but she kept thinking of Gracie and Lottie. Philip was kind enough to them – at least he brought them little gifts whenever he was out in town, and he never failed to allow money for Margaret to buy what the family needed. So, she was sure he would provide for them. Still she wondered what kind of life would they have growing up above a dance hall? Even as she was embracing the girls of the house and praying for them and trying to witness to them, Margaret knew that she must do everything possible to protect her daughters from spending their lives in such a place.

She could not imagine what would be the solution. She could remember many men who had been left widowers with small children back home. They quickly found wives, sometimes quite young women, who would step in and raise the children. Until the man could remarry, the women of his family, his own mother and sisters, would usually help him so that he would still be free to run his farm or his business. Unfortunately, neither Philip's family nor her own were anywhere near. She wondered if his mother, who both he and Joseph so often spoke of, might come from Italy to help him raise his family. He wouldn't even talk about that possibility.

The more she considered the doctor's suggestion, the more she thought that Tennessee would be better for them. This thought began to be always on her mind and she looked for a chance to suggest it. She got just such a chance one rare morning as they all prepared to go down for breakfast together.

Margaret was feeling particularly weak on this particular morning. Her forehead glistened with perspiration as she went through her morning routine despite the fever. She could ignore the fever and the fatigue, but there was no ignoring the persistent cough. It stopped her while brushing Gracie's hair and again as she tried to lace her own boots. Philip stepped from their bedroom and looked carefully at her. She was never sure what those looks meant, but feared it meant she was making too much noise and disturbing him.

"You are worse today, no?" he asked.

"I don't know; you've seen how the coughing comes and goes."

"I think it comes more and more with each passing day. You are sweating now?"

"Yeah, the fever's worse today."

Philip stood staring at her for a moment, then his eyes refocused on Gracie who was seated gently rocking Lottie's

Beth Durham

basket. He almost smiled as he considered the little girl who had stepped so readily into nursemaid's shoes.

Margaret watched his eyes as he considered his family. She tried to read what was going through his mind. "Philip, we've gotta' be making some plans, don't ya' reckon?"

He nodded without a word.

"Doctor Brown mentioned that some doctors are treating consumption by sending patients to the mountain. Do you think that it might be helpful for all of us to return to my family's farm in Tennessee?"

Again, he nodded. He was avoiding looking at her at this point, studying his shoes instead. After a moment, he left the room without another word.

Two more weeks passed. Margaret began to see color in the leaves that were visible from their third floor apartment. The hint of fall that usually brought such joy was troubling instead. She wanted to believe Philip had not forgotten their discussion and she absolutely believed that God would provide a solution.

So, when Philip entered the apartment, while she sat sewing, and brought up the subject on his own, she simply breathed a prayer of thanks.

"I have bought tickets to travel to Tennessee; you will leave on the 15th of October," he announced.

Margaret quickly counted the days; her needle froze in mid-air as she suddenly realized the timeframe. "Two weeks? Oh my, can we be ready by then? Thank you, Philip. I know this is the very best solution for our family." Tears came to her eyes as she thought that he had given up so much of his dream for the benefit of his wife and children.

"Yes, you have prepared the staff to work without you

through the winter so all you should have to do is pack bags. Now I have gotten you passage all the way to Chattanooga, but you will have to go to Nashville first. Where do you suppose they would prefer to pick you up?"

Margaret's mind began to spin as she thought of what would be necessary to take and she would need to contact the family and even though she'd prepared the stock and inventory, she really must speak to each of the girls one more time in hopes of planting a strong seed of the gospel in their hearts.

Then she paused in her planning, "Philip, what will happen to your business? Will Joseph be able to manage it? You aren't turning it all over to him, are you?"

Philip stifled a snort. He had less faith in Joseph than he liked people to believe. "No, Joseph cannot manage on his own. I will stay here and run things."

"Stay?" Her voice was a mere whisper. It never occurred to her that he would send her away.

"Yes, I will stay. You go to your family for the winter months and in the spring when you are stronger you will be back home with me. Like I said, the tickets take you all the way to Chattanooga. If they prefer to pick you up in Nashville, you could just cash in the remaining fares."

Philip picked up his ledger book and seemed to bury himself in the accounts while Margaret tried to sort it all out in her head. Lottie began to stir and as Margaret picked her up to change and feed her she tried to pray through this turn of events.

In the end, she clearly realized that for both her own health and for her daughters, she would have to get out of the city and that the very best option seemed to be returning to the farm. It broke her heart to think of leaving her husband for months – or maybe for good. Nevertheless this was the way he wanted it, and she really had to think of Gracie and Lottie.

And so she resolved herself to Philip's ideas and began planning the trip.

It was morning before she found both time and energy to write to her Mama. Her letter was very brief. She had not previously told her family that she was ill. Now, she needed them to understand, yet she did not want to cause undo worry.

Dear Papa and Mama,

I trust that you are all doing well. We are having a miserably hot summer, but we are soon looking forward to the cooler temperatures of fall. I read in the papers of the Reconstruction the Union is forcing upon The South and I am praying that the hardships are not reaching to Elmore community.

My health is not currently very good and I find myself needing the fresh mountain air of Tennessee and the strength of my family. And so, Gracie, Lottie and I will be traveling home in two weeks' time. Would it be possible to meet me in Nashville? I will leave Chicago on the 15th and would expect to make Nashville by the afternoon of the 19th.

We are most eager to see all of you and for you to meet these precious daughters that God has blessed us with. Lottie of course is too young to understand. Gracie however is a bundle of excitement knowing that she will soon be with her grandparents and aunts and uncles.

Your Loving Daughter,

Margaret Berai

Margaret had to prepare not only for the long train journey to Tennessee but also several months away from home. She was now so weak that she could only work for short times and would have to rest for longer and longer periods.

She began packing a large trunk Philip had until Candy, whose demeanor toward Margaret was greatly changed now, advised her that smaller bags would be easier for her to handle. She even brought a beautiful black Gladstone bag to lend to Margaret.

"Oh Candy, I can't take that. You know that I will be gone for months and frankly there is no knowing whether I'll even be strong enough to return in the spring. What if I couldn't get it back to you?"

Candy placed her hand gently on Margaret's arm, "That bag is the least of my worries." In that moment, Margaret realized that her ministry had truly born fruit. Even though she had not heard Candy pray a sinner's prayer, this hard, working woman had clearly felt the love of God through Margaret. Margaret breathed a prayer of thanksgiving to her Lord for giving her continued peace in this transition.

Each of the girls brought something for Margaret or the children.

Margaret also packed her grandmother's carpet bag. In a small silk reticule that Philip had brought her, she packed all of her handkerchiefs including new ones that Babe and Lula had embroidered for her. Pearl gave her a small bag of penny candy for all three of them. Mrs. Walsh had a large bouquet of mint wrapped in muslin, which Margaret packed for easy access on the train; the tea did seem to help a little with the coughing.

The evening before they would leave, Margaret was checking the bags again when Philip came into the apartment. "Do you have everything in order?"

He stood very close to her. This surprised her because he had been increasingly withdrawn from her as the consumption overtook her body. Now, he placed his arm gently around her waist and pulled her head under his chin.

"I will miss you, Philip."

He took a deep breath in and began to stroke her temple. She knew that he loved the feel of her hair and wished she could loosen it from its bun for him. "It will be a long winter without your warmth beside me."

Margaret had been so focused on one day at a time that she had not really thought of the long winter months. Now, she looked for something positive, "Maybe you can join us at Christmastime?"

Every mention of Tennessee seemed to drive Philip from her. And now, he stepped out of their embrace and seated himself at the little desk.

Margaret blinked slowly, chastising herself for ruining the moment. She dropped down on a low stool in front of Philip and took his free hand in hers. "Philip, I will pray for you every day that we are apart. " She just sat with him, silently praying for the words to say that would lead her husband to a saving knowledge of Jesus Christ. "Philip, we have to realize that I'm not long for this world. And I want you to know that my fondest desire is to know that you will meet me in heaven."

Philip adjusted his position in the chair, cleared his throat and turned the page of the ledger book. She knew that he could hear her; she had learned that he was listening even when he didn't want her to realize it. How she wished he would look at her now and talk with her about this most serious subject.

"I'll leave the bible that Father Michael gave me. Have you ever read through the book of John?"

He answered only with a 'hmmf.'

"You know what? I'm going to put my bookmark right here at the beginning of John and maybe you can read it. It is such a beautiful telling of the love that Jesus has for us. I think if you would read it for yourself you would understand what I mean."

Without looking up from his work, Philip answered, "I will be sure to go to Mass regularly and light a candle for you. You sound just like Mother, I think her last words as I climbed on the ship for America were, 'Be sure you are in Mass every week'."

Margaret still didn't really understand Mass. She didn't know what the priest was saying and even the people in the congregation responded strangely. After growing up with a father who wished more than anything to be able to read God's word, she always found it strange that Philip's answer was always Mass, or that the priest would read for him. She never saw him pick up their Bible.

Realizing she could do no more, she inserted the bookmark and left the precious book on the table by his chair. Moving around their apartment in final preparations, Margaret's mind prayed without ceasing for her husband's salvation.

Margaret had not returned to the train station since she arrived in Chicago four years ago. On the morning of their departure, Philip had arranged for a roomy carriage to be waiting at the front door. The entire household was lined up at the door to see them off. Gracie and Lottie were squeezed and kissed and passed down the line for attention from everyone. Joseph gently embraced Margaret and bowed as she stepped through the door.

She was going home and she couldn't have been more thrilled at the knowledge that she would be in the bosom of her family within a few days. Yet tears streamed down her cheeks as Philip lifted her into the carriage.

For the first time, she realized that she loved these people as she loved her own family. Joseph had indeed become her brother and each of the girls seemed like her own sisters. She blushed slightly at the thought of these women as her sisters. Her mother would gladly take a switch to one of her girls who even flirted with a boy, much, much less drinking and dancing and entertaining men alone. This thought led to a fear of going home; would Mama chastise her for her own behavior with Philip?

Philip pulled her from her thoughts, "Margaret, you are in your own world again."

She smiled and placed her gloved hand on his. "I'm sorry dear. I know I need to enjoy these last moments with you." She smiled across at Gracie sitting opposite her like a half grown lady. Daisy had helped to dress her this morning and she had arranged ringlet curls around her face below the knitted cap that was tied on her head.

Gracie had never ridden in a carriage and she was engrossed with all of the sights around her. As she asked questions about everything, Philip would absently say, "We'll go see that," and Margaret imagined Gracie was making a list of all of her father's promises. Lottie squirmed in Margaret's arms trying to climb through the open window, oblivious to the danger.

The Rock Island depot was crowded with people. Margaret could hear the hissing of the steam engines even before they entered the building. Philip had already made arrangements for their passage so he handily grabbed the two bags, food basket and Lottie's sleeping basket. This left Margaret to maneuver her two daughters' through the crowd and try to keep up with him. He had blessedly gotten them a private compartment and Margaret quietly wondered what that must have cost.

"Oh Philip, thank you so much for this compartment. It will be hard enough to manage these little girls even in here." As the words came out of her mouth, she wondered if she had betrayed some of her fears to him. She didn't want him to realize how scared she was to attempt this journey alone with their daughters.

Philip either missed her concerns or he simply dismissed them. Having stowed their bags in the compartment he turned to say his goodbyes. "You have some money for the journey? I want you to be able to eat when you are hungry. "

"Yes, I have the bills that you gave me last night. They're in my reticule." She lifted the beautiful bag and admired it for just a moment.

"I will send money periodically. Write if you need anything extra. Also, do you think you have enough to help your parents with household expenses?"

She was nodding, even before he finished. Margaret was struck by his concern for her family; he had known them less than a week but he was willing to send a bit of his growing fortune to care for them. She reached out to lightly touch his sleeve as he bid his children farewell.

Philip stooped down to Gracie's level and wrapped his long arms around the tiny frame. "Ciao – uh, good-bye Gracie. You have a good time with your grandparents. Take care of Mommy, okay?"

The little girl nodded vigorously but immediately turned her attention back outside the window, where she was amazed by all of the people and activity.

Margaret had Lottie in her arms and Philip reached for her little cheek. "I love you Lottie."

He wrapped his arms around Margaret in a gentle

embrace. Placing his cheek against hers, he bid her farewell. "Margie, I love you. I will be very eager to have you home again with me."

Margaret was frozen for a moment by her husband's unusual affection. She could not remember him ever saying he loved Lottie before, in fact he rarely even said her name. Her heart yearned for him and she wondered if she should leave but a tiny movement in her arms immediately reminded her she must think of her babies.

"Good-bye, Philip. I'll write you as soon as I'm at Papa and Mama's house."

Philip stepped out of the rail car and Margaret soon saw him on the platform searching the windows. She waved and held back both tears and coughing until the train pulled her out of his sight.

During the initial ride to St. Louis, Lottie slept a great deal as she was lulled by the gentle rocking of the car; when she was awake, Margaret allowed her to crawl around their compartment, thankful again that she had this space. Gracie was enthralled with the landscape that zoomed past their window.

When the porter came to ask for their orders for the dining car Margaret felt overwhelmed by the idea of even walking that far. She managed to feed all three of them from the treats Mrs. Walsh had packed and she found the gentle rocking of the train lulled her to sleep.

Chapter 23

Margaret and Gracie watched the sunset on the second day before the conductor passed outside the compartment announcing their arrival in St. Louis in fifteen minutes. Margaret had hoped that she could remain in this compartment but the conductor's answer disappointed her. She would have to move the children to another train. He consulted a sheaf of papers pulled from his tunic and announced that the Chattanooga train would not leave St. Louis for several hours and he doubted she would be able to immediately occupy her compartment on that train.

The disappointment settled upon her like a lead weight. It seemed an insurmountable task to move everything, including the children. At this point, she was so weak that lifting Lottie was becoming difficult.

She closed her eyes and breathed her favorite prayer, Lord, help me.

Instantly, there was a pecking at the compartment's door and the porter peeked in asking, "Shall I take your bags into the terminal, Ma'am?"

She could scarcely answer as she fought a wall of grateful tears. The "Thank you" that she breathed was woefully inadequate.

"Come Gracie, can you carry the food basket?"

But the porter overheard her and managed to get the basket as well, leaving Margaret with only her small reticule,

Lottie on her shoulder and Gracie's hand in hers.

As they stepped down onto the platform, the now familiar hissing of the steam engines and the rush of people threatened to knock her off her feet. The porter loaded her luggage on a wheeled cart and started into the station, so she followed. Inside, he showed her to an open space on the long wooden benches and excused himself. He returned after only a moment to tell her that her connecting train would not be available to load for about four hours.

The man looked compassionately at Margaret. "Will you be okay until then? You look very weak."

She smiled at his kindness, "Yes, I'll manage just fine." Silently she added, *For them*, as she unconsciously drew her babies closer to her.

Gracie tugged at her mother's sleeve and shyly asked if they were going to eat supper. Margaret felt the reticule securely on her arm and was comforted that there was money there to feed her daughter. However, she was unsure what would be available at this hour. Looking at the bags on the cart, she knew that she could not manage them. Something inside her told her it would be okay and she responded to Gracie, "Well we've got to eat, don't we?"

Looking around, she saw no prospect for food, and wondered if the ticket agent could direct her. She stood with Lottie in her arms and swayed a bit as she reached for Gracie's little hand. By sheer willpower and the grace of God, she did not stagger as she approached the agent.

He looked through the barred window a bit skeptically at her, but as he looked closely, his contempt changed to pity as he realized she was really quite ill.

"Is there anywhere I can buy some supper for myself

and my daughter?"

Leaning out as far as the cage allowed, he began pointing down the length of the depot and explaining where she could get meat and cheese and maybe a glass of milk at this hour. If she wanted a full meal, she would have to wait for her train to arrive. After giving her the directions he seemed to realize she would never be able to make the trip through the depot. "You have a seat on the bench and I'll have the boy come to you."

She smiled genuinely, thanked him, and made her way back to the seat near her bags.

As promised, a tiny boy with an oversized basket soon appeared filled with a vast assortment of foods. She chose a small loaf of bread and a good chunk of cheese. There was a quarter-sliced watermelon wrapped in paper and fried pies. The boy did not know what the pies were filled with, she took one anyway, knowing she would enjoy any fruit. She bought too much for their simple meal but hoped she could replenish the food basket Mrs. Walsh had sent them with. Paying the young boy, she gave him an extra penny, 'just for you, okay?' Beaming, he ran back down the length of the waiting room.

The big clock in the center of the depot told Margaret they would have plenty of time to enjoy the foods. The porter had told her she could probably board the St. Louis – Evansville – Nashville train around eleven and it was just before nine now.

Margaret pulled a small cloth from the basket, only slightly soiled from their earlier meals on the train. Placing it between Gracie and herself, she set out the items she'd bought and took Gracie's hand in hers.

Softly, she prayed, "Thank you Lord for your bountiful

provision. Please carry us in your hand on to Tennessee and our family. Bless Philip and the household in Chicago. Amen."

Gracie squeaked an "Amen" louder than Margaret thought she should have, then she reached for the hunk of cheese.

"Gracie, let's break off a small piece for you. You feel like you can eat all of that, don't you?"

Margaret knew Gracie was hungry but as they ate, she admired the little girl and marveled at what a good child she was. She had not complained on this hard journey and had done everything she could to help her mother.

Lottie began to stir and Margaret took the baby on her lap and broke off tiny pieces of bread for her to nibble.

After eating her fill, Gracie's eyes grew heavy and her hands dropped into her lap still holding the last of her portion. Margaret eased the food from the little fingers and leaned Gracie against the bench, making her as comfortable as possible.

By the time Margaret had Lottie settled back in her basket and the remaining food wrapped and stowed in the basket, she heard the stationmaster's booming voice as he walked through the depot. "Evansville and Nashville, Evansville and Nashville. Boarding now for Evansville and Nashville."

A quick glance at the big clock told Margaret they were a little early. It was only a quarter till the hour and they were already boarding. She smiled, hoping that meant she would be home with her family fifteen minutes sooner.

The food and the rest together had strengthened her, but now the task of loading bags and babies threatened again to overwhelm her. As she placed the food basket on the cart and began waking Gracie, a porter appeared offering to take the bags.

"Thank you, I was wondering how to manage it all."

"No problem Ma'am, that's what we're here for. You just manage those two beautiful ladies. Do you have your ticket?" Seeing the papers in Margaret's hand, he headed toward the platform, 'Just follow me then."

As they reached the train, still belching white smoke just below the platform, the porter led the trio to a door and offered his hand first to Gracie then Margaret as they stepped up into the car.

The train car was much like the one she and Philip had ridden in four years ago from St. Louis to Chicago. It had rows of seats wide enough for three adults and many of the seats were turned so that passengers were facing their neighbors. It was filling fast and seemed chaotic with everyone up and moving about.

Margaret turned to the kind porter, lifting her tickets. "I believe I had a private compartment booked, didn't I?"

The porter held the tickets for closer examination but explained, "There are only a very few private compartments on this train. " Handing the tickets back to her, he shook his head apologetically, "No Ma'am, I'm afraid your ticket is for the coach car. Which of these bags would you like to keep with you and I will load the others in the baggage car?"

In Chicago, Margaret had expected nothing more than this coach car in which she and her daughters would have no more space than a bench seat with her bags under her feet. Now, after the luxury of the private compartment, Margaret reeled for a moment from this surprise. Recovering, however, she straightened her shoulders and looked at her bags as though she could see their contents. "I will definitely need the food basket and the baby's basket. Oh, would it be possible to keep both bags under my seat?"

The porter nodded slightly, "You can keep them, but you wouldn't be able to move about the train very easily."

A small smile danced at the corner of Margaret's mouth and she looked down at her children. Returning her gaze to the porter with unspoken sarcasm she said, "I don't think I'm going far from this seat."

Situated on the rail coach with her daughters on either side, Margaret tried to relax. She had thought she was rejuvenated after rest and food at the terminal, but the effort of getting onto this new train had completely drained her strength. And now the coughing returned. She wished she had a pot of hot water to make Mrs. Walsh's mint tea. Of course there was none available. She tried desperately to stifle the deep, wheezing coughs but to no avail. Pulling handkerchiefs from her reticule, she covered her mouth to hide any hint that she might be bleeding.

All of her traveling neighbors would know well the symptoms of consumption. In fact, she suspected one look at her pale complexion, sweaty brow and hollow eyes would leave no doubt of her condition. As she shyly looked around the car, she saw no one especially concerned. Likely, all had been touched by the plague of consumption; hardly a single family escaped its wrath.

Noticing her weakened state, an elderly woman seated nearby offered to help with Gracie and Lottie. However, Margaret felt compelled to protect them and politely declined the offer. She was terribly exhausted and she felt like she might faint if she didn't sleep soon. Still she refused to allow sleep. She felt Gracie could wander off or Lottie could fall from her precarious perch on the upholstered seat. She talked to Gracie to keep herself alert, until Gracie fell soundly asleep with her head against her mother's arm. She turned to Lottie and found her also asleep. Looking out the window at the pitch black night she turned again to her ever-present Lord. And she prayed.

She prayed for her daughters. She once again entrusted their care and protection to God. She prayed for her husband that he might surrender to Jesus' saving grace. She prayed individually for each of the girls in Chicago. She prayed for gruff old Mrs. Walsh. She prayed for her family in Tennessee. And she prayed that God would see her home to the farm and to safely entrusting her daughters to Mama.

Right now it felt that she would not make it that far. Her own strength was failing fast. She put herself completely in the hands of The Lord and found rest in that surrender.

She was sure she had not slept, certain that she refused to let down her guard over the children. When Lottie began squeaking and lifting her little hands up toward her mother, Margaret could not remember the hours on this train. Leaning over the still sleeping Gracie to see out the window, Margaret could see the horizon streaking with pink and orange as the sun began to peek out. As she patted Lottie's back trying to give her a few more moments of sleep, she used her free hand to dig into the food basket hoping to reach the now-warm milk she'd placed there last night. Lottie would be hungry when she awoke and Margaret didn't want her getting upset and waking everyone on the train.

Margaret had Lottie sitting up and sipping the milk straight from the small bottle when she spotted the conductor making his pass through the car. With a smile she drew his attention, "Can you tell me the time, Sir?"

Like a machine, he pulled the shiny watch from his vest pocket and reported, "Quarter of seven, Ma'am. We'll be in Evansville by ten o'clock, right on time." The watch case snapped as he tipped his hat with the other hand and continued toward the end of the car.

Margaret rolled her shoulders, attempting to unknot the muscles. Although Gracie had scarcely moved, Lottie was squirming to get down and play. Margaret nestled her on her blanket in a corner with her doll and she was content for the moment. She dabbed the perspiration from her brow and took a sip of the warm milk Lottie had left. And she prayed.

The conductor was announcing their imminent arrival at Evansville before she knew it. Once stopped, the train seemed stationary for only a moment. Yet, there was a flurry of activity all around Margaret. Passengers got off, others got on the train. From the window she could see people moving up and down the platform pushing carts and carrying trunks. And then she heard the "All aboard" that signaled they were leaving. Leaving Evansville and heading home.

She was thinking of home now, home with Mama and Papa and the familiar farm around her. She was feeling more anxious about facing them with every turn of the great iron wheels. Sure, Mama's letter had acted as though nothing had happened but Margaret would still be apprehensive until she saw their faces and felt them wrap her up in their loving arms.

She had never been to Nashville, but if Papa would be waiting for her, she would consider her journey complete. She closed her eyes and imagined his face breaking into a broad smile as he saw his daughter coming from the train.

A tear escaped as she again battled shame that washed over her every time she thought of how badly she must have hurt him. She reached out in prayer and was immediately reminded that she had repented of this sin and God had forgiven it. *Thank you Lord that you have cast that sin into the depths of the sea.*

Chapter 24

By the time the conductor began chanting 'Nashville', Margaret was almost numb. Her eyes were dry and she felt as though they were propped open with sticks. She had to shake her head to make herself start to move.

"Gracie, we're home. We have to get off the train when it stops."

"Home?" Gracie was looking out the window at the fast approaching town. This looked nothing like the farm that she had heard so much about. In fact, she'd heard so many stories about their Tennessee home that she was sure she would know it immediately. Now it was obvious she didn't imagine this.

Margaret smiled, realizing the reason for Gracie's confusion. "Well, we're in Tennessee anyways. And your grandpa will surely be waiting to take us on to Elmore. "

Margaret made quick work of packing the food basket and the bits that they had pulled from the bags over the last day, all while trying to hold Lottie in place.

As the train rolled to a stop, Margaret sat on the edge of her seat. She had forgotten to worry how she would manage children and bags and baskets. She forgot about her intense fatigue and the constant effort to draw a deep breath. She was practically home and that was all she could think of.

No porter was available to help her with her bags, so she put the food basket on Gracie's arm, Lottie on her shoulder and one bag on each arm. As she stepped to the platform, her exuberance failed her and she stumbled under the weight. A strong hand caught her arm before she dropped poor Lottie. She looked up to thank her rescuer but froze at his face. It was older, yet unmistakably it was her brother Paul.

"Paul?"

"Yep, it's me. Come to carry you home." He lifted her effortlessly down from the train car, as she held securely to baby Lottie. Then, grabbing the bags from Margaret's arms he looked around seeming to assess if he had everything. "Is this it?"

"Well, I left Lottie's basket in the car because I simply couldn't carry it."

Leading Margaret by the arm with Gracie holding tightly to her mother's hand, he positioned the family against the wall of the depot and strode back to the train car. In a moment he was back, carrying Lottie's basket. Margaret marveled at the man that approached her. He had seemed like such a boy when she left home and now here was a full-fledged man coming to her rescue. It seemed obvious that he had taken on a lot of responsibility at home that had really caused him to grow up. She wanted to know all about him but she had so many questions to ask him, she hardly knew where to start.

Paul seemed to have just realized that Gracie was hiding among Margaret's skirts. In the flurry of activity, catching the falling Margaret and trying to secure all of the bags, there had been no opportunity for greeting. Now, he bent to Gracie's height, "Well now, who would this one be?"

The head alone appeared among the draping fabric, "You know I'm Gracie. Are you Uncle Paul?"

"How do you know that little lady?"

Gracie looked up at her mother as though questioning

whether she got his name right. Her confidence grew and she stepped out in full view. "Mama called you Paul. I know all about you and Grandma and Grandpa and Aunt Mary and Aunt Cathy. We are all excited to see you."

The smile threatened to consume Paul's face. He reached a work-roughened hand out to pat the little head, "Ever'body at home is excited to see you, Miss Gracie!" Standing, he turned his attention to the baby, taking her from Margaret's arms. "And you would be little Lottie. What a sweet girl you are. Margaret, you have beautiful children." He looked deep into Margaret's eyes and despite the genuine smile she offered him, he was troubled by the sunken, hollow eyes. He knew he had to get her home to Mama.

"Alright, let's all come along. I've got a borrowed surrey waiting outside so we can make the best possible time getting you home." He pointed and moved all at once, "It's just out here. I made it down here in just over a day. 'Course I was pushing the ole' mares pretty hard and it was just me. We won't drive so crazy today."

As happy as Margaret was to see her brother, she was still looking around for her father. She followed her brother as she asked, "Where is Papa?"

Paul talked as he worked. He seemed very eager to get on the road. He soon had the bags tied securely on the back of the surrey and Margaret and Lottie seated in the back seat. He lifted Gracie onto the front seat beside him and in one smooth motion swung himself up and grasped the reigns.

"Papa's at home. I asked if I could come instead. It would be a pretty hard trip for him. I've been sleeping on the ground for two nights." He clucked to the horses, flicking the reins, "Walk on girls. I kind of knew I was comin' early, but didn't want to take any chance that you would be waiting in Nashville by yourself with the two babies."

Her voice was growing weaker, still she had to know, "So he didn't refuse to come? He does want me at home?"

Paul cast a searching glance over his shoulder, he thought that maybe he hadn't understood his sister, after all, she was speaking awfully faintly now. "Of course he wants you home. They – Papa and Mama - can hardly wait."

Margaret let out a deep breath that she felt she'd been holding since she stepped off the train. When Papa wasn't on the platform with Paul, her mind began fabricating reasons. By the time she managed to ask the question, she had convinced herself that Papa must have disowned her. She whispered a soft, "Thank you," to God for this was surely another prayer answered.

Paul skillfully turned the carriage out into traffic and walked the horses as quickly as possible. "I don't know my way around this town you know, but I've driven out a couple of times to try to find the best way around. I've never seen so much horse flesh, have you? Well, I guess that's silly. You've been to the big city, there's no telling what you've seen."

Margaret dropped her head. She had no grand adventures from the 'big city' to report. She only wanted to talk about home, the family and the farm. "I guess with the war's end, things are getting back to normal at home?"

Now Paul's voice was as faint as hers, "Things will never be normal again Margie."

"What? Matthew is home isn't he? He wasn't seriously injured?"

"Well his body's whole. He walked in one day last summer and we scarcely knew him. He'd been makin' his way home for a month, scavenging for food along the way and hiding from Union patrols. "

"Hiding? But the war is over."

"Even after the Generals said it was over, some of the Yankees still thought it was okay to kill Rebs. Anyway, he walked in barefoot and rail thin. Mama doctored his feet for weeks and finally he can walk right. He's just not the same Matthew we sent off to fight. He's different."

Margaret took the news like a physical blow. Of course war would change a man. Still it hurt to think that Matthew had to suffer. She thanked God that he had not died like so very many others, or come home maimed. Really it was nothing short of a miracle to have him home and whole as she'd seen many vets along the streets in Chicago limping along on crutches or with one sleeve hanging empty. She simply had no energy left to speak these thoughts.

After a few moments of silence, Paul wondered if Margaret had fallen asleep. He glanced back to find her head up, but eyes just staring ahead. He looked again at his sister and felt a new urgency to get her home. He prayed, *Lord, she looks worse than Matthew did when he first got home.*

They drove well into the night, Paul pushing the horses as hard as he could. As the light faded, he had to slow the team. He had hoped to make twenty miles up the Walton Road and be ready to start the climb toward the plateau at first light. However, Margaret's train had not arrived until after five and by the time they were loaded in the surrey it was nearly six o'clock. There was just not enough time to make that kind of distance now.

During his wait at the depot, he had kept the horses watered and fed so they would be ready to travel at a moment's notice. Gracie had not been hungry when she got off the train so he shared his fruit and cheese with her, but could not entice Margaret to eat anything as she fed Lottie instead. He promised to find an inn before the night was over and get them a hot meal. He was thinking Margaret was in no condition to sleep under the wagon as he had, so he would have to get her a decent place to get decent rest.

He pushed the horses as hard as he could and estimated they'd covered almost ten miles when he saw the lights of a roadside stand where he gently tugged the right reign to pull the surrey off the road. After ensuring there was a bed for Margaret and hot food for all, he returned to help the little family get inside.

Margaret pulled a roll of bills from her reticule and pushed it into Paul's hand. "Pay for whatever we need tonight, and tomorrow we'll try to buy everything we can carry that is needed at home."

Paul squeezed the bills in his hand seeming to measure their value. "Where did you...? How did you...? I haven't seen this many greenbacks – ever."

"Philip wanted to help out at home. He will send more as time goes along, or if we need anything in particular."

Shaking his head, Paul took Lottie in his arms and steadied Margaret as she stepped from the carriage. "It will be a blessing for the family. We don't have much and everything is awfully expensive since the war."

As they made their way into the low building, Margaret had to lean on Paul to walk. Realizing how weak she was, he knew he needed to do something. "I will ask inside if there is a doctor near and I'll see if he can come look at you tonight."

She squeezed the arm that was supporting her, "No, you

sleep. We must leave at first light. I just need to get home to Mama."

It was all that she said for the rest of the evening. She fed her children, rocked Lottie to sleep and passed out between them. Despite the money Margaret provided, Paul did not take a bed in the inn. He slept on the seat of the surrey and woke again and again wanting to check on Margaret. Once he even stepped into the inn and the innkeeper's wife checked on Margaret and reported they were all sleeping well, although she'd been hearing Margaret coughing through the walls.

After his fitful night, Paul was indeed up at dawn, feeding his horses and preparing for a very long day's travel. The innkeeper's wife, seeing his preparations, had a hearty breakfast ready by the time he entered the building. She also knocked gently on Margaret's door and knew her guest was awake by the coughing that answered her.

"The woman?" she asked Paul.

"She's my sister, coming home from the north."

"Husband dead in the war?"

"No, he's still up there, working."

"She ain't doin' no good, you know that?"

Paul dropped his head. He did know it, but surely didn't want to hear it. "Yeah, I wanted to get her to a doctor this morning. She insists we push on toward home. Our mama will doctor her when we get there."

The old woman nodded her head as she kept on at her work.

Gracie shortly came bounding into the room. She had made fast friends with Uncle Paul during their evening drive and was excited to see him again. "Uncle Paul!" she announced as she ran into his arms.

"Good morning Gracie. Are you ready to eat a big breakfast?"

Holding onto his neck, she nodded her head vigorously. "Oh yes, I'm starving!"

He laughed. Gracie made him laugh and he was excited to have her with them at the farm. But when Margaret walked into the room, his face froze. She looked as haggard in the morning as she had the night before. Holding Lottie, she looked as though she might faint at any moment.

Paul rushed to the doorway and took Lottie from her. "Can you eat something this morning Margie?"

Margaret smiled at the childhood nickname. Philip had picked it up, but no one else ever called her 'Margie' – well, except for Joseph; it wasn't pleasant when he used it. "I'll try," she answered Paul.

"Did you get any rest?" he asked her from across the rough plank table.

"A little."

Gracie chimed in, "I slept in a big bed with Mommy and Lottie slept on the other side of her. Daddy said it's hard to sleep with Mommy because she coughs so much, but I slept just fine."

Gracie now had an adult-sized plate of biscuits, salt pork and eggs in front of her. She dug in with her fork without making much progress. Paul used his own knife and cut the pork into little girl sized pieces and mashed the egg with her fork. "You'll never eat all of that, especially if you keep talking," he winked at her.

Identical plates were placed in front of Margaret and Paul. Paul was concerned for his sister but knew he must sustain himself for the day. "We're ready to get on the road as soon as you are. The horses are fed and harnessed."

Margaret was feeding Lottie tiny bites from her own plate. "I can leave immediately after we eat. I want to get home."

"Are you sure we shouldn't find a doctor before we try to get up the mountain?"

"No, Paul, please get me home."

The tone of her voice broke his heart. He swallowed the rest of the food, gulped the hot coffee before him and headed outside to re-tie the bag Margaret had taken inside for the night. He looked eastward imagining he could see the mountains they would have to climb through to reach their home on the Cumberland Plateau. He spoke to the distant mountains, or to God, or just to himself. *It's more than a hundred miles, there's no way to make it in one day.*

With the small family loaded and the horses making the best time they could, his mind said it again and again, *How do I make a hundred miles today? There was just no way for a team to do it. Even if they knew the road, they wouldn't have the stamina to go that far. Could I ever change the team?*

If he made it to Sparta, he could borrow horses from Daniel Cox. Paul felt it would be a miracle to see Sparta today – that was a good sixty miles and most of it steeply uphill. He couldn't even imagine how they could make it to Crossville or Elmore community. *Lord, maybe that's what we need, a miracle. I have got to get Margaret home and I don't much think she can stand a night outside.*

The whole party was quiet as they drove. Margaret seemed to have no strength to talk, although she coughed frequently. Paul was deep in thought, and prayer. Gracie and Lottie seemed to sense the seriousness of their journey and while their eyes darted all about their new surroundings, they did not ask all of the questions children are known for.

From his earliest memory, Paul had been learning to drive a team and manage animals. Papa was always gently reminding his children to 'stop and let her blow' after the horses had climbed a hill or plowed a few rows. He had learned that the Bible taught a righteous man would take care of his animals. These teachings were second nature and he automatically slowed the team to a fast walk periodically, allowing them to catch their breath. Where the road was particularly steep and deep ruts were washed down it, Paul got out and led the horses.

They made good time and the animals, which were accustomed to both tender care and hard work, were eager to perform when Paul asked them. Mid-day arrived and both his stomach and the high sun told him they should take a short break. Unfamiliar with the road, he didn't really know how far they might be from a town so he found a shady spot that promised a water source and pulled the team off the road.

Hopping down from the surrey with Gracie in his arms, he set her on the ground and reached to the rear seat for Margaret and Lottie. Lottie had fallen asleep and, looking at Margaret, he wasn't sure if she was asleep or fainted. Leaving them for the moment, he took his bucket and along with Gracie went toward the water. He was thrilled to find instead of a muddy creek there was a spring.

After watering and graining his horses, he returned to the spring and brought water for the family. Back at the carriage, he woke Margaret, offering her the cool water. "Here Margie, this will feel good on your throat. I know it must get sore coughing so much."

Margaret was still drowsy but took the pewter mug

gratefully. She simply smiled her thanks.

"Do you want to get down and stretch your legs a bit?" Paul asked her.

She just shook her head.

Lottie began to stir in her basket. Paul wasn't sure when Margaret had settled her in there, but she was ready to be up now.

Margaret reached a trembling hand to stroke the little head. Turning to Paul, she asked, "Can you feed Lottie?"

With a quick nod, Paul stepped to the other side and gently picked up his niece. He spread a blanket on the ground and opened the food basket they had restocked at the inn. Paul made the meal a joy for the little girls. He pointed out birds that flew by and told them the names of each of the trees surrounding them. He kept his tone as light and happy as possible, but his heart was heavy.

As they packed the leftovers and blanket in the basket and secured it for the rest of their day's travel, Paul heard the approach of a horse. His hand went to the squirrel rifle he carried under the seat and his eyes were glued down the road. The approaching horseman had similar concerns as he slowed and watched the parked carriage.

The stranger pulled his horse to a stop alongside them and greeted Paul, "The spring is a fine place to cool the beasts, ain't it?"

Paul nodded, "Yeah, we've enjoyed the cool water and the shade. We're just about to head out, got a long way to go."

The man swung out of his saddle with canteen in hand, "Where ya' headed?"

"Crossville."

He whistled, "Sure is a long way. You'll never make it

tonight, will you?"

"Not without a miracle. I'd be willing to drive it, but my horses have been going hard since early this morning. Where are you headed?"

"Sparta."

Paul saw a moment of hope. "Do you know Daniel Cox?"

"Don't think so. Is he there working in the mines?"

"Yeah he is. Daniel just might bring me a team to switch out if I could get word to him."

The stranger looked at the mound of blankets in the back of the surrey with a woman's head bowed over them. He looked back at Paul. "I could try to find him."

"Mister, I would sure be indebted to you if you could. Just tell him Paul Elmore is trying to get Margaret home and she's awfully sick. If he'd drive his team out then we could make it all the way to Crossville tonight – it'd be late, but we'd make it."

They had stepped over to the spring as they talked and the stranger filled his canteen. He looked at Paul and past him at Margaret slumped in the back seat of the surrey. "Elmore?"

"Yes Sir, Paul Elmore."

"Yeah, I'll do that for you. Are those your kids?"

Paul followed his gaze to the little family, "No, it's my sister and her children. They are trying to get home and like I said, she's awfully sick."

As though to prove he was telling the truth, Margaret began coughing hoarsely.

With a nod of his head, the stranger swung into his saddle, looped the canteen over the horn and picked up the reins. "I'll get to Sparta just as fast as I can."

Beth Durham

Without chance for another word, he laid his heel into the horse and was off.

Paul stood frozen for a moment. It seemed miracle enough to meet someone on their way to Sparta. And if Daniel came out with a fresh team, it would seem like the impossible had truly happened.

Not willing to waste a moment, and encouraged by this potential help, Paul headed out behind the stranger. The man was already out of sight as they were well into the climb to the plateau. Paul continued to drive his team as steadily as before, praying and hoping that this miracle would pan out.

280

Chapter 25

The setting sun behind Paul cast a gorgeous golden light around him. He was tired. Accustomed to hours in the field, to holding a hoe or driving a team he was surprised how tired his arms and hands were. And the upholstered seat that had seemed like such a luxury when he borrowed the surrey in Crossville now felt like the grating board Mama gritted corn on. Still, he knew he could not stop. Trying to get a good look around him in the quickly fading light, he estimated he was several miles from Sparta.

As the horses trotted along, Paul bowed his head both from fatigue and disappointment. He heard Margaret moving behind him and a glance told him that she was shivering and trying to wrap the shawl and blankets more closely around her. Her fever must be rising again and she hadn't spoken a word for hours now. With every passing minute the sky was darker. He knew he couldn't ask his team to do much more today. He saw a creek running near the road and stopped to water them.

Without the plod of the horses' feet and squeaking harness, he heard another team approaching fast. In the growing darkness, they were upon him before he could make them out. He was looking up to greet the fellow traveler when he recognized Daniel Cox. He was so happy he dropped the water bucket out of Jewel's mouth, but recovered before all the water was lost.

With a hand on his horse's forehead and a gentle word

of apology for depriving her of water, he waited for enough quiet from the new team to speak to his friend.

"Daniel, you are a miracle from heaven, brother."

"Well you knew I'd be coming, din' you?"

"I guess my faith was fading with the light, and for that I am truly sorry."

"So, what are you waiting on Paul? Let's swap these horses. I'll take care of graining and watering your team. You just get on your way. This pair here knows their way through Sparta on the worst day. Just give them their heads and they'll get you up to Crossville and even home to Elmore."

It took them only minutes switch the harness to the fresh team and hitch them to the surrey. Daniel peeked into the back seat to speak to Margaret. She smiled and reached out to squeeze his hand but was then taken with another bout of coughing.

With the fresh horses, Paul seemed to have fresh spirits. Waving at his friend, he clucked to the horses and they stepped into a trot immediately. He would use every minute of dusky light in that fast gait and let them rest and walk in the darkness. "Lord, give us a good moon tonight."

Paul tried to remember what phase the moon was in, but his exhausted mind couldn't even remember yesterday. Something inside reminded him that God controlled the moon and the clouds that often shrouded it. "Where is your faith, Paul?" he spoke under his breath.

Paul was trying to think of the landmarks he ought to be able to see, even in the moonlight, and guessing how far they had come when he realized they had reached the turn north in Crossville. "Well that's got to be a miracle." Whether he was talking to himself, the horses, or God, it roused Margaret.

"What's that Paul?"

"Margie, we are in Crossville!"

"Oh, glory to God!" Her voice broke and then she was coughing again. Even in her silence, Paul knew if she hadn't fainted away she would be singing praises in her heart.

He knew there was a well at the square and though he didn't want to take the time, he had to care for the animals. So, he gave them a good drink and looked up into the night sky to estimate their time. God had indeed blessed him with a nearly full moon tonight and it was beaming down directly over him. He spoke to the horses head he was holding, "Midnight. Well, it will be a very early morning for Mama and Papa, but they will be happy for it I know."

The remaining miles up The Stock Road went both quickly and slowly. This road was most familiar to Paul and least familiar to the Cox team. Although they could see their way quite well in the bright moonlight, they were naturally less confident about their footing and therefore slower. Then, as they approached the Elmore farm, no doubt sensing Paul's - and maybe even Margaret's - excitement, they matched the pace they'd set when Daniel first hitched them to the surrey.

Paul had hoped to reach the farm by sunrise but the sky showed no color as they turned down Elmore Road. He announced to his passengers, "We're here. We've made it home!"

No one responded to him. The children had been sound asleep for many hours and Margaret, he believed, was unable to answer him now.

But he drove on. The fast drumming of iron-shod feet on the hard packed earthen road made a distinctive ringing and he knew if there were a window open anywhere in the house, this would serve as an alarm. As soon as it was in sight, he fixed his eyes on the house and watched for light. They did not disappoint him. Before he was in shouting-range, a tiny light appeared and he knew someone had turned up the oil lamp on the kitchen table.

The horses did not slow until they were upon the house. Papa stood in the doorway waiting to identify the early morning visitor. "Mama, it's our children come home."

Mama appeared in the faint light beside him as Paul stopped the surrey expertly in front of them.

Bessie Elmore rushed immediately to her daughter, slumped in the back seat. She began unwrapping the form and reached her hands in to touch Margaret's face. Without a word, Margaret's hand clasped her mother's against her cheek.

"Papa, help Paul get her in the house. Take her to my bed." She was inside the doorway immediately and shouted, "Mary, I need you child!"

Mama had thought she would have to wake Mary but the eldest daughter appeared immediately, for she had positioned herself at the top of the steep stairs when she heard the approaching horses.

In minutes Mama had water boiling, a medicinal tea steeping, broth cooking and bread and cheese on the table for a very quick meal. With everything underway, she realized she had grandchildren to meet.

While Lottie slept through the flurry of activity, Gracie was standing beside the door, her eyes the size of dinner plates and giant tears forming at their corners. She had been so excited to meet her grandparents but this was all very scary.

Bessie dragged a low milking stool very close to Gracie and dropped herself onto it. "Hello Gracie, I am your

Grandma."

Gracie fell into her grandmother's arms. Exhausted and terrified, the little girl knew she was safe with this woman her own mother had told her so much about.

For a long moment Bessie held little Gracie, stroking her hair and holding back tears. Then, she knew that she had work to do and handed Gracie into Mary's eager arms. Carrying the tea and broth into her bedroom, Mama prepared herself for the greatest nursing challenge she had ever faced.

As she entered the room her eyes met her husband's and read there how gravely ill their Margie was. She sat down on the edge of the bed and listened to her daughter's breathing. Margaret was not awake, and even in her sleep she coughed periodically and her brow glistened with sweat. "Get me a pan of cool water and a cloth. We have to get this fever down more than anything."

Mama talked to Margaret as though she were wide awake even though there was no response at all. "Margie, you didn't tell me what was wrong with you. This is consumption. I can't believe you are already coughing like this. Surely you didn't get sick the moment you left us, but usually consumption would take longer…" As she chatted away, she bathed Margaret's head with cool cloths and laid a plaster on her chest.

Throughout the early morning hours, Mama sat by Margaret's bedside alternately talking to her and praying for her. No one in the house had really been asleep since the first sound of hoof beats announced Paul's return. As the morning brightened, Jesse and Catherine made their way downstairs. They knew the situation was serious enough that they'd have only been sent back upstairs if they'd come down sooner. Now, they were eager to meet their nieces and start the day's work.

At the crack of dawn, Matthew quietly arrived in the barn on the premise of beginning morning chores but he first checked for any sign of the borrowed surrey. When he found the carriage backed into the barn, he ran to the back porch and had to stop himself from tearing in. Mama had warned all of the family that Margaret wrote she was ill so they would need to give her quiet rest for a few weeks. Matthew was trying hard to follow his Mama's orders.

Mary was in the kitchen, keeping the firebox filled, the tea kettle steaming and jumping on the tiniest task that Mama called out. As her siblings entered the kitchen she immediately put a finger to her lips to quiet them. They moved close to her and she tried to prepare them, "She is awfully sick. It's a lot worse than Mama expected. Consumption."

Only Jesse wasn't familiar with the disease. The last neighbor who suffered with it passed on while he was still very young. The other children, Matthew and even Catherine, remembered and they were immediately terrified for their dear sister.

But Mary hadn't trained at her mother's heels for twenty-three years for nothing. Mama's practicality was deeply rooted within her. She turned her brothers and sister to the task at hand. They would not mourn Margaret prematurely. "Cathy, your nieces are asleep on pallets in the front room. They had a long, hard ride yesterday, so I don't know when they will be up, but you will need to do for them when they do wake. Why don't you go ahead and get Gracie's things setup in our bedroom upstairs. Lottie will probably stay down here with Mama and Margaret."

Turning to the boys who knew well the needs of the farm, she only smiled and promised breakfast in due time and they were off to care for the stock.

It was late morning before Margaret roused. "Mama, is that really you? Or is it an angel?"

Mama laughed. It was good to hear her laugh. "Child, if I'm the best looking angel heaven has to offer, you might as well stay on this old earth for a while."

Margaret reached for her mother, seeming to want to touch her to convince herself that she truly was home. "Then Paul got us home? Where are Gracie and Lottie?"

"They are well cared for, you know that. They are both sleeping out in front of the fireplace."

"Weak as I feel, you can't know how good it feels to be home."

"Margie, we are so happy to have you back. Let me get Papa. He's been by your side all morning long and just stepped out to the porch for a bit of air."

Margaret desperately wanted to hold her there, but Mama would know what was best.

She was gone only a moment and then both of her parents were there.

Margaret had planned what to say to them. There was so much to ask forgiveness for, and so much to ask them to do. Now she struggled to find the starting place. "Mama, Papa, can you – have you forgiven me for rebelling against you?"

"Shh, shh, we will not waste any energy on that stuff. How dare we refuse to forgive what the Lord already has forgiven. "

Amid gasps and coughs she tried to explain, "Oh Mama, I thought I could come home and get better. The doctor in Chicago said that some doctors are sending patients to mountains because the air is better. So, we had hoped that I would improve here, but on the trip home I just got weaker and weaker."

"Shhhhh, don't waste your energy. The sun has come out bright and beautiful today and I'm going to get the boys to carry you outside in the air. That will help your lungs."

Lawrence Elmore looked at his wife with a mixture of terror and anger. No one took sick people outside when they had lung troubles. It would probably kill her. As Bessie stepped into the kitchen to get her sons, Lawrence followed her.

Before he could say a word, she proved she had read his mind. "Lawrence, can't you see that it is probably too late for her to heal from this disease. If she had come home sooner, if the trip hadn't been so hard on her, only the good Lord knows what could have changed this. We just need to make her comfortable. And you know that staying in the stuffy house is never helpful when you have breathing trouble. It's going to be quite warm today and I won't let her get chilled. Let her enjoy the sunshine and the smell of leaves and the sound of corn shocks rustling. That's the best thing we can do for her."

Lawrence Elmore had long since learned the wisdom his wife carried. He rarely argued with her and this was no time to start. He went to the barn and asked Matthew, Paul and Jesse to come inside and help him.

Lawrence and Matthew had carried their share of coffins and somehow expected that kind of weight as they lifted the feather tick Margaret lay on. She weighed no more than a child and a small gasp escaped from Papa when he realized it. These men knew that in both livestock and children, weight meant health and stamina. Realizing how little Margaret weighed somehow told them how short her time would be.

By the time the men had Margaret outside, Bessie and

Mary had pulled Jesse's small bedframe downstairs and arranged it in the sun near the spring house. Catherine made a thick pallet of blankets for Gracie and Lottie. The little family was settled in the sunlight and Catherine sat with the children on their blankets with the homemade toys that each Elmore child had played with and loved. She began to tell them stories, using the cornhusk dolls as characters and Gracie squealed with glee as her aunt moved the dolls about.

Margaret made no sound except to cough, which she did with great regularity. Mama sat at her bedside alternating between giving her sips of cool water or hot herbal tea and praying over her. Margaret desperately wanted to talk to her mother but Mama wanted her to save her strength.

Catherine rose to carry Gracie and Lottie inside for a bit, "I need to change Lottie and I think we should get Gracie a little snack, don't you?" Catherine was looking down at Gracie's upturned face for agreement.

Margaret reached for them, "Let me love them for a minute, please."

Catherine was hesitant to put Lottie's weight on her frail sister, but with one nod from her mother, she settled the squirming baby in her mother's arms.

Margaret beckoned to Gracie and she clamored up onto the bed.

"Do you girls know how much your Mama loves you?"

Lottie responded only with, "Mamamama," which escaped around the fingers she was chewing.

Gracie quickly responded, "You know I love you too, Mama."

"Please always remember that. Now, you go in with Aunt Cathy and be very, very good girls. Listen close to your

Granny and your aunts. They love you too."

Gracie hopped down and began to skip toward the back porch with Catherine following as quickly as she could while carrying Lottie.

Margaret could wait no longer to talk with her mother, "Mama, we need to talk." She paused to cough then to catch enough breath to continue. "I'm not going to last much longer, am I?

Bessie bowed her head for a moment; she could not lie to her. "You are very weak, sweetheart."

"Gracie and Lottie, they can't go back to Chicago, not the way things are now."

Bessie didn't understand. "What do you mean?"

"Philip's business, they can't grow up there. They need the same kind of upbringing you gave me." It was all she could get out, and her mama could see that.

Bessie waited for Margaret to go on, realizing that the conversation was going to take a long time and wondering how much breath Margaret had left for talking.

"I wanted to come home because I thought it would help me, but that's not all. If I died, I knew they couldn't grow up there with just their father."

"Was he unkind to them? To you?"

"No, not really. He is not like Papa is with his family, although Philip loves his children. It's the business."

Bessie's face showed her confusion. She didn't really want Margaret to waste her energy talking and she wasn't following what her daughter was telling her. "What do you mean?"

Margaret coughed as gently as she could, "I thought it was going to be a restaurant – a really fine place for people to come eat."

"A restaurant? Well I guess that's respectable Margie."

"But Mama, when we opened the business... I didn't realize until it was too late... then Joseph hired all these... Mama, they don't just serve food." She closed her eyes and took a deep breath, which brought on more coughing. It was very hard to admit to her mother where she'd been living. She could see the confusion in her mother's eyes. Finally, she just blurted,, "There is strong drink and – there are women."

Bessie only expressed her shock with a very quickly drawn breath. Without a moment's hesitation she said, "No, my granddaughters will grow up on this farm. They won't have much, probably not even as much as you had, but they will be loved and taught the Bible and that will be the best thing for them."

Margaret smiled. Her face settled into a look of peace and contentment. Bessie realized immediately that all that had been holding her daughter on this earth was a drive to protect her children.

Bessie began to hum and to caress Margaret's brow as she had done when she was a child. She knew Margaret had said all she needed to, all that she could.

The sun was still quite high and warm with a gentle Indian summer breeze when Bessie knew that her precious Margie was no longer with her. Bowing her head she allowed the tears to flow freely.

Bessie sat by the bedside as was their custom, her little girl would not be left alone until they buried her. And Bessie knew that would have to be very soon. She had a large linen napkin in her apron pocket which she unfolded and placed over Margaret's face. As she knew, the cloth lay perfectly still over her nose and mouth; no air escaped to cause it to flutter.

Catherine started toward the pair with the children in hand but saw a straight look from her mama while she was still several yards away and skillfully distracted Gracie and Lottie, heading them to the barn instead.

Alerted by Catherine, Lawrence quickly came to his wife's side. "I don't understand how she could be taken by consumption. We are a strong family."

Bessie shook her head. "It's something in the city."

"Nah, that Dunlap man across the ridge died from consumption a few years ago and he'd never been to a bigger city than Crossville." The thought of Crossville as a city caused a quick chuckle, despite the grave situation. "Then one of his kids came down with it; that girl will never be a strong one."

"I know that people everywhere have it, but there was something about the city that caused Margie to get sick. No matter how, the Lord has called her home and we have to take care of the body. Are the boys coming?"

"Yeah, they'll be along directly."

As their papa expected, his sons came out to help them within minutes. Bessie was giving directions as there was much work to be done.

"We need to bury her tomorrow morning at the very latest."

Lawrence disagreed, "We need to let the neighbors come in."

"No, we have her two little girls to think of now. I can't work on getting them strong and healthy until we've taken care of Margie. We need to get a box built."

Paul raised his hand, he felt like he had failed his sister and his whole family somehow by bringing her home in such a weakened state. "The least I can do is build the coffin. Papa, there's some sawn lumber in the smokehouse, right?"

Lawrence nodded.

After the men had carried the straw tick back to its place in her bedroom, Bessie directed her family to the chores that would need attention. Matthew's wife Lou had arrived and she and Mary helped her remove Margaret's clothes and lovingly bathe the body. The dress was brushed and smoothed and the body was redressed. She found a quilt that could be used to line the coffin when Paul had it finished.

Matthew was dispatched to tell the preacher and arrange his presence tomorrow morning. He would also ring the church bell and alert any neighbors he could see. In this way, the community would know what the Elmores were facing and turn out to support them.

When her mother no longer needed her, Mary went to find Catherine and her nieces to help Catherine in explaining where their Mommy had gone and what was going to happen to them.

The day had started long before daylight and it was nearing midnight before Margaret's body was arranged in the parlor in her coffin. The bed linens had been completely stripped and placed on the back porch for washing as soon as the funeral was over. The house was scrubbed from top to bottom both in anticipation of neighbors arriving tomorrow and at Mama's insistence for the health of her family.

Lawrence and Bessie greeted the preacher before breakfast was cleared. He understood the dark circles that surrounded their eyes both from lack of sleep and mourning. No stranger to death, he knew these strong Christian people would weep over their daughter but they would recover for they knew she was in God's hand – really had been all along.

Lawrence wanted him to know Margaret's heart at her time of passing. "She had truly repented you know. Her first words to us were asking *our* forgiveness."

Brother Miller nodded. He had been concerned for Margaret after she left home and had prayed for her along with his congregation. Now, his focus was on the family and his purpose was their comfort. Lawrence Elmore seldom required a strong shoulder so he would certainly provide it for him today.

Many neighbors turned out and the kitchen was brimming with food. Well before noon, as much of the crowd as possible gathered in the tiny parlor, the kitchen and on the front porch. They listened as Brother Miller read the twenty-third Psalm, and then prayed over the family and the neighborhood that suffered the loss of this dear sister in Christ.

Neither the Elmores nor their church family believed in 'putting on' mourning. As they walked solemnly to the family graveyard, their grief was genuine. In fact, Lawrence and Bessie struggled to maintain their composure as they heard the dirt ring hollowly against the pine box.

Bessie knew that her little Margie was far better off in heaven today than here suffering, but it was hard to let go of the child she had birthed and raised. She reflected on the last four years, missing her daughter and worrying about her well-being. Then when she started to receive letters, she had rejoiced that Margaret had repented of her rebellion and was again seeking to follow the Lord.

Bessie's eyes fell on little Gracie, whose big eyes darted from one sad face to another trying to understand all that was happening. Bessie was reminded that she had no time to mourn the dead for she had to serve the living. And these two beautiful children needed her love now.

She lifted her chin and squared her shoulder, emotionally preparing for the rest of the day and the days to come. She looked to her husband to share her resolve, "Lawrence, we have two precious granddaughters to raise."

He nodded and wrapped his arm around her shoulders. They had faced so much together;   surely they could endure this. "With God," was his only response for that was how they would face it, and how they'd raise the children. Bessie understood his response as only a lifelong mate would.

In the days that followed, Margaret's name was mentioned often. The family was accustomed to sharing and remembering stories from both the near and distant past. None of them held resentment toward Margaret and they all missed her acutely. So it was easy for her daughters to grow up hearing about their mother.

Bessie tried to write her son-in-law frequently to tell him how his daughters were fairing. Philip sent money every few months; never a lot of money, but the Elmores were thankful for anything. Bessie and Lawrence had never been accustomed to wealth; they managed with what they had and what they could grow. And in the years after the war, cash money was especially hard to come by. The United States government called it 'reconstruction'. For the families of the Confederacy, it felt more like retribution, for their treatment certainly seemed severe. Now, with two young mouths and their own advancing age, any help from Philip was appreciated.

As Gracie and Lottie grew toward adulthood, they naturally asked more about their mother. Bessie never hid that Margaret had acted in youthful rebellion when she ran away from home. And she took every opportunity to teach the blessing of forgiveness and to remind them that Margaret had in fact asked God to forgive her rebellion.

These girls knew from childhood the precious gift their mother had given them by bringing them home to Tennessee. Neither would ever see Chicago again, and only Gracie had the faintest memories of the dance hall. Really, she remembered the girls working there who all played with her and brought her candy, especially Daisy. And she had a distant memory of time with her mother while they lived there.

When they had well mastered their letters, their grandma would ask them to write a few lines to their father, which she included in her letters. His responses to them were short and never especially warm. However, they were so loved by their grandparents and uncles and aunts that they never missed warmth from Philip Berai.

Lawrence and Bessie taught Gracie and Lottie from the wisdom of years on the farm in that rugged corner of the Cumberland Plateau. They taught them from Bible wisdom gleaned through a lifetime of study. Each of their granddaughters eventually came to accept Jesus as her Lord and Savior. Bessie prayed with Gracie when she asked Jesus to save her. Lottie had prayed on her own and came to her grandparents with both the announcement and with questions. In each instance, Bessie lifted thanksgiving to God; Margaret's work was complete when her daughters were saved.

Epilogue

Thirty-year old Lottie forced open a rusty gate, taking in the whole area. Grass had grown up higher than the split rail fence she knew had always been in place around the family graves. She waded through the sea of green wondering if she'd even be able to find her mother's grave. Her feet seemed to remember the path she had walked with Grandma so many times. She first passed Grandma and Grandpa's graves. The stones in this area were newer and farther from the trees. Small, unmarked stones gave evidence to babies whose lives were measured in hours or days. And then there was Aunt Lou's grave, and Lottie knew from the family's stories that there lay Lou with her infant son; the delivery proved too much for either of them. She could see the break in the grass now where she would find Mother's stone.

Grandma had taught Lottie and Gracie to remember the dead, to honor their family heritage by good upkeep of the graves. Now Lottie felt a moment's shame that the grass was so high. Then she spotted the patches of flowers surviving in the green mass. Over the years they had brought flowers from home, sometimes planting different varieties. Lottie missed Grandma at these times. It was easier when Gracie could join her.

Today, Gracie's services had been required at the bedside of another expectant mother. She served as midwife to their whole community and Lottie knew how comforting it had been to have Gracie at her side when her own babies came; so she could not deprive other mothers from the same solace.

She could hear her children now. Daniel always gave her a few minutes ahead of the family to walk among the stones, and among her own memories. Lottie breathed a quiet prayer of thanksgiving for the godly man she'd married. Daniel Ingle was a simple man, but honest and hardworking. He loved Lottie and each of their children and above all, he loved The Lord. She could hear him quietly talking with the children as they came behind her. Eight year old Dewey was her little man; he walked beside his father as though he too carried the responsibility for this family. Sweet Ida Francis didn't take her eyes off her Mama, looking for any opportunity to offer the comfort of her little girl hugs. And Daniel had Tabitha by the hand and Tom in his arms. Poor Tabitha getting little notice as Tom cooed and clamored for attention.

They were a good family and she longed for Grandma to know how she and Daniel yearned to raise them in the fear and admonition of The Lord. Whether it was premonition or daydream, she could see Dewey leading his local church as pastor, Ida raising a houseful of children following the patterns of parenting Lottie and Daniel taught her by example. She saw Tabitha working with lost people in some unknown mission field and Tom, well just entertaining and bringing joy wherever he turned with his instant smile and constant antics.

As the children reached her side, Lottie began to tell them the story of her mother. They had heard this story many times, but both Gracie and Lottie were committed to retelling it often lest their children forget and make the same mistakes. Just as these little ones learned bible lessons and basic elementary education, they learned the price of a rebellious spirit.

Lottie took Daniel's hand and bowed her head as he began to pray, "Dear Lord, we come before you here in this field of stones. There is no life here, and no spirit, for the souls of these loved ones are at home with you. These folks knew a lot of hardship, and they loved you through it all. I thank you, Lord, for Lawrence and Bessie Elmore who struggled to raise children who would follow your commandments and love your word. I thank you that Margaret, rebellious in her young life, saw the benefit of her Christian upbringing before it was too late and managed to bring my sweet Lottie, along with her sister, home to grow up in the same godly home she had known. I know you have used that final act of repentance and sacrifice to bring Lottie to me. Help us to instill in our own children your word and the love for you that we enjoy. We pray in the name of our blessed savior, Jesus Christ, amen."

The End

A Note from the Author

Margaret Elmore's early life was rich and blessed, even though she could not see it; despite a humble home, she was surrounded by love and godly teaching. Still she rebelled and found herself in dreadful circumstances with no easy way out. This is a situation many of us will experience and Jesus addressed it in a parable recorded in Luke chapter 15.

Jesus said the boy's father saw him and ran to him while he was still far away. We understand that God is watching for his rebellious child to return to him and if you only turn your heart from the rebellion and desire to return to him, God will reach out to embrace you. If you are in that situation today, I beg you to talk to The Lord right now and begin that trip back home to Him.

Repentance, and the subsequent forgiveness God promises, do not immediately change the situations we've gotten ourselves into. Margaret faced tough choices when she looked around and realized she was far from where God would have wanted her. He led her to *bloom where she was planted* and to spread His word to people that might have no other opportunity to hear the good news that God loves them and Jesus died for their sins.

Margaret's life may seem like a tragedy on the surface but I believe if you look deeper you will see that she was a strong witness to the working girls in the dance hall as well as her unbelieving husband. And in the end she gave everything to get her own daughters to a place where they could grow up learning about The Lord. Her ultimate success can be seen in Gracie giving of herself as a midwife and Lottie raising a godly family.

God longs to use all of us, no matter where you are or what mistakes you have made.

About the Author

A native of Tennessee's Cumberland Plateau, Beth Durham's novels draw both characters and plots from the region's rich oral history. She now lives near Chattanooga, Tennessee with her husband and children.

Beth writes Christian fiction and blogs weekly at www.TennesseeMountainStories.com about the legends and lessons from her beloved mountain home.

Other Titles by Beth Durham

Available at Amazon

Made in the USA
Columbia, SC
26 August 2021

43797106R00183